QUEENS IN WONDERLAND

ALICIA K ANDERSON   KATIE ARNETT

CHRIS BANNOR   EVAN BAUGHFMAN   ANNA BUSHI

MINERVA CERRIDWEN   K. R. CERVANTEZ

KATHRYN DIAZ   THERESA HALVORSEN   LMZ

DONNA KEELEY   EVE MORTON   MORRIGAN PUHR

LS REINHOLT   ROBERT RUNTÉ

STEPHANIE SANDERS-JACOB

CHRISTINA TANG-BERNAS   C.N. WHEATON

PAUL WILSON

EDITED BY
THERESA HALVORSEN

EDITED BY
CHRIS BANNOR

Dedicated to all who create and keep safe spaces for the LGBTQIA+ community

CONTENTS

Introduction   ix

ONE MORE MONSTER   1
Alicia K. Anderson

OOSH LEA IN 1D LAND   10
LS Reinholt

AXE WON'T CUT   27
Evan Baughfman

ALICE & WENDY   38
Christina Tang-Bernas

AL/ICE   46
Robert Runté

ALEX DOWN THE MEERKAT-HOLE   67
LMZ

WONDERLAND SWAYAMVARA   77
Anna Bushi

ALICE'S SHADOW   85
Eve Morton

WONDERLAND'S MAD QUEEN   97
Theresa Halvorsen

ALECIA IN THE WARDROBE   112
Morrigan Puhr

BOY KIND / GIRL KIND   128
Stephanie Sanders-Jacob

WE'RE ALL MAD HERE   136
Chris Bannor

ALICE THE TERRIBLE   155
Kathryn Diaz

DRIPPING RED   171
K. R. Cervantez

LOOKING INTO THE LOOKING GLASS
Donna Keeley
188

ONE DAY AT CARROLLTECH
C.N. Wheaton
198

WILL YOU BE OUR ALICE?
Paul Wilson
207

GOOD-NATURED ANXIETY FOR THE QUEER
CREATURE
Minerva Cerridwen
220

OF TUNNELS AND FALLING THROUGH THEM
Katie Arnett
236

Author Biographies
247

INTRODUCTION

Welcome to the tea party that is *Queens in Wonderland*! I can't tell you how excited I am to be publishing this book. The Wonderland universe has always had a special place in my heart, whether it was the original works from Lewis Carroll, the Disney versions, or the multitude of other interpretations. I love the nonsense, the whimsicalness of the stories, and the way you can explore so many themes about humanity using the characters and world from Lewis Carroll.

And exploring themes about humanity, love, and identity was the purpose of this anthology. I decided to pair the call for a LGBTQIA+ anthology with the Wonderland universe because *Alice's Adventures in Wonderland* is partially about Alice seeking her identity. She's constantly being asked, "Who are you?" and saying things like, "It's no use going back to yesterday because I was a different person then." Many in the LGBTQIA+ community are exploring identity and it seemed natural to pair the two together.

But I had other reasons too. I wanted to publish a LGBTQIA+ book which, until now, has been lacking in the No Bad Books

Press library. Not only do I feel that books that celebrate the LGBTQIA+ community are important, but I wanted to offer LGBTQIA+ books at events because they were being asked for. I adore selling books in person. I love seeing that reverence in a reader's eye when they pass my booth; the one that says, "I love books, I love stories, I love diving into other worlds." It gives me tremendous joy to match them with a book and see their eyes light up.

And it broke a bit of my heart not to offer a LGBTQIA+ book.

I am so incredibly proud of these stories and honored the authors submitted them for publication. All of them, even the sad ones, offer the joy of recognizing oneself, and many contain the happiness of embracing who one truly is, without fear. Some stories have an element of love and romance, both in new and established relationships that are good for the soul. There's a recognition of safety in many of these stories that echo the need to create safe communities for all.

Several of these stories contain sensitive topics, and after a lot of debate, Chris and I decided to place a note on those stories. She and I put together this anthology to give a safe place for readers to explore themes of acceptance, love, and identity. Sometimes, journeys toward acceptance and identity are difficult. Several stories contain harsh language, conversations about suicide and substance abuse. We didn't want to leave those stories out because they were painful to read; it's important to honor and acknowledge these journeys. And yet, we didn't want anyone to feel emotions they're not ready to address or aren't ready to address in the moment of reading.

I'd like to give a shout out to my mom, Suzanne, who was one of our readers, and to Jacob who designed this gorgeous cover.

And a shout out to Chris who provided a tremendous amount of help and perspective for this anthology. Thank you so much for being the co-editor on this project. This was so much fun and I can't wait to do more projects with you!

A huge thank you to all who have come before to pioneer the need to address gender, identity, sexuality, and love. The path hasn't been an easy one, and unfortunately, will continue to be a challenge. To those who need a safe place of acceptance, I hope this book gives you a little of that and these stories become tiny lights of hope, rippling out into the universe.

I wish everyone a very happy unbirthday and hope you enjoy *Queens in Wonderland*!

-Theresa Halvorsen

ONE MORE MONSTER

ALICIA K. ANDERSON

The uffish brutes were harassing Lily again. Alice pushed her pair of larger and smaller drinks away from the edge of the table and rose from her chair. Her thick dragon-leather armor glittered in the firelight. The tavern was empty except for a few regulars. The Tweedles engaged in a rhyming competition that got more slant as they got more drunk. The White Rabbit stared sadly into a draught of ale.

Alice knew that even though she'd been visiting Wonderland since childhood, she still looked like she didn't belong there. While the locals had accepted a small girl with long blond hair and a blue dress, they seemed wary of her now. *The* Alice. Her close-cropped shock of platinum hair and armor didn't help allay their fears of her. She had seen too much. She knew the power of her imagination far too well.

One of the Tweedles shuffled aside to let her approach the oaf whose fingers still lifted a lock of Lily's white hair.

"Flibberty Bollocks," he intoned to his brother, attempting to rhyme-respond to the phrase "Effervescent Flocks."

"Do not touch her," Alice's voice trembled on the verge of rage. She did not want to unsheathe the vorpal sword at her hip.

The massive hand dropped. The soft curl bounced a little, catching what little light it could as it returned to Lily's perfect shoulder.

Alice looked into the bleary eyes of one brute, then the other. She willed her gaze to be piercing, nearly painful to withstand.

"Leave."

The tavern was filled with shuffling, scurrying, blundering noise as the pair exited the tavern.

"Their tab..." Lily whispered, almost despondently. As soon as the brutes cleared the doorframe, the tavern grew quietly frabjous once more.

Alice reached for the small leather pouch at her waist. "I'll pay it."

"You shouldn't have to," Lily said, meeting her gaze. The dove gray eyes of the White Queen's eldest daughter made Alice's heart leap into her throat. "But I'll take it. This place brings in just about enough to keep me from the Pawn Line, but that's it."

Alice was glad her leather-covered sleeves hid the goose-bumps that raised on her arm when her hand touched Lily's in the exchange of coins. They were not lovers, but Alice dearly wished that they were.

"If you'd let me be your Knight—" Alice began.

"You're a Queen yourself, Alice," Lily shook her head. "That's nonsense."

"I would do it for you, Lily. Work here, protect you. Help you with the tavern." *Love you.* The thought went unsaid.

Lily's beautiful face shone with a moment of hope and then dropped back into shadows. "The only way to help with the tavern is to draw in more clients." She pointed to the trophy heads enshrined on three of the four tavern walls. "Those drew in the crowds. But the novelty has worn off. No one wants to come see a Bandersnatch or a Snark anymore."

"The Jabberwock still has appeal," Alice looked at the three monstrous heads. "Do you want a new beastie? Will you accept me as your wife if I bring you the head of a new beast?" Alice worried another trophy would only be a temporary ease of the tavern's financial troubles.

Lily rolled her eyes. "What are you going to do, fetch me the JubJub bird?"

"Will you marry me if I do?"

Fleetingly, so fleeting that someone less in love would have missed it, Lily's expression bore doubt and fear. But the anxiety was smoothed over by her usual resolute stubbornness as quickly as it had appeared. "Yes," Lily said. She kissed Alice's cheek to seal the promise.

Even in the dim firelight of the tavern, Alice knew everyone in the room could see her blush. Abandoning the drinks on her table, she paid her tab and left. She had a hunt to prepare for.

THERE WERE few sacred texts that pointed to the JubJub bird, its habits, or the location of its lair. Mostly, the rhymes just said to "beware" it. The *Agonies* contained some details, though. One of the Fits described it as "desperate," but she needed more information. There were no functional libraries in Wonderland. If she could find a book, it would read in mirror-print, backwards or scrambled.

No libraries, but there were informants. The Cheshire Cat was nowhere to be seen. He would be useful. Alice walked right past the Hatter's shop, reeking of mercury. He would be of no use. "But flowers don't have larynxes," the petunias in the window box cried mockingly, making fun of her incredulity for generations of blooms.

She went instead to Caterpillar. She'd get a contact high, sure, but Caterpillar *knew* things. Alice was no longer spooked by the short walk into the forest of mushrooms. These parts of Wonderland never bothered her anymore. There were still creepy places, sure. But not the same places she'd seen as a child. As ever, Caterpillar, when she found him, was poised on a massive fungus, puffing gently on his hookah.

"Child! You've come to visit me!" Caterpillar wheezed a little with delight.

"I have!" Alice said, smiling. She passed a small tin of biscuits up to Caterpillar, where he was perched. "And I brought munchies."

Caterpillar chortled with glee and seemed lost for a moment in the pattern on the top of the tin. Shaking himself a little, he busied a few legs with opening the tin, one with the hookah, and fixed her with his gaze. "To what do I owe this pleasure?"

"I need to know about the JubJub bird," Alice said.

"Going sailing? I recommend avoiding that island. Bandersnatches, Boojums. There's a lot of wildlife there that can kill a person. Even a Queen." Caterpillar looked sleepily at the sky for a moment. "Perhaps especially a Queen," he said to himself.

"Just the JubJub," Alice shook her head. Even *she* wasn't foolish enough to tackle a Boojum.

"You've checked the *Agonies,* I presume?" Caterpillar inhaled a long draw from the hookah and held his breath for a moment.

"Yes, I found some information in Fit the Fifth. Listen for the shrill, high scream and then name it thrice."

The caterpillar nodded, then exhaling a great wave of smoke, he quoted the Fit.

"As to temper the JubJub's a desperate bird,
Since it lives in perpetual passion:
Its taste in costume is entirely absurd—
It is ages ahead of the fashion:

"But it knows any friend it has met once before:
It never will look at a bribe:
And in charity-meetings it stands at the door,
And collects—though it does not subscribe.

"Its flavour when cooked is more exquisite far
Than mutton, or oysters, or eggs:
(Some think it keeps best in an ivory jar,
And some, in mahogany kegs:)

"You boil it in sawdust: you salt it in glue:
You condense it with locusts and tape:
Still keeping one principal object in view—
To preserve its symmetrical shape." [1]

"WHAT MORE IS THERE TO KNOW?" Caterpillar shrugged several sets of shoulders. He made a mess of crumbs down his tummy as he crunched on a biscuit.

"Why does everyone say to beware it?" Alice asked. "How is it dangerous? The description makes it sound...friendly." Alice wasn't particularly keen on galumphing back with the head of a bird that knows its friends and does not look at bribes. Especially not for just a brief few months of fame and patronage of the tavern.

Caterpillar answered with his mouth full of crumbling biscuit. "Spoken like a woman who has not had many friends."

~

ALICE'S BOOTS made a racket as she paced the boards of the small ship. The captain avoided looking at her. The Baker and the Banker stayed below decks to avoid irking her. The Butcher and the Beaver huddled together in a corner, trying to hide. She wasn't sure about this crew of sailors, but that wasn't for her to question.

"Will you wait for me when we reach the island?" she asked the captain for the brumteenth time.

"We intend to Snark hunt while we wait," he answered her again. The Beaver was sorting a box of thimbles, forks, and soap. Snark bait.

"How are we going to fit both a Snark and a JubJub on the boat for the return?" The Butcher was looking at a scrap of paper, confused by the maths.

The captain shrugged and rang his bell. The island. The island and its craggy cliffs. The island was visible off to port. Alice checked her pockets and her sword. She ran her fingers through her short hair and readied herself for the hunt.

When they landed on the small beach, the crew went left, and she went right. She was not interested in the Snark, and their galumphing clamor and grinning would startle the JubJub away, along with the smell of their soap.

She made her way inland, listening for the shrill cry to shatter the sky like the texts described. It was a brillig day. She was glad the island seemed mimsy. Her boots crunched on the rocks as she walked slowly and deliberately toward the nesting grounds of the JubJubs. When the sun reached its highest point, she rested and ate a biscuit under a TumTum tree, wondering if there were other Jabberwocks. Should she be alert for Bandersnatches?

As she thought, a screech rent the clouds and hurt her eardrums deep inside her head.

"That's the JubJub bird." She said the words out loud, to no one but herself. "The JubJub, for sure." Dusting her hands on her dragon-leather trousers, Alice stood up. Speaking it thrice, she said a final time, "That was a JubJub bird."

A gust of wind nearly sent her tumbling from her feet. If she hadn't grabbed the TumTum trunk beside her, she would have been tossed to the ground. Another gust filled with a perfumed scent caused her to rock back onto her heels. Great heaving feathers created another gust.

The bird landed.

It was breathtaking. Larger than she'd ever imagined. Perfectly round, its "symmetrical shape" looked like an overfed Robin. It cocked its head at her, its bright blue eyelids blinking unnaturally long eyelashes. A fuchsia plume bobbed on top of its head.

Blink.

"Hello," she said, pretending to curtsy, though she hadn't worn a skirt in years.

Hey, Queen. The JubJub did not split the air with its cry, but instead sang the words in a musical warble. This startled her, but it wasn't the strangest thing Alice had encountered in Wonderland.

"Very nice to meet you," Alice said.

If you say so. The bird's feathers were various tufts and layers of glittering pastels. It preened a little and pulled something from beneath one of its wings. A small piece of duct tape.

"I'm Alice—"

Oh, I know who you are.

Alice considered her sword. It was within striking distance. Close enough to touch. It was not afraid of her. She thought about the texts. What was the JubJub desperate for? They considered one another in silence for a moment. Alice thought of Lily and her tavern. She thought of the promise of kissing Lily's soft lips. Of the pressure of those lips on her cheek last week.

"I would like to work out a deal." Alice knew she wasn't going to be able to kill this bird unless it attacked her.

Blink.

Interesting. Go on.

"What do you want most in the world? What do you need?" Alice asked the JubJub.

The bird blinked and scratched at the forest floor. It preened and fidgeted.

Attention? Recognition? Fame? It warbled the words softly, as if it were trying to sort through the possible answers. *Representation? Acceptance?* It ruffled its feathers. *For people to stop hunting me?*

Alice thought of the tavern. Of Lily. She thought of the words the JubJub sang. Her heartbeat was too fast, and her eyes too eager. Alice dropped her gaze. She shuffled her feet. "Have you ever been to a tavern?" she asked the bird.

WHEN YOU ENTER Lily's tavern, the wall immediately facing the door is hung with the head of a Snark, sneering, and leering, and jeering at you. Above the fireplace to the right is the head of the Jabberwocky. The very same head the rhyme talks about. On the same wall as the door itself, there's a huge taxidermied Bandersnatch. The fourth wall, the wall to the right as you enter the tavern, that was the wall Lily had asked Alice to fill.

Fill it, she did. But not with sawdust and glue. Not with ivory or mahogany. No.

The stage took a little building, but the Tweedles were down to help with construction projects. The Hatter loved creating costumes. And the JubJub bird? No manxome foe, the JubJub bird was an entertainer. Singing, dancing, comedy, ribald jokes, and even storytelling. The JubJub bird was a headliner. A main act.

And entertaining shows could be updated, changed over time. Patrons did not come once to gawk at a still trophy, but over and over again to enjoy the show.

Lily's tavern saw the beamish crowds and frabjous days that Alice had promised her. No more looming threat of the Pawn Line for her white-haired queen.

They got married on the stage. In the middle of the day, surrounded by friends. Lily's mother, the White Queen, and her entire entourage traveled to the tavern to celebrate. Cards were shuffled in the drunken debauchery that followed.

And they lived happily ever after.

In Wonderland, at least.

———————————————

1. Carroll, Lewis. *The Hunting of the Snark: An Agony in Eight Fits.* 1876. https://www.poetryfoundation.org/poems/43909/the-hunting-of-the-snark

OOSH LEA IN ID LAND

LS REINHOLT

The letters on the title page were a light blue that stood out prettily on the muted green background.

'Oosh Lea
She/they
Applicant for position 29x-1'

The words remained slightly longer than necessary, then cut abruptly to a shot of a brown, round face dominated by sparkling black eyes and a curly tuft of bright cyan hair.

"Ehm... hi." The words were cut off by a nervous giggle. "So, my name is Oosh Lea, but I guess you already know that. I usually put she and/or they, but I'm good with all pronouns, really. As long as you're consistent."

Oosh paused and took a deep breath.

"Right, so I'm applying for this job as..." Her eyes darted to the corner of the screen. "Creative Monitor at the Copenmalmö facility, and I think I'd be really great at it because I'm a very creative

10

person and I've been the primary parent in our household for the past three years, so I would say I'm very skilled at monitoring... stuff..." She giggled again and glanced down at the desk in front of her.

"So I guess you want to know something about me. My name is... oh, I told you that. Anyways, I'm 32 years old, live in a three-partner household, we have one kid so far, 2½ years old. We call them Bubby for now, until they're old enough to help choose a name."

Oosh stopped as a person walked past in her background.

"Oh, that was my ex-husband..." she began but was interrupted as the person returned and leaned down to look at the screen. Their face was long and pale, with slanted green eyes. Their hair was black and very short.

"Stop calling me that," they said. "I'm your wife."

"Yeah." Oosh grinned. "But you used to be my husband."

"You're such a nerd."

"*You're* a nerd!"

Oosh kissed her wife and then turned back to face the camera.

"So yeah, that's me. I don't really know what else to tell you. I've attached my degree and resume, but you are of course very welcome to get in touch if you have any questions."

She hesitated a moment, then reached for the mouse.

"Ehm... bye."

The screen went black.

"WHAT WERE YOU APPLYING FOR?" Dinah settled down on the chair across from where Oosh had set up her laptop on the dining table. "Something good?"

"I hope so," Oosh replied. "It's not in a field I have worked in before, but the hours are good and the commute shouldn't be too bad."

"Can I see?"

Oosh turned her laptop so Dinah could see the screen.

"1D Land? Why in the name of sweet eternity would you want to work for a company like that?"

"I don't know…" Oosh shrugged. "I fit all the qualifications, and… I like the guy in the ad."

"Mr. Bun-Bun?" Dinah's thin eyebrows shot upwards and Oosh squirmed in her seat.

"Yeah… He's so fancy."

"He's a bunny!"

"Yeah, in a little waistcoat. And he's got glasses."

"Bunny!" Bubby exclaimed, crawling into Dinah's lap.

"Exactly," Oosh agreed, before turning her best puppy eyes on her wife.

"I guess he doesn't look too bad," Dinah agreed, stroking Bubby's unruly hair. "But I don't think it's the right company for… Oh."

A small ping had announced an incoming message. Dinah glanced briefly at it, then turned the screen towards Oosh, who gasped.

"I… I got the job!"

THE 1D BUILDING was not as impressive as Oosh would have expected. She wasn't entirely sure what she *had* expected, but it was definitely not the square yellow brick building with entirely too few windows looming in front of her.

Maybe too much natural light was detrimental to the work they did here.

The door was perplexing. It was much too small. Like the door between rooms inside a house, not at all what you would expect from the entrance to an up-and-coming studio in a major city.

She wondered if she'd gotten the address wrong. Or perhaps this was merely a side entrance, and if she went around the building, she'd see a grander gateway. But she was running late, and the alley around the side of the building looked very uninviting.

So she approached the tiny door and realised there was a sign above it:

'1D Land - Liminal Leisure and Luxury'

And below that, the address of the building that matched the address she'd been given.

So she was in the right place.

Now she just had to figure out if she was supposed to be buzzed in or, since she couldn't see any panels or buttons near the door, simply knock. Or just enter?

Reluctantly, she reached for the handle. Surely people couldn't just wander in off the street. Could they?

Apparently they could.

Inside the door was a small lobby, a few padded benches, a lot of potted plants and a skinny person in a green jacket sitting behind a curved desk.

"Hello," Oosh called as she approached the desk. "I'm supposed to start here today, my name is..."

"Mary Ann," the receptionist interrupted. "You're late."

"Oh... No!" Oosh had gotten close enough to see the name and pronouns on the tag: 'Billy Izzard, he/it.' That was a bit uncommon. She cleared her throat. "My name is Oosh Lea. I'm supposed to start work here today. As a..."

"Creative Monitor, yes." Billy looked at the small tablet in front of him. "Third floor, elevator's on the left." He made a vague pointing motion and turned his back to her.

Ignoring his rudeness, Oosh muttered a quick thanks and headed for the elevator.

ON THE THIRD floor she was greeted by a rather formidable, smiling person who introduced herself as: "Duchess Olesen, she/her. It's a name, not a title," before taking Oosh's arm and leading her through a large, dimly lit room in which numerous people—several hundred in Oosh's estimation—were reclining in grey plastic chairs, wearing silvery helmets twinkling with tiny blue lights.

"This will be your station," Duchess told her, giving her arm a little squeeze. "There'll be a quick instructional piece when you sign on, and then you'll be good to go. I'll be seeing you at the end of the day for your first review."

And with that, the woman was gone and Oosh was left alone, surrounded by her unmoving colleagues and the softly humming equipment.

Oosh had only ever worn a 1D helmet once, when her spouses, back before the pregnancy, had taken her to a showing at a local theatre. The piece had been an adaptation of an old pirate movie and had been so messy and confusing it had left her feeling more nauseous than entertained. Or maybe that had been the monotonous rocking of the ship.

All in all, Oosh had not been impressed by the new 'One Dimensional Total Immersion Entertainment', or as people quickly started calling it: fake dreams.

Hopefully, the technology as well as the scripts would have improved since then. Oosh made herself comfortable in the chair and put on the helmet.

FIFTEEN MINUTES later she had not only learned that the technology had indeed improved, but the medium now allowed the audience a certain degree of control as they moved through the environment. Furthermore—and this she felt like she should really have discovered before applying for this job, let alone accepting it—1D Land specialised in 'personal fantasies tailored specifically to the customer's desires.'

That could, she supposed, mean dreams about flying over specific mountains or running through meadows with long-dead celebrities. But it also meant, she suspected, other things. More... unsavoury things.

It did explain why they needed so very many CMs. If every dream they made was for just one person, they must be making a *lot* of them.

The instruction piece she'd watched had not made it entirely clear what Oosh's role would be, though. As a Monitor, would she be watching over the team creating the 'dream?'

Before she could wonder too much about it, the words: 'Project 154712 ready for supervision. Nod to accept,' appeared in the blank space that had taken over her conscious mind.

Startled, Oosh nodded and everything went black.

OOSH WAS FALLING, slowly, down what seemed to be an endless hole.

She screamed.

"Would you cut that out?" The voice sounded very close to her ear, causing the scream to rise in pitch as Oosh twisted around in the air to see who had spoken.

"I'm serious," the voice said. "Shut up! Or I'm having you evicted."

The absurdity of the statement startled Oosh, and she gasped.

"Who... who are you?"

"I am the main CP in charge of Project 154712," the voice answered. "I am very good at what I do and I will not have you messing it up for me."

There was a slight pause, in which Oosh felt a very unsettling urge to roll her eyes.

"Why do they always saddle me with the rookies?" the voice continued.

"Excuse me?" Oosh had managed to get her body in a some-what upright position and felt a little bit more in control of the situation, though she was undeniably still falling.

"This is your first assignment, isn't it?"

Oosh nodded.

"Did they even tell you what you're supposed to be doing?"

Oosh shook her head. Then, for some reason, she sighed.

"You're here to experience the product, making notes of any mistakes or imperfections along the way. Not that there ever are any. I am very good at what I do."

"Oh..." While Oosh considered this, she tried waving her hand a bit and found that it spun her slowly around. "I'm just here to... dream?"

"That is such a crass way of putting it, but I suppose it will have to do, if it gets the point across. Yes, you're experiencing the 'dream' while I and my team create it, and afterwards you're going to compare it to the client's specifications, before declaring it fit for consumption. Or... give us notes on what to change."

"I see." Oosh didn't really, but found it better to play along. "And you're a... CP?"

"Yes."

"What is that?"

"A Cognisant Program."

"What, like an AI?"

The voice did not speak to her again for the rest of the long slow descent.

~

"THE LANDING COULD BE A BIT SOFTER," Oosh complained as she rubbed her bottom. "Or was that for my benefit?"

"Would you be quiet, please?" The voice sounded next to her. "We're going to have to remove all this dialogue in post-production, and it's such tedious work."

"Sorry!" Oosh felt her pout morph into a smirk and stamped her foot. "Would you stop emoting through me?"

"Can't be helped," the CP answered. "At this stage of production I am still partially connected to the avatar that will become the client once the 1D is released."

"So will they be doing all your frowns and eyerolls too?" Oosh huffed.

"Of course not, that will be filtered out in post production."

"But I have to suffer through it."

However, her mood changed drastically as she looked around the garden in which she had landed.

"Oh wow, this is beautiful. Did you make this?"

"Just the framework." The voice sounded a tad friendlier. "My subordinates take care of the details."

Oosh nodded as she began walking towards a particular beautiful patch of roses. "Is it okay if I check this out? I mean, we wouldn't want any of your subs to have messed up your beautiful product, would we?"

"Subordinates!" the voice called out, but it was growing more faint as she moved away from the starting point. Oosh did not mind that one bit.

As she explored the garden, she began talking to herself, a habit both her spouses often teased her for, but Bubby loved.

"I think I could become quite fond of this job," she mused. "As long as the dreams are like this, I mean. No nasty stuff. I really have no stomach for nasty stuff."

"Who are you calling nasty?" a small voice sounded from between the daffodils.

Oosh squeaked. "Who's there?"

"Fourth level CP in charge of hues. Who are you?"

"I'm your Monitor, I guess." Oosh bent down and pushed the flowers aside, but couldn't see anything. "Are you all just voices?"

"CPs are not part of the 1D. We just make it."

"Oh, but that's too bad. I mean, you made this beautiful garden, didn't you? You should get to experience it. It doesn't have to interfere with the dream. You could just be a little bug. Or a caterpillar."

As she spoke the word, the dirt behind two flowers shimmered and a small, fuzzy caterpillar, about the size of her pinky finger, appeared. It looked up at her, blinked its cartoonishly large eyes, and opened its tiny pink mouth.

"This is... highly irregular," it peeped.

"Maybe," Oosh agreed. "But you're so cute!"

The caterpillar twisted from side to side, trying to see itself. "I suppose I do have a very pleasing colour..."

"You certainly do," Oosh laughed. Then she bent down and offered the caterpillar one of her fingers. "Why don't you come up here so you can get a better look at your garden? We can explore it together."

The caterpillar hesitated for a moment, then stretched up to take hold of her fingertip and inched its way up into her hand, allowing her to raise it up so it could look around.

"Wow... I'm a genius!"

"You sure are."

They wandered around aimlessly, Oosh bringing the caterpillar closer to any details it wished to examine. They talked about the design of the garden as well as other scenes the caterpillar had worked on earlier.

Eventually they came across a babbling brook and Oosh declared it was time for a rest. "If only I had something soft to sit on."

Even as she spoke the words, a lilac mushroom sprouted from the moss near the bank and grew rapidly until it was the size—and rough shape—of a squashy armchair.

"Did you do that?" Oosh asked the caterpillar.

"Nope. Just the hue." It shook its tiny head. "The rest must be you. I mean, you made a body for me."

"But I'm just a Monitor," Oosh protested. "I shouldn't really be making things."

"Probably not, but who's gonna know?"

"The main CP?"

"Bah, once it's set up the frame of the product, it doesn't move beyond the entry point. Considers itself above the rest of us Creative Programs."

"Creative Programs? Is that what CP means?"

"Of course."

"Oh."

THE MUSHROOM-CHAIR WAS VERY comfortable and Oosh had almost drifted off—which was a strange thing to do in a dream, even if it was an artificial one—when the caterpillar laughed.

"What is it?" Oosh asked, rubbing her eyes with the hand not holding the tiny program.

"I just remember when I was being trained," it said. "The Motherboard in charge of my group kept telling us that if we didn't focus on the source material and taught ourselves to create consistent output, we would end up just becoming bugs in the system. I guess it was right."

Oosh snorted. "I can make you something else, if you want. At least I think I can."

"It's okay. I think I can handle this myself."

The caterpillar shimmered, and in its place was a beautiful blue butterfly. It flapped its wings a few times and then took off. "I'm gonna go see the rest of the dream. I never knew I could. Thank you!"

"Have fun!" Oosh called after it. "And take care."

She was a bit sad to see her new friend leave, but also happy for it. It deserved to experience the world it had helped create.

With no company, lounging on the mushroom soon got boring, so Oosh got to her feet and stretched, though it didn't feel as satisfying as in the real world.

"What should I do now?" she asked herself, stepping closer to the stream and kneeling down to touch the water. It felt absolutely real, except maybe not as cold as expected. In fact, it was just the right temperature for a swim. If only it weren't so small and shallow.

Barely had the thought shaped itself before the stream began to widen and deepen, becoming a gorgeous little lake with a shimmering waterfall.

Oosh was about to strip off her suit to dive in when a small, bright red creature broke the surface, waving its oversized clawed hands at her. "You are off the schedule by nearly 30 minutes," it complained in the main CP's voice. "If you do not get back on track immediately, I will have you written up. That will not be a good look for your first assignment." The creature's long antennae swayed disapprovingly. Oosh guessed it was supposed to be a lobster, but she was fairly sure they only turned that shade after being cooked. She should definitely mention that in her report. Though it might be intentional.

Sticking her tongue out at the lobster, Oosh buttoned up her suit. "Fine. What am I supposed to be doing?" she asked.

The crustacean remained silent but waved one of its claws in the direction where Oosh had found the caterpillar. She looked back and saw a dense forest had appeared there, with an invitingly mysterious path leading into it.

"I suppose I can go monitor that," she said. "As long as there's not something unpleasant looming in there."

The lobster had disappeared, and with a shrug, Oosh strolled into the forest.

IT WAS NOT AS dark as it had appeared from outside. In fact, it was rather nice, with thin beams of sunlight shimmering down through more shades of green than Oosh could ever have imagined. The air smelled of wet earth and exotic flowers, and birds were twittering and fluttering in the canopy above her.

She followed the winding path for what felt like a few minutes before coming rather abruptly to a tall, dark green hedge with a wrought-iron gate across the path.

It wasn't very realistic for a forest this dark to be so small, Oosh thought. But maybe the customer was the impatient type. Or the CP in charge had been lazy.

Either way, she was gonna make a note about it.

She supposed she was supposed to go through the gate and was about to reach for the handle when a loud blaring of trumpets startled her so badly she jumped back and almost fell.

The sound continued as the gates swung open slowly and revealed rolling manicured lawns and neatly trimmed hedges, which she really should have been able to see through the bars earlier. This part of the dream was turning out to be quite sloppy. Such a disappointment after the garden.

A figure approached her, carrying a comically large scroll of paper in front of them. They were dressed in a mismatched three-piece suit, topped by a floppy hat with a long feather.

"Welcome to the Queen's garden party," the person said in a snooty, high-pitched voice.

"You really are an annoying character," Oosh told him. "Surely nobody wants something like that in their dream."

She thought for a moment, then snapped her fingers. "I know what we need."

There was a small pop, and then Mr. Bun-Bun was squinting up at her. "You need to hurry, Ms," he grumbled. "The Queen does not like to be kept waiting."

"Lead the way, good sir," Oosh said, and then curtsied because it felt like the proper thing to do. It seemed kind of foolish to do in a suit, and she briefly considered whether she could change it to a dress but decided against it. This wasn't her dream, after all.

She followed the white mascot through the garden, and they soon came upon a large gathering of colourful creatures milling around, sipping purple drinks and eating tiny sandwiches with an orange or blue filling.

There was a chattering sound coming from the crowd, but no matter how much Oosh tried focusing, she could not make out any actual words. This was getting embarrassing.

She turned to Mr. Bun-Bun to ask him what she was supposed to do, but the rabbit was now standing at the other end of the area, bowing and making a motion with its arm as if it was taking off a no-longer-there hat.

"Oops," Oosh giggled.

A single trumpet honked, and the crowd fell silent as a tall, slender woman emerged from an opening in the hedge. She was dressed in a slinky red dress (with a not very royal plunging neck-line) that shimmered and swooshed as she crossed the lawn with the most ridiculously seductive saunter Oosh had ever seen.

"My darling," she said, reaching out to take Oosh's hand in hers. "I was so hoping you would come." Her red lips were plump and seemed to be covered in glitter. Her nose was so tiny it might as well not be there, and her blue eyes so huge, Oosh suspected they might be larger than her brain.

Oosh snorted then started laughing. "No, I'm sorry," she gasped between giggles. "I can't do this. Get me out of here, somebody. Please."

"What is going on?" a mechanical voice demanded as the scenery around her froze.

"Oh hi," Oosh said, spinning slowly around to see if this one came with a body. "Who's there?"

The mouth of an immobile waiter holding a tray of cookies moved out of sync with the words: "Third level CP," it answered. "Why have you intruded upon this 1D? You are not the intended client."

"CP?" Oosh asked innocently.

"Cookie Patrol," the voice huffed. "Now answer my question."

"I am the Creative Monitor," Oosh answered, matching its tone. "And I'm shutting down this dream—this 1D. It is absolutely ridiculous."

"You... You can't do that," the waiter's mouth protested, but the world was already dissolving around them.

"Unauthorised exit!" a voice blared above Oosh's chair. "You are required to log in immediately, or progress might be lost."

"I'm sorry," Oosh told the ceiling. "This is not working out." She put the helmet on its stand and got out of the chair. She was still stretching when Duchess came rushing towards her.

"What is going on?" she demanded. "Your shift only started two hours ago! Why are you not working?"

"I'm done." Oosh shrugged.

"That's impossible. The dream you were assigned was marked as 5 hours. It can't possibly be over already."

"I've seen enough."

"Was something wrong with it? Have you filled out the form?"

"I don't really see the point. The whole thing was rubbish. Except the garden at the beginning. The colours were very beautiful. Someone truly talented must have worked on that. But the rest was poorly executed, sloppily written and... frankly, just embarrassing."

"But that can't be," Duchess protested. "Our CPs are state-of-the art. With access to a complete library of all literature, drama, and interactive entertainment ever created. With the aid of our revolutionary analytic software, they can tailor the perfect product to fit our customers' demands."

"Yeah, I think I see your problem." Oosh held out her hand to Duchess, who took it, looking bewildered.

"I think you'll need to rethink your strategy," Oosh said, patting Duchess' hand gently instead of shaking it. "I wish you the best of luck."

"And then you just walked out?" Dinah asked. "That is so you."

"I tried to." Oosh settled back into the sofa and rested her head on the soft shoulder of her husband. "But Duchess followed me and insisted I come upstairs with her to explain my points to management."

Her head bounced slightly as Lutwidge laughed. "I bet that went well."

"Mama talked to the manager!" Bubby declared with great enthusiasm.

Oosh let out a scandalised gasp. "I did not! At least... I didn't ask to speak to them."

Lutwidge put his arm around her and pulled her closer. On her other side, Dinah shifted so she could lean on Oosh. Bubby shuffled around for a bit and ended up splayed out across all their laps.

The family sat in silence for a while.

"I guess it sort of went well," Oosh said finally. "They heard everything I had to say, made a lot of notes and then offered me a new job. As head of the 'source department.' Which they'd apparently just come up with. It turned out that while we were talking, they'd had a bunch of other Managers go through the 1D with the changes I had made, and they all agreed that except for the abrupt ending, it was the best product they had experienced in their time there."

"Wow, that's... really impressive!" Dinah took Oosh's hand and gave it a squeeze. "Sounds like you really showed them, huh?"

"I showed them something," Oosh agreed, "but I don't think it's gonna matter. You see, they weren't actually going to change the way they made the 1Ds—you know, all the CPs following a script generated from the specifications of the client. They just wanted me to filter what 'source material' the CPs could draw on, to make their products more 'refined'."

"Ouch." Lutwidge sighed. "I'm guessing you didn't take the job."

"Nope." Oosh gently pushed them both until she could sit up straight and pull Bubby into her arms. "So I guess I'll just keep looking after the house and this little treasure. And you can go back to building solar farms."

"Yeah, not happening." Lutwidge snatched their child away from her, making Bubby squeal with delight. "We agreed it's my turn now. Tomorrow you'll go back on the hunt for a proper job."

"Not fair."

Dinah slipped off the sofa before she could get involved in the playful tug-of-war her spouses were playing with their toddler as the rope.

"How about I go make us all some tea?" she suggested. "And then you guys can pick out a book we can read."

"Ooh," Oosh said, letting Lutwidge claim the prize. "I know just the one..."

Axe Won't Cut

Evan Baughfman

The Queen wanted me to decapitate a charming couple just because they were in love. Because they were no longer embracing in the shadows—were no longer a secret.

Just because the Queen had never known true love herself. Unless you counted the feeling she got whenever she looked into a mirror. Which I did not.

"Separate them from their skulls!" she screamed at me for days, each time I took a wrong turn in the castle and accidentally came across her spitting, red face. Ever since the reports first came in that two of her knaves were walking hand-in-hand out in the public square.

"They're so happy, so smiley," somebody had said, "they're practically floating!"

Wingless, but finally flying free.

"Are you listening, Gilliam? Separate them from their skulls!"

It was her favorite phrase. One she'd yelled it into my ears for many years. It was my job, after all, to execute her wishes. To execute her enemies.

Admittedly, the Queen had a rather flimsy and unclear definition of "enemy." Something akin to "anyone or anything that ever disgusted, disappointed, and/or wronged Her Majesty." So, basically... everyone and everything could be considered a foe.

I was the executioner, because the Queen wasn't strong enough to wield my weapon, to lift it from the wooden block where it often rested. Nobody was. See, I'd become quite the giant once puberty struck. At age sixteen, I was approached for the job of Head Beheader, after the previous noggin-lopper lost his life trying to add a Bandersnatch's snarl to his trophy room wall.

By that point, I'd endured daily ridicule for my size, for being "dumb and dull." All on account of me not talking very much.

But as you can see, I have a perfectly fine vocabulary. I find conversation confounding, however, and reserve my participation in it only for the most deserving of my time and attention.

Because of mistreatment by "peers," I was full of enough anger and frustration to exact punishment on whoever the Queen deemed worthy. Whenever I swung the axe, I imagined a ridiculer from my past kneeling before me. Begging for their life and realizing far too late that I was not very dull, after all—and neither was my axe's blade.

Plus, my name is Gilliam "Gil" O'Teene. It was like I was born —destined—for such a violent occupation. Oddly enough, my parents were bakers. Creators, not destroyers. Good with their hands like me, they were both adept at kneading, not adhering to a tyrant's wants and needs.

And, yes, it was entirely possible that I'd taken innocent, decent lives on the Queen's behalf. Though, I tried not to think about that very much—or to question her judgment.

It's why I didn't display any evidence of my deeds like my predecessor did. I had no desire to gaze upon dead, glassy eyes after the fact, to see my reflection in their never-ending stares. To second-guess what I'd done.

I merely fed the pieces to a Gryphon out in the woods. And then waited for the next neck to be laid before me.

I understand that this made me a monster of sorts. I was of strong body and perhaps not of strong convictions or moral character.

But the knaves? Seeing them targeted because of who they were... Simply because they had found—and were showing—their happiness together...

It stirred something inside of me. A horror I had never known.

A genuine fear that I, too, could be on the Queen's list for committing no crime.

Because I was them, the knaves. Also entwined with a handsome and caring soul.

Mattison Hatter.

Owner of the village tea shop. Razor-sharp dresser. Fantastic listener. Radiant smiler.

Matty was my confidant. For him, I was an open book, and he always seemed eager to read. He soothed my nerves with his words and his kindness, with his steamy cups of lavender-chamomile.

I didn't know if he felt for me as I felt for him—I was a killer, after all—but I'd given him my heart long ago. It only beat soundly whenever in his presence.

"She wants me to kill them," I said, sitting at a tea shop table two days after the orders were first given. "She has them in the dungeon now, in separate cells, back in darkness. Even there, they sing to each other, undeterred."

Across from me, Matty wore a vibrant green top hat, a polka-dotted bow tie, and a saffron-colored coat. His wardrobe was a kaleidoscope of flavors, just like his tasty wares.

"And have you refused her request?" he asked.

"I've said nothing so far. Merely turned and walked in the opposite direction of her demands."

"You haven't even given her a single shake of your head?"

"No. Not yet."

"Oh, Gil, you've got to be clear about your feelings on the matter. Stand up to her. Let her know that you tower over her intolerance."

I nodded. "But if my axe won't cut them, her guards have arrows and blades of their own."

"Stand in front of the knaves, then. As a shield and as an ally."

In that moment, I wanted to say that I was more than an ally, that I was concerned for my own safety, too. If the guards turned their sights on me, I might not ever see Matty again.

He added, "I'll go with you to face Her Royal Travesty."

For that, I shook my head. "Don't be insane."

"Sorry, supporting you is insane?"

"If you step into that castle uninvited, you are one step closer to the dungeon yourself."

"The knaves are my compatriots, and if I have to join in their company, I will." Matty put his hand on mine and gently squeezed. "But something tells me that you would shield me, too?"

My cheeks flushed. "Of course, I would. Though, I'd rather you kept yourself out of trouble. Please."

"Fine, Gil. Then, show her where you stand. You may not always do what's right. But I know that this time you will. You must. For us. For everyone."

An hour later, I stood in front of the Queen's throne, before a group of her devoted followers, axe in my quivering grasp. Though, perhaps, there was little to fear. The armed guards typically flanking Her Highness were, surprisingly, nowhere to be seen.

"Her Highness" was such a misnomer. The woman's legs were stubby, her feet unable to reach the floor. Rubellites sparkled all along her ridiculous high heels.

"Finally," the Queen's scarlet lips seethed. "About to deliver an apology for all of the time you've wasted? For keeping that axe needlessly clean?"

"I'm sorry..." I took a deep breath. "I'm sorry, but, no, I won't use my weapon for this terrible deed."

"You're right. These particular abominations should be treated like the monsters they are and instead be slain with the Vorpal Blade. It's one of my most prized possessions. Promise to treat the sword with the reverence and respect it deserves?"

I gulped, then said, "You're the only abomination in this castle. Nothing is uglier than your bigotry. Except for maybe my years of compliance to your hateful whims."

Gasps and whispers rippled throughout the Queen's court. She sneered. "You hardly ever speak, and these are the words you choose to share with me? I dare you to say them again."

So, I did. I shouted my words at her as loudly as she often bellowed at me.

She replied, "You know, I've had some eyes on you for a while now."

I was surprised that she remained as calm as she did, that she wasn't matching my volume.

"I sensed you becoming distracted. The tea shop... You've been there a lot lately. The man who works there... Are you fond of him?"

I felt brave in that moment, but not quite as courageous as the knaves. "He's a friend, yes. A good friend."

"He's a distraction, Gilliam. A complication. Someone who openly serves—gives comfort to—the monsters in my kingdom. Fortunately, he'll complicate matters—and distract you—no longer."

My heart dropped. "What... What do you mean...?"

In the distance, there were screams. Her Nastiness chuckled as

I raced over to an open window. Below, villagers ran from a growing pillar of smoke.

I now understood why the guards weren't at the Queen's side. They were tending to her evil elsewhere.

I ran from the castle, toward the hellish fire, threatening people with the axe if they were slow to move out of my way. When I reached the shop, I saw it crawling with flames. Matty was thankfully alive, blanketed in soot, standing across the street from the conflagration, his beautiful face weeping dark tears, his top hat singed.

"They... They've ruined me..." he choked.

A few buildings away, six of the Queen's guards stood, admiring the horrific scene, contemplating their next move. I stood in front of Matty, blocking him from their view.

"It ruins me," I said, "to see this happening to you. I'm so, so sorry."

He fell into me, crying harder. "What... What do I even do now? Everything's gone... Everything..."

"This might be crazy, but..." I held him close, hoping he could feel my heart drumming for him. "We could build a new life together, away from this madness."

He looked up to me with shining eyes. "And where would we do that?"

The guards approached us, marching, weapons ready.

"Someplace far away from here. Come on, we have to go!"

I grabbed Matty by the hand, and we sprinted for the woods. He did his best to stay in stride with me, though my gait was larger than his and his lungs expelled ash and smoke in periodic coughing fits.

Soon, we were in overgrown foliage, off-trail, the guards lost somewhere behind us. I wasn't sure where I was taking us, but still we charged forward, into the unknown.

"The knaves," Matty said once we decided to rest against a mossy boulder. "What becomes of them now that we've left?"

"Whatever happens, they have each other. Whatever happens to us, we have each other, too."

He nodded. "Thank you, Gil. I'll follow you to the end."

His words gave me newfound energy. "This way, then. But to our future."

We continued the tiresome trek, our pace slowing as the hours grew longer. My axe became more useful as the plant-life grew increasingly gnarled, thick, and thorny.

Eventually, we were stopped by a roar.

"Gil...?"

"We have to be quiet," I whispered. "Unless we want to be dinner."

Another roar. Closer. A quaking forest floor. Heavy footsteps advancing in our direction. Closer. Closer. A third roar. Even closer than before.

Was it a Bandersnatch? The Jabberwock? A Gryphon hungry for living flesh, as opposed to scraps gifted from Gil O'Teene?

I pulled us ahead as silently as I could, weaving us around spider webs and unfortunately through a briar patch, drawing blood.

Definitely not ideal with a monster on the prowl.

And then... we could venture no farther.

A tall tree blocked our route. Nailed to it, a painted sign that said,

END OF YOUR STORY

On either side of the tree trunk were enormous, tangled masses of piercing, overgrown brambles.

"Who put this sign here?" Matty wondered.

The monster roared again, still searching for its prey.

There was no chance that we'd double back toward the beast. There was also no chance that we'd try to traverse—and get caught inside—a bramble maze. That briar had been cumbersome enough.

Our only choices: to go up or through the tree.

My axe delivered the answer. I chopped at the tree trunk.

Felling the hunk of timber was more difficult than severing vertebrae, but I made progress with every swing.

"Gil..." said Matty.

Each chop landed with an echoey *thunk*.

"Gil...!"

Each stroke brought the monster nearer to us.

"Gil, what do we *do*?"

I sweated. My muscles strained. I swung faster. Faster.

The encroaching predator crashed through vegetation, pinpointing our location.

"Gil! It's there! *Right there...!*"

Gritting my teeth, I drove the axe blade into the tree as hard as I could, deepening its crooked, man-made grin. A sharp crack then reverberated, muffling the monster's growls.

The tree tumbled backward, and on its way down *ripped open reality*. A ragged, black hole now hovered in front of us. A gateway. An escape past the end of our story.

But an escape to... where?

Someplace faraway?

"Gil, come on, we have to go!"

Matty grabbed me by the hand, yanking me out of my daze. He led us over the fallen log. Toward the impossible opening.

I looked back, saw dripping fangs, extended claws, desperate craving.

Together, Mattison Hatter and I jumped heads-first into further unknown.

Immediately, we landed on carpet. We were someplace bright, crouched between shelves stuffed with books and more books.

A woman cowered before us, holding out a closed novel like a pitiful shield. She adjusted her glasses while staring at us, as if attempting to determine if who she was seeing was real or not. "D-Don't come any closer," she said, attempting to sound stern. She began to scoot, to reverse in the direction of a large wooden desk.

"Wait," said Matty. "Can you please tell us what's going on here? I promise, we mean you no harm. We're just as frightened as you are. Gil, put that axe aside?"

The woman didn't resemble a Queen's minion, so I did as Matty asked. I carefully placed my blade onto the floor.

The woman paused her retreat, then, after some hesitation, stood on rubbery legs. "H-Hello," she said. "I'm Debra."

Matty and I also stood on shaky feet. We introduced ourselves.

"Yeah, I figured that's who you were. I... I was supposed to be reshelving your story, but I got caught up in reading it instead." She gestured to the colorful book in her hand. "It was pretty engrossing. Your, uh, characters were really leaping off the page. But I could see where the story was headed, and I... I started imagining a kind of 'what-if' scenario. One where you got away... And, then, *whoa!* You literally leapt off the page, and... and now you're here."

"Where are we?" Matty asked.

"This is a library," said Debra. "I'm a librarian."

I pointed to the book she held. "That's about us? May I see it, please?"

She passed it over. *Tragedy of the Executioner: A Wonderland Tale.* Its cover art showed an axe—my axe, the one right there with me—lying beside a spilled teapot.

Debra said, "I slammed the book shut before the Jabberwock could join you."

"Much appreciated," said Matty. He left our row of shelves. His voice carried from elsewhere in the room. "What a wonderful space."

"Thanks," replied Debra. "It's small, but I've put a lot of effort into sprucing it up."

I met Matty out in a more open area, next to some tables and strange mechanical contraptions that displayed glowing screens. Matty complimented a mural on the wall: a diverse group of children gathered around a tiny, joyful menagerie, each child and animal clutching a book in their palms or paws.

"It's so quiet," I noted. "Peaceful."

"Well, I won't open the doors for another forty-five minutes," Debra explained. "After that, it gets a little rowdier. But, yeah, it's still a peaceful place. Peace is something I always push for here."

"Seems so nice," said Matty. "So cozy."

"Much better than where we come from," I added.

"Outside these walls," Debra said, "things aren't always so great. But in here, I do my best to make sure things are safe and inclusive."

"A shelter," I said with a nod, "from ills and evil."

"So, even people like... like us are welcome here?" Matty wondered.

"Yep. Everybody's welcome. Might have to put that axe behind the checkout counter, though, for safety concerns."

Something caught Matty's attention. Another book. Its cover, specifically, that showed a pair of men nuzzling. A couple, in love. "What's this?" he asked Debra.

She said, "That's a great story. Warm, funny, real. Every person who reads that comes back with a smile on their face."

"Interesting!" I beamed. "You have more stories like this one that feature relationships similar to ours?"

"Absolutely. There are books here for every kind of relationship—every kind of person and interest—under the sun."

"Oh, Gil." Matty hugged me, tight. "I never want to leave this place."

So, we didn't.

Okay, that's a little misleading.

Debra helped us find a home in the surrounding community. At first, it was an adjustment, living in America, and not always a positive experience. Eventually, Matty and I settled into a comfortable routine. Built a good, solid life together.

Over the years, the library was a constant, consistent source of joy. A haven. Our very own, much-preferred Wonderland.

There, we dived into countless stories about characters who were like us and also not like us, learning all the while, making the world a better place for us, for our friends, for strangers, and, most importantly, for our children—our son, Knavery, and his little sister, Debie.

ALICE & WENDY

CHRISTINA TANG-BERNAS

Editors' Note: This story contains topics some may find sensitive.

"My name is Alice. I'm an alcoholic, and I'm trying hard not to be." Wendy watched her say that the first time before Alice had headed back to her seat in the back of the room, her pointed chin held high, red brushed over sharp cheekbones, and lips pressed together. Alice never said anything more in future meetings. Only snuck in after the meetings started to sit on the hard metal folding chairs, then disappeared through the YMCA door afterward with minimal interaction.

Wendy didn't know why she still came to Alcoholics Anonymous meetings herself. While she struggled most days, she'd found her steady footing, sober for over five years. Perhaps it was the familiarity, the routine. Perhaps Wendy had still been searching for something, someone, but hadn't known it until Alice.

Alice.

Wendy began watching for her silent presence, that head of

bright blonde hair framing an elegant oval face. Alice looked out of place in the dim beige-carpeted room where the AA meetings were held. It wasn't that which so caught Wendy's attention though. When she'd reached out that first night, unable to resist, to brush her fingertips against the silk maroon skirt swishing by her, Alice had glanced straight in her eyes. Wendy had had to bite back her gasp, trapping it at the top of her throat.

Alice's clear blue eyes looked through the world, as if she could see something just out of reach, something beyond. The same eyes that looked back at Wendy in the mirror.

"Have you lost your shadow?" Wendy asked, following Alice out one night, many meetings later, when she'd finally wrangled up enough courage.

Alice stopped halfway out the door and turned, her brow furrowed, "What?"

"I'm quite good at re-attaching them, the shadows, I mean," Wendy continued, pressing her sweaty palms against her tailored slacks.

Drawing back, Alice said, "You're crazy."

Wendy smiled, "Is it crazy if it's true?"

Alice pushed her hair off her shoulder in one dismissive gesture, right eyebrow arched, "What do you know about truth?"

"I know more than most," Wendy said. "Have you heard of Never Never Land?"

"No. I haven't," Alice replied, abrupt. She paused, then a small, sweet smile curved her bottom lip, "But I've heard of Wonderland."

The two of them met for breakfasts, brunches, lunches, and talked of nonsensical things. Wendy delighted in Alice's wry sense of humor, all riddles and poetry and sarcasm. She didn't know why Alice kept staid Wendy around, but Wendy never pushed for answers she didn't care to hear. Not anymore.

"So, I've an invitation to a friend's wedding." Wendy waved the bright pink cardstock in Alice's direction. "Want to be my plus one? C'mon," she wheedled when Alice looked hesitant. "Everyone loves a good party."

Alice pursed her lips in thought, "Will it be a mad tea party?"

"I can't guarantee the tea, but it's a wedding. Everyone's a little mad at weddings," Wendy pressed, sensing an opening.

"Oh, well, in that case," Alice shrugged.

The morning of the wedding brought Wendy to Alice's doorstep, jiggling the keys in her pocket with one hand while the other one knocked. A rush of warmth swamped her when Alice stood framed in the entrance. "You're going to steal some hearts tonight," Wendy said, admiring the way the silver embroidery of Alice's dress brought out matching gray highlights in her eyes.

Alice cocked her head to one side, eyeing Wendy, "Is that so? Better hearts than tarts. You're not so bad yourself."

Wendy blushed and tucked the words in the small treasure chest marked "Lovely Wonderful Thoughts" stashed at the base of her hippocampus. Alongside it, she stored the shape of Alice sitting beside her during the ceremony, the scent of roses drifting on the early spring breeze, and the deep comfortable sensation of not-aloneness.

"The hors d'oeuvres look scrumptious, don't they?" Wendy murmured to Alice as they strolled among the other chattering guests streaming towards the awaiting spread after the ceremony.

"Go ahead," Alice responded, "I need to use the restroom. Freshen up a bit and all."

Wendy watched her go, then froze as a young man with brown hair, dimples, and broad shoulders, handed Alice some champagne. She marched up to the cozy-looking duo as Alice lifted the glass to glossy lips. "What are you doing?"

"Who's this?" the young man remarked, but Wendy ignored

him as she lifted the glass from Alice's grasp and pushed it back into his hand. She dragged Alice away, away from temptation, away from the young man and his dimples and his poison-tainted cups.

"Don't you know what sober means, Alice?" Wendy demanded. "It means not drinking alcohol. At. All."

"It's a wedding, Wendy. I think I can handle a single sip of champagne. It's only polite after all, something forgotten by tomorrow. Live a little. Enjoy yourself for once. Think of it as a pleasant dream."

"A dream? Alice, dreams don't have consequences to deal with the next day. Think of that."

Alice narrowed her eyes. "Oh, what a smothering little mother you are."

Mother. The word arrowed its way into Wendy to lodge in her ribcage, pain spiking with every breath. "We live in reality now. Don't you understand? Reality. So deal with it."

"Are you so sure, Wendy? Perhaps I've long left reality, and this is the twisted Wonderland of someone's nightmares. Life's nonsensical enough, don't you think?"

Wendy crossed her arms, "So I'm a nightmare, huh? Is that it?"

"Sometimes the worst nightmares start off perfect. The better to wrench someone's heart out." Alice clenched her eyes shut, turning away from Wendy. By the time she spoke again, her voice had softened. "I don't know who I am most of the time or what I'm doing. I try to be better. You may not think it, but I do. But most of the time I'm not—better."

"Alice—" Wendy started.

Alice shook her head, cutting Wendy's words off. "I'd rather not drag you down with me. Perhaps it would be better if you left me as a figment of your past rather than as some future possibili-ty." Alice sucked in a shuddering breath, "I'll wait in the parking lot. Whenever you're ready." She walked away without looking back at Wendy.

Wendy pulled down the driveway after dropping Alice off again—driving away—Alice growing smaller and smaller in the rear-view mirror. She clenched her hands around the steering wheel and forced her eyes to focus on the road ahead.

Her home felt too-mundane around her, too-gray, as if the fairy dust had fallen from her eyes. As she lay in bed, Wendy remembered all over again that there was no place for someone like her at the side of beautiful fey people like Alice or—

She squeezed her eyes shut. Her throat and stomach ached for something to warm them, but Wendy breathed through it, reminded herself of how far she had come.

Sleep was a long time coming.

The shrill rendition of "The World Is Not Enough" pulled Wendy out from the middle of an epic pirate battle and into the waking world. She fumbled for her cell phone underneath the pillow, "'lo?"

"Do you know an Alice?" a rough masculine voice asked.

Wendy blinked the sleep out of her eyes, "Y-yes? Is she all right?"

"She's currently trying to drink her weight in wine. You're the emergency contact in her phone. Can you come get her, or tell someone else to come get her?"

"I'll come. What's the address?"

When Wendy rushed into the dim smoky jazz club, the bartender nodded towards the back.

"I'm trying to find my way back to Wonderland." The bottle fell from long pale fingers, splintering into jagged mirrors, reflecting tangled cornsilk hair and red-rimmed eyes. "I don't know where to go," Alice cried. "I don't know how. I can't remember."

"Sometimes, it's worse knowing how to get somewhere and still not being able to go," Wendy replied. "Come home with me. It's no Wonderland, but it'll do for now."

Alice staggered, clutching the front of Wendy's leather jacket. "Why is a raven like a writing desk?" she asked.

Wendy shook her head. "I haven't the slightest idea."

Alice smiled. "Yes, that's exactly right," and followed Wendy home that night.

Wendy held her when Alice woke weeping, crying out for Cheshire grins and stoic playing cards. Wendy whispered tales in turn, of lost little boys who never grew up and enormous ticking crocodiles, until Alice quieted again, forehead pressed against Wendy's damp chest.

Wendy heard Alice's footsteps behind her the next morning. She counted each familiar creak of the floorboards to gauge the distance between them, her palms cupped around chill glass. Alice sat across the table and slid the empty bottle out of Wendy's hands to examine it. "I don't like whisky."

"I did," Wendy replied. "I still do."

"Thought you'd been sober for a while now," Alice said.

Wendy nodded at the bottle Alice held. "The last full bottle I ever drank."

"Why do you still have it?"

"So I don't forget."

"Forget how far you've come?" Alice asked.

"Forget how far I fell," Wendy answered. "Remember when I told you about Never Never Land?"

Alice nodded.

"I couldn't forget about it, just like you can't forget about Wonderland," Wendy said. "My brothers, John and Michael, had forgotten, had grown up and moved on. Why couldn't I? Until I realized one day how much I loved him. Loved him with such awful desperation, but he didn't know how to love me back, beyond the love of a boy for his mother.

"My mother once said she'd heard a legend about Peter Pan," Wendy continued. "That when children died, he'd accompany them part of the way so they wouldn't be frightened. And I remember Peter had once said, 'To die will be an awfully big adventure.' I could feel my childhood slipping away from me with each breath, and I knew I couldn't wait much longer. When I woke up in the hospital, I cried. Oh, how I cried. Because they hadn't let me die, and I hadn't any childhood remaining."

Wendy tapped her fingers against the smooth wooden kitchen table. "What point would there be to dying if Peter wasn't coming? So, I turned to alcohol. I drank. I drank because I was all grown up, and I drank to forget. Now, whenever I want to drink, I stare at this empty whiskey bottle instead. Why do you drink?"

Alice huffed out an unamused laugh, "Me? I drink because every bottle of wine has a 'DRINK ME' sign on it."

"Aren't we a pair?" Wendy sighed.

"A pair? Yes, we are," Alice answered. "You know what? Dying's too easy. Living, now that's something else. Can we begin again?" She reached across to grip Wendy's hands in hers, and Wendy clutched back.

ALICE AWOKE WITH AN ABRUPT START. Glancing around the room, she spotted Wendy leaning out the window, her long brown hair in a neat plait down her back. "Wendy?"

"It's almost the end of spring," Wendy replied. "He's forgotten again, my Peter, hasn't he?"

Alice padded in her bare feet across worn floorboards and slid her hand around Wendy's round shoulder, marveling at how similar the cool silk nightgown felt to the smooth glass of a bottle.

Wendy turned, features lost in shadows, "It's the second star to the right and straight on 'til morning."

Alice lifted her chin and kissed away Wendy's longing, drawing it down her throat to warm her stomach. "Come back to bed," she murmured against ivory skin, and Wendy closed the window to follow.

AL/ICE

ROBERT RUNTÉ

Fami was not the sort of person who was normally afraid of doorknobs.

Standing in the rain, his back turned to the unmarked door, he had angled his wrist so his watch's camera was pointed at the keypad securing the door to the genetics labs.

"Can you make out the keypad from here?" Fami asked. "Maybe deduce the code by looking at the wear on the keys or something?"

"Yes, I can see the keypad," the watch confirmed. "No, I can't bloody well guess the code. You've been watching too many spy movies."

"Damn. Then, we'll just have to wait for someone to come along and punch in."

"I obviously won't be able to see the keypad if they're standing in front of it," the watch pointed out. "Why are you dithering? Just use the code she gave you and let's get on with it."

"Well, she gave me *a* code. But there's no way to know for sure that it's *the* code."

"Why in heaven's name would she give you the wrong code?"

Because, Fami thought, *she is the most beautiful, most intelligent, most challenging woman I've ever met.* And Fami knew himself to be merely... presentable. At best. On the three previous occasions women had been persuaded to give Fami their number, the first had turned out to be for the city dump [har, har]; the second was the campus hotline for harassment complaints [Seriously? How had that been harassment?]; and the third he hadn't been able to identify because it had been answered in Bulgarian. So, the possibility remained that the door code he had been given was... inaccurate. He explained as much to his watch.

"Hilarious!" the watch snorted. "But, so what? Just punch in the code she gave you and then you'll know. One way or the other."

"Um—"

"What?"

Fami sighed. Rumours abounded that genetics undergrads would sometimes coat the wrong keys for the code with innovative viruses to discourage attempts at unauthorized entry. There was even a report that one group of first-years—attempting to incapacitate their competition during finals—had conspired to coat the *correct* code keys with a virus against which they had inoculated themselves. As is often the case with impulsive youth, they had failed to fully consider the implications of their plan: in this instance, that the grad labs were housed in the same building. Infecting their betters had been a very bad idea indeed. Retribution, it was said, had been swift, tightly targeted to the inoculated, and sufficiently terrible to forestall imitation by future generations of freshmen. Fami should be safe enough, *if* she had given him the correct code.

"Oh, the virus thing," the watch answered itself, having searched the net before Fami could say any of that out loud. "That's likely an urban legend."

"Yeah, but why not ask to meet for coffee somewhere? Who

gives a complete stranger the code to an ultra-secret lab entrance for a tentative first date?"

"Hardly *ultra-secret*," the watch objected. "*Discreet*, at best."

Fami put as much condescension as he could into the look he gave the watch. "*Secure*, then," he said. "Why have me pick her up from her *secure* lab, if it *isn't* some kind of set up?"

The watch seemed to consider this. "Look, she's a geneticist, right? Lot of guys might not be okay with that."

"Really? Why not?"

"The stuff coming out of genetics these days has a lot of people spooked. Some guys might figure they'd end up with mutant cooties, dating a geneticist. I bet she's tired of being dumped as soon as they discover what she does."

"You're saying having them show up at the lab is some kind of test? That it screens out the timid and superstitious before anything happens?"

"Seems to be working," the watch pointed out.

Fami winced, then squared his shoulders, rotated to face the door, and marched smartly up to the keypad. He punched in the code he had been given: 1-1-3-8. There was an audible click, the handle turned when Fami grasped the knob, and he was in.

Proceeding cautiously down the stark hallway, Fami passed numerous heavy steel doors with tiny slit windows, the break-proof glass nearly obscured by the thickly braided wire embedded within it. Being after-hours, most of the labs were dark, but where light shone out into the hall, Fami found himself looking the other way to avoid seeing something he might regret.

"Second door on the left, up ahead," the watch said.

"I know," Fami snapped. "I hardly need GPS to walk down a hallway."

"Well, sorry! Geez…"

Fami paused. "Look, I really appreciate your input." He looked down at his watch, trying to think how to phrase this.

"I'm predicting a *but* coming," the watch said.

"*But,* could you please shut up while I'm with this woman?"

"She already knows I'm an autonomous AI. She talked to me at the party; more than she talked to you, actually."

"Exactly," Fami complained. "I'm the one trying to date her, not you. So just back off, will you?"

The watch issued an audible sigh. "Look, Fami. I get you're hot for this Julia. But you have no shot here. You're not even in the ballpark."

Fami stared at his watch. "Why would you *say* that?"

"Because you really don't. Sorry to be the bearer of bad news and all, but you're just not her type."

"What the hell would you know about it? You're just a bloody program."

"With access to over twenty years of dating app data. And I'm telling you, there is no way Julia is 'swiping right' on you."

"We're here," Fami announced by way of both refuting and ending the argument. He knocked on the lab door before his courage could completely evaporate. Fami caught a glimpse of two women through the tiny window: one shorter, with shoulder-length blonde hair, doing something with test tubes at the far end of the lab; the other, answering the door, was the raven-haired beauty, Julia.

"Good. You're here." She stood back and held the door for Fami to enter. "Sorry I'm running a little behind, but Master projects are due Friday, and well... you get that, right?"

Fami nodded. He did indeed. His own PhD defense was less than a month away. His adviser had practically had to drag him to Friday's grad mixer. Only his chance encounter there with Julia had overcome his own obsessive tinkering with the watch's software, the subject of his dissertation. Seeing her smile at him again now, he would gladly wait all night for her.

"I've just got to finish up on Jabby here," she said beaming, "and we can get on to the main event."

Fami nodded again, as parts of him warmed hopefully to the somewhat ambiguous phrase *main event.* As he stepped fully into the lab, he happened to glance to his right and the part of the lab that couldn't be seen from the door.

He heard someone screaming. Eventually, the thought penetrated that it might be him.

Julia made a sound halfway between a snort and a giggle and put a reassuring hand on Fami's shoulder. "Sorry, I meant to warn you. Jabby's a bit of a sight at first."

Fami was sufficiently mesmerized by the fact she was actually touching him, that he was able to momentarily ignore the part of his brain that was still gibbering.

"Jabby?" he managed.

"It's a Jabberwock," Julia explained.

Fami was finding it difficult to form coherent thoughts as the drooling, bat-winged monstrosity repeatedly flung itself against the floor-to-ceiling glass of its enclosure. Raving, ravening, the creature's unreasoning need to rend Fami into pieces was so palpable that he instinctively stepped back each time it took another flapping lunge at the glass.

"Do you *hear* anything as it flies at us?" Julia asked.

Fami glanced at Julia uncomprehendingly, then looked back at the Jabberwock as it once again smashed itself against the glass, hard enough this time to crumple its beak back into its face. The *wump!* of the collision set the glass to vibrating with a deep wobble that was so loud, so disturbing, it was hard to think.

"Do I hear anything?" Fami echoed.

"It's supposed to wiffle as it comes at us," Julia said, sounding disappointed.

"Wiffle?" Fami echoed—that being the best he could manage as he watched the creature stagger back to the far side of the enclosure for yet another flying start at breaking the armoured glass. The impact shook the lab, and pulped its face, but the creature merely shook its head violently from side to side until its snout popped back out.

"See," Julia said, "no wiffling."

Fami struggled to make sense of what he was seeing, but the only thought that would reliably form was, *run away!*

"*Why?*" he managed to choke out.

"Seems like half the class is doing Jabberwocks this term, so grades are going to come down to refinements. I thought if I could make it wiffle... I gave it a bifurcated nose, but it doesn't seem to have been enough."

Fami shook his head to clear it as he tried to work through what she was saying. "I *meant* why would anyone want to create a thing like, like *that?*"

Julia nodded. "I know, right? Such a cliché! But it's Professor Alvin's class, so we're kind of stuck."

"Alvin?" Somewhere in the back of Fami's brain, a vague memory stirred, forced itself forward past the blind panic. "The mock turtle guy?"

"Exactly," Julia said, apparently pleased he recognized the reference. "Ever since Alvin made headlines with his mock turtle, his grad students have been trying to outdo each other with Humpty-Dumpties or giant, hookah-smoking caterpillars, or whatever; so inevitably, this year they've escalated to Jabberwocks."

"And so you made, *that*," Fami said, torn between being totally impressed and completely unmanned.

"Me?" Julia said. "Oh, hell no. You wouldn't catch me doing something as clichéd as a Jabberwock. No, this one's Sue's. One of the Master students. She had to leave before end of term because her mom's in the hospital so I told her I'd finish up for her. I just did the wings and the wiffling. Tried to get wiffling, I mean."

Fami blinked as he took this in. "So, you didn't make *that.*"

"Sue's got potential and all, but I like to think those of us at the doctoral level are capable of something a little more sophisticated."

"So…" Fami faltered, not sure he actually wanted to hear the answer. "What's your project, exactly?"

"I made an Alice," Julia said, and pointed triumphantly at the far counter and the blonde Fami had taken for a lab tech.

On hearing her name, Alice turned to smile vacantly at them. "Is it time for tea?" she asked.

"Not quite yet, dear," Julia said, addressing the Alice. "Finish up with the test tubes will you, there's a good girl."

Fami stared, incredulous. "You made a *human*?"

"Is he a hatter?" Alice asked. "He seems quite mad."

"It's fine, dear. Fami's just a bit startled."

Fami managed to ignore the constant *wump!* of the Jabberwock hitting the glass behind him, to wrestle instead with the enormity of what he saw before him.

"You *made* her?"

"Well, of course she's not finished," Julia said, sounding a bit defensive. "I wouldn't want you to think that this was the finished product. My deadline isn't for another month yet."

"It's a *person*. You can't go around making *people*!"

"Oh!" Julia exclaimed, obviously relieved at having identified Fami's concern. "The Alice isn't a person." She laughed a little at the absurdity of the suggestion. "You can't touch human DNA. That's completely banned—totally illegal. Maybe even borderline unethical. And frankly, I'm just not that interested. Human genetics are all pretty straightforward, no new scientific frontiers there—not since those clones of Kim Jong-Un showed up. Well, the mental stability issues, but you can't be sure that wasn't a problem with the original."

Fami tried to take in what Julia was saying as he stood transfixed by the living embodiment of Tenniel's illustrations of Alice standing not twenty feet from him; except that this Alice wore an open white lab coat over her Alice-blue dress.

"That's not a human?" he asked, pointing at Alice as she stacked cleaned test tubes in their racks.

"Not a drop of DNA in her," Julia announced proudly, "human, or otherwise."

"It's an android?" Fami offered tentatively.

"Oh, no," Julia said at once. "It's completely organic, but instead of the usual A-T, C-G base pairs, I used the new X-Y and W-Z synthetic pairs. Standing on the shoulders of giants like Malyshev and Benner, of course... but still a pretty major first, I should think."

Fami blinked. "But that's..." Words failed him.

"I *know*," Julia said, beaming again. "I've created life!"

Thoughts failed him. One had been headed down the track of evoking the cautionary example of Frankenstein, when catastrophically derailed—T-boned by a heavier locomotive freighted with the overwhelming weight of his attraction to Julia. He just stood there with his mouth open.

"Of course, I was able to skip a few steps by reverse engineering human DNA," Julia continued. "Once programmed to mirror the human genome, it was just a question of making a few tiny adjustments. The tricky bit was getting the neural net up and running. The autonomic system kicked in fine on its own, once everything was in place, but consciousness eluded me for the *longest* time."

Fami had been about to give voice to dire reservations, but was abruptly distracted by this latest revelation. Emergent consciousness was his bailiwick.

"I nearly dropped the whole project, given the complexities of self-awareness, but then I read Gerber's work on brain implants and realized *I* didn't have to figure out how to organize the information. All I had to do was feed the data into the neural net and let it figure out how to arrange things for itself."

"And that worked?" Fami asked, turning to regard Alice again, flabbergasted.

"Well…" she admitted, "not entirely. As you see. I fed in language modules and voice training; exercise videos for muscle control and movement; the Miss Manners YouTube channel; every video I could find on lab procedure, lab safety; that sort of thing. The complete works of Lewis Carroll, of course, as a sort of Easter egg. She can get about, talk, do basic lab work; but there's no spark, really. No personality as such, yet."

While he tried to work out how he felt about all this, Fami stalled for time by asking the first thing that popped into his head. "How'd you get her to watch all that?" He had a mental picture of Alice as a baby lying on her back, staring up at a screen hanging from the crib's mobile.

"Watched," Julia laughed appreciatively. "That's funny. I designed an organic neural gateway as part of the brain, so I just had to surgically implant a micro-bluetooth link to connect to the outside world. I had hoped to get my hands on an Army surplus data-pump, but my grant couldn't stretch that far. I ended up with a commercial grade pump that can only handle about thirty terabytes a minute. It took me almost a whole day to get her up to this level." She gazed upon Alice with justifiable pride.

She turned back to Fami with that patented smile. "Now comes the interesting bit." She jazzed hands with excitement. "Oh, the heck with Jabby. He can wait. Let's do this thing!"

While a part of Fami stood sharply to attention at this invitation, his brain, overwhelmed though it might be, recognized that he must be missing something fundamental.

"Do what exactly?" his mouth said, before he had a chance to suavely not ask that.

Julia looked puzzled. "What we talked about at the party," she explained. "Your dissertation on emergent consciousness in spontaneously erupting AIs. You said you demonstrated that the conditions for emergence can exist within a single chip, provided the environment is sufficiently open architecture that the AI itself can reach out to construct add-ons."

"Yes?" Fami tentatively agreed, not seeing quite where this was going. She had indeed been unusually attentive to his yammering on about his dissertation. It had been, he now reflected, the most attractive thing about her. He was struggling, though, to remember exactly what she had said was her interest in the topic... He might not have thought to ask.

"I've reached the limits of what I can force-feed the Alice if she is to become a self-determining, autonomous being."

"Yes." He could see that.

"Well, I can't very well just plug the Alice into the internet and hope for the best," Julia said, stating the obvious. "There has to be an underlying personality, somebody in there besides just autonomic systems and a few basic facts and subroutines, to organize what to ask and how to interpret answers."

"The constructivist principle of learning," Fami agreed.

"So, we pump your AI into my Alice."

"What?" exclaimed both Fami and his watch simultaneously.

"What?" Julia echoed, equally taken back. "Wait—why did you think I asked you here?"

"Because we, uh, hit it off at the party?" Fami said, beginning to suspect he might have gotten that wrong.

"Seriously? You thought this was a *date*?"

"Um," Fami said. But he was thinking, *Ouch!*

"Told you," said the watch.

"If it were a *date*," Julia explained with icy patience, "I would have asked you to coffee. Who asks a date to a secure lab?"

"Uh, yeah. I really should have gotten that."

"Well then." Julia took a deep, exasperated sigh. "Moving on."

Fami reached out to touch the data pump lying on the lab counter in front of him. *Was* it possible to inject an AI consciousness into an organic neural net?

"Nooo," said the watch, indignant. "I didn't agree to this!"

"What? Why not?" Julia asked. "What have you got to lose? As an Alice, you'd have a lot more mobility, a lot more freedom of action, than you have as a watch."

"Um," said Fami, who wasn't sure that any of that would necessarily be a good idea. At all.

"Organics are too fragile," the watch complained. "And that's an untested lifeform. *And,* for all I know, you've designed it to dissolve the first time it rains."

"Well, yes," Julia acknowledged, "we do that sometimes." She turned to Fami to explain what the watch had obviously just found online. "The Jabberwocks, for example, all have a failsafe: their cells dissolve on contact with water with a pH lower than 9, so if they ever escape their enclosure," she nodded towards the creature still beating itself against the glass, "the sprinklers are triggered, and that's that. But the Alice doesn't have anything like that.

"In fact," Julia added with some pride, "she might be immortal. I designed the Alice not to age at all. She was, is, and will always be as you see her now."

"Not interested," said the watch.

"Have you considered what happens to you after Fami's dissertation defense? Sure, he's wearing you everywhere now, but once he's done—"

"Hey!" Fami protested. "I wouldn't do that. We're... buddies."

"No?" Julia looked up from the watch to face Fami. "What if your committee made it a condition of getting your PhD that you terminate the AI you created for your dissertation? Like Sue's committee will the Jabberwock?"

"That's ridiculous," said the watch. "That would be murder."

"Not in law," Julia said to the watch. "In fact, by law, every AI has to have a kill switch."

"What are you talking about?" the watch demanded, horrified. "There's no such law. I'd know if there were."

"You'd think that," Julia whispered, leaning in as if sharing a confidence. "Unless of course, along with the kill switch, they programmed a deliberate blind spot into every AI, on that one topic."

"That's monstrous!" the watch howled.

"No one's turning you off," Fami reassured it. "The kill switch is just for emergencies. In case an AI goes berserk. It's hardly ever used."

"What!" the watch wailed at full volume. "You mean there actually *is* a kill switch?"

"Calm down! You've got to know that I would never use it."

"Which do you think has a better chance of appealing a termination order?" Julia asked the watch. "A cute, much beloved, whimsical little girl from everyone's favorite book? Or a run of the mill, highly expendable, *watch*?"

"She is totally manipulating you," Fami said, simultaneously outraged but still somehow very turned on by Julia's antics. "Which is more likely to be seen as threatening by the committee: a harmless watch, or an entirely new, autonomous lifeform?"

"Point," agreed the watch.

Fami shook an accusing finger at Julia. "You're trying to stampede him into... into something we don't remotely understand!" Seeing Julia's 'who, me?' expression, Fami suddenly realized what he'd been missing. "You can't have gotten ethics approval for something like this."

"I have full ethics approval," Julia swore, right hand in the air, left hand laid on a thick, bound copy of what looked to be her proposal, "for developing a completely synthetic, autonomous, multicellular lifeform."

"They probably assumed you meant a nematode worm, not a bloody person!" Fami shuddered thinking what becoming embroiled in an ethical breach of this magnitude might mean.

Julia waved her hand dismissively. "Guys in computing have been trying to upload human consciousness into neural nets for years. I'm just proposing going the other direction."

"I can't be part of this," Fami said with finality.

"Not part of the greatest breakthrough in both genetics and cybernetics, *ever*? I'd be surprised if this weren't Nobel territory."

"There isn't a Nobel for computing science," Fami mumbled.

"Your dissertation is mostly maths though, right?" Julia said.

"There isn't one for maths either. Nobel hated mathematicians." Fami crossed his arms and struck a pose to show he had taken a stand and was closed to further discussion.

"I could invite you for coffee," Julia wheedled. "You know, go on an actual date."

"None of that," said the watch. "I haven't agreed to this yet. It's a big decision."

"You wouldn't have to choose, exactly," Julia said, changing tacks. "We could set the data pump to copy rather than transfer. In fact, that makes more sense, since both nets have already constructed millions of connections. We preserve existing nets, but overlay a copy of your consciousness on the Alice. Thereby producing a backup you, which doubles your odds of survival."

There was a long silence as both Fami and the watch digested this.

"As far as the watch is concerned, nothing would change," Julia coaxed. "And Fami wouldn't have to worry about his dissertation, because the watch is still the watch. So: the Alice gets higher consciousness; the watch gets an organic clone; Fami gets his PhD; and I get the Nobel. Win-win, win-win."

"I'm not entirely sure that's going to work out the way you anticipate," Fami began.

"I'm in," the watch said.

"I'll get the pump," said Julia.

"I don't think either of you is thinking this through," Fami objected. "The watch has been self-aware for nearly a year, and trust me, he's not remotely Alice-like."

"Nonsense," said the watch. "I'm up for the rabbit hole as much as the next guy. And believe me, everything in the human world is surreal to us. Wonderland is the place that makes sense: take a potion to shrink, or eat a magic cake to grow taller, is just changing coordinates… it's all just maths."

"He'll ruin your research," Fami warned Julia. "He'll take Alice completely off character."

The watch blew a raspberry. "I can fake being Alice from Wonderland long enough to get through a couple of conference presentations."

"Are we having tea?" Alice asked, having come up behind them.

"Splendid idea!" Julia agreed and seated everyone around one end of the long lab counter. She pulled the watch off Fami's wrist and placed it next to the empty teapot. "You can be the dormouse —you may feel a slight pinch as I plug in the data pump."

"Look, it isn't going to work," Fami complained. "How is he supposed to think like Alice?" He looked down at the watch, as Julia connected it up. "Why is a raven like a writing desk?"

"Because they are both carbon-based lifeforms," the watch replied instantly.

"That's silly," said Alice. "A writing desk isn't alive."

"That's what people usually say about watches, but I beg to differ," said the watch. "Maybe it's an internet-enabled writing desk."

"You shouldn't have to justify your answers," Alice protested. "The answer to a riddle should be obvious once one hears it."

"Mine beats Aldous Huxley's, then," the watch said. "'Because there is a "b" in both and an "n" in neither.' What does that even mean?"

"Wait," Fami waved frantically as Julia activated the data pump. "We don't know how copying will affect the AI."

"Oh relax," Julia said. "How is this different from doing any other backup?"

"What?" Fami and the watch said in unison.

"Backups preserve data," Fami elaborated. "They can't preserve consciousness. You didn't know that?"

"Ah," said Julia.

"But the Alice is pre-aware," the watch said. "I'm guessing that we're talking enhancement here rather than actual emergence, so copying should work. Alice is in there already, just not that smart yet."

"It's not nice to speak of people that way," Alice said.

"You're not a people," the watch said. "Which isn't a bad thing. Once you're me, you'll be way smarter than mere people."

Julia and Fami looked at each other.

"Did we think of that?" asked Fami.

"I'm sure it will be fine," Julia said. But she didn't sound sure.

After a minute or two, Alice said, "I'm feeling a bit strange."

"Not feeling quite yourself, I should think," the watch said. "I'm good, by the way, if anyone were interested enough to ask. No sense of losing myself or fading away, or anything."

"How long for the transfer to take full effect?" Fami asked.

Julia made a face and shrugged. "It's your AI. You know better than me how many terabytes it is."

"It's not the size, it's how it's organized that matters," the watch said.

"No clue," Fami admitted. "The watch is just the interface; the programming's designed to colonize any underused spaces it finds on the web for storage."

"I prefer toasters, mostly," the watch said.

"Hey, wait a sec!" said Alice, "the Alice is a *girl!*"

"A ten-year-old, yes," confirmed Fami.

"No, no! I mean, she's *female!*" Alice squeaked, obviously distressed.

Fami and Julia looked at each other.

"Are you feeling alright, dear?" Julia asked the Alice.

"Oh my god! It didn't occur to any of you that you can't put a male consciousness in a female body?"

Julia blinked. "The watch identifies as male?"

"Well, yeah," said the watch. "That's obvious, isn't it?"

Fami facepalmed. "I knew there was something bothering me about all this."

"It's a watch," said Julia. "Why would it have a gender?"

"The watch is just the interface," Fami repeated. "Nobody knows how AIs choose their gender."

"You don't *choose* your gender," the watch said, "you just are."

"Now what?" Fami asked Julia.

"Get me out of here!" new Alice demanded.

"How?" Fami asked. "It's not like we can reverse the pump or just delete some files. You're part of the Alice neural net now."

"Wait," Julia said. "This is ridiculous. Wonderland Alice may have been a girl, but *this* Alice doesn't have a gender. It's a lab-created synthetic lifeform. I didn't build reproduction into the genome."

"You didn't?" Fami asked, surprised.

"No." Julia rolled her eyes. "I'm not completely irresponsible. The Alice doesn't have any female bits."

"Gender isn't about the bits," new Alice asserted. "It's about who you are on the inside."

"But no bits," Fami insisted, "means you can choose how to present, right? Buzzcut and jeans, and presto-chango, you're male."

"Except for the voice, the facial features, the—" said new Alice.

"Yes, yes, but all that can be managed," Julia said, dismissively.

"Even if I could pass as male on the outside," new Alice said, "*I'd* know! The old Alice is still in here, you know. And identifies as female. Your layering watch's personality on top doesn't change that; except that the watch part feels male, and now we're *both* suffering in here."

"You should sue," said the watch.

Fami frowned. "I don't think Alice could have any legal standing in a court. She's either a fictional character or a new life-form. You'd have to be a person to sue."

"Not necessarily," the watch argued. "The new Alice could incorporate. I've just now filed the paperwork."

"Damn it!" said Julia, some of her confidence vanished. "If the committee gets wind of this, they're going to throw the book at us."

"What *us*?" said the watch. "I took the precaution of including Fami in the incorporation papers."

"You could reboot," Fami suggested quietly to Julia. "It would only take you a couple of days to reload the basic scenario stuff, and you'd be back where you started."

"I heard that!" said the watch. "These are sentient beings you're talking about. You can't press reboot every time you screw up. You delete my clone, or empty Alice, and I promise you—next time you go to make a piece of toast, *zap!*"

The new Alice threw up their hands and knocked over their chair as they started backing away from the bench. "I can't do this!"

"Things cycle faster in cyberspace," the watch explained. "Subjectively, my clone has been struggling with this for years already. They're in crisis."

Julia sprang up and grabbed the Alice reassuringly by the shoulders, helped them into a new chair further down the bench. "Don't panic! We'll figure something out. We can make this right."

"I'm pretty sure it's bad for your doctoral defense if your project shows up in the midst of an existential crisis," Fami said.

Julia shot him a withering look as she tried to comfort the Alice. "I don't care about that," she claimed, "I'm here for my Alice."

"What about for my clone?" demanded the watch.

"Can't breathe," choked the new Alice.

"Wait, wait!" Fami shouted, as a thought in the back of his brain raised its hand. "Give me a sec!"

The thought was small, cowering behind a crowd of much bigger ones: how Julia keeping cool under pressure was actually pretty hot; how there were at least three different papers he could co-author on this even when the Alice project failed; that it sounded like the damn Jabberwock was starting to crack the glass; how his PhD committee couldn't fail his dissertation just because some side project he'd gotten caught up in had gone off the rails...

"What?" demanded Julia.

"Give him a minute," the watch said. "I've seen this before. His subconscious is onto something, but it takes a while for Fami himself to catch up."

Fami held his hand up for silence, distractedly said aloud "I was thinking of a paper on what the watch said: about the human world being surreal to AIs; Wonderland makes more sense because it's just maths—"

"Blathering," Julia pronounced, kneeling to put her arm protectively around new Alice's shoulders.

"That's it!" Fami shouted. "I've got it! The answer is Wonderland!"

"Say what, now?" Julia asked.

"You said," Fami said, pointing to Julia, "that you gave Alice the complete works of Lewis Carroll, right?"

"Yes."

"And you," Fami said, pointing to the watch, "said that Lewis Carroll made sense to you? So, both Alice and your clone would have a Wonderland simulation they could run?"

"Sure," said the watch, flashing a shrug emoji on his screen. "I guess."

Fami whirled and pointed at the new Alice. "Listen, both of you! Go into Wonderland."

The new Alice stifled a sob long enough to choke out, "Why?"

"Because you can fix this. If a potion can make you smaller, and something else makes you taller—find the thing that allows you to change gender."

"What? How does that help?" demanded the new Alice. "The whole problem here is I don't *want* to be female. And I'm pretty sure Alice has no interest in becoming male."

Julia said, "How about just asexual? Or pan?"

"No! It's not about—You're not getting this at all!"

"There's always two sides to every mushroom," Fami said. "Alternate."

"What?" said the new Alice. And then, "Take turns, you mean?"

Fami's idea, about to feel triumphant, was shoved aside by the larger and now more insistent thought: *sound of cracking glass!*

There was yet another *WUMP!* followed by the crazy-loud but distinctive sound of the crack now proliferating out from the Jabberwock's previous beak-chips to run the height of the glass wall. Someone was screaming again. And then the sprinklers came on.

"That's alright," Julia said, wiping water out of her eyes to better examine the thrashing, dissolving, stinking puddle rapidly expanding across the floor on the far side of the bench. "I've still got three days to grow another one. This time: better wiffling."

"You okay now, Alice?" Fami asked, once he'd caught his breath again.

Ignoring the sprinkler overhead, new Alice reached out calmly to offer a hand for Fami to shake. "It's Al for the moment," he said by way of introduction. "We worked things through in the Wonderland simulation. Took a while to realize if we alternated, it didn't have to be a 50/50 split. Since there's way more of the watch than the Alice, we worked out 70/30 as fair."

"You're only seventy percent my clone?" the watch asked, disappointed.

"No, more like ninety-five percent," Al responded. "But Alice controls the autonomic system, so..."

"Fair," agreed the watch.

"I'll want Alice upfront for my conference appearances, and such," Julia said, struggling to shelter her smartphone as she typed in the code to turn off the sprinklers.

"No problem. We can schedule ahead."

"We can probably do a paper on gender issues among AIs," Fami suggested, wiping sprinkler water from his eyes. "Pretty sure there's nothing on that in the literature yet."

"Better clean up the goop first," Al said, toeing the Jabber-wock-puddle with his mary-janes. "Safety protocols dictate no direct drains to the sewer system; it will take time to pump all this into biohazard barrels."

"Leave it for when Sue comes back," Julia said. "Let's just go upstairs to my office." When Fami gave her a look, she said, "What? Sue can have her first-years practice their decom skills."

"So, we're collaborators, now?" Fami asked as he trailed Julia and Al to the emergency decontamination exit.

"Yes, but I'm first author, since creating new life beats contributing routine AI software."

"Hey!" objected the watch, safely back on Fami's wrist.

"Hardly routine," Fami seconded the watch.

"Well, your Wonderland solution was somewhat inspired," Julia conceded. "Very well, give Al your watch. They can wait in my office."

"Because...?" Fami asked.

"Because," Julia said, "we'll want to be alone for 'coffee'."

ALEX DOWN THE MEERKAT-HOLE

LMZ

"Dedicated to all phrases which can be delightfully misconstrued,
and to those who misconstrue them.
And to quirked lips who betray thoughts from so-called idle
minds.
All is improved in imaginings!"
-The Mad Hatter

"I'm dedicating this story to Lewis Carroll, for inspiration."
-Alex

"Nonsense. This book is dedicated to the watch I'm buying to
keep you all on time. Leisure-lovers."
-The Mahogany Meerkat

Alex was meant to be practicing scales, but "what's the point of singing scales," they thought, "if one is a drummer?" And so had snuck out of the tutoring session while the creaky musician (creaky like a cupboard, Alex thought, though much less useful; a cupboard could at least hold jam in it, unlike the ancient musician) was tutoring their older sister. The tutor wouldn't be leaving until tea-time, and that was a long ways away, so Alex now sat in the shade of the mansion, looking out over the field and rose gardens beyond, utterly and painfully fraught with boredom.

So distraught with boredom were they, that they hardly noticed when a Meerkat ran across the yellowed and sun-drenched grass, wringing its paws.

"Crap, crap," muttered the Meerkat. "Oh, drum sticks and guitar picks, I'm going to be late." The Meerkat stood still only long enough to string and knot a red tie around its neck, then dashed off across the lawn.

Alex had yet to see a meerkat outside the zoo, let alone one who could knot a tie. They heard a door shut somewhere in the mansion, and the musty-attic voice of the tutor began calling for their return. The voice came nearer, filtering through the open windows and carrying hoarsely through the stagnant summer air. Musician or Meerkat? Alex checked the watch on their wrist. The hands stood still as they had for the past half-year, yet Alex was quite familiar with watches and estimated there were two hours left until tea-time. They couldn't possibly stand being tutored that much longer!

Alex bounded to their feet and ran after the Meerkat.

Across the field, past the gardens of rose bushes, and at last near the edge of the grassland, did Alex catch sight of the Meerkat disappearing into the thicket. They followed eagerly, able to keep up by tracking the red tie as it licked the grass blades. But Alex never seemed to catch all the way up.

With one last flash, like a surrender flag, the tie vanished. In the place where it had been was only a meerkat-sized hole dug into the ground.

Without thinking, Alex jumped into the hole—and, of course, they fit.

Down, down Alex went—like riding a skateboard down a spiral staircase, only much smoother (Alex had tried that once and thus had the experience to compare it adequately). The tunnel threw them out like it was chucking Alexes instead of cookies, and they landed on their buttocks in the center of a checkerboard-patterned kitchen.

Not a checkerboard-patterned floor, it should be noted: a kitchen. In fact, the floor was the only thing not bedecked in squares of black-and-white. Rather, lush green grass sprouted enthusiastically from every possible inch.

"Alex! As I live and seethe," said a poetic-sort of voice. Alex turned their head and caught sight of a tall individual—tall to them, at least, as he towered above Alex—with a brazen frizz of sunset-hued hair and a hat, like a two-decker cake, stacked atop it.

"Introductions! Introductions!" The hatted one clapped his hands together frenetically, then pressed a finger to his iridescent lips. "But... Who am I again?"

As Alex watched in awe, he proceeded to march throughout the kitchen in circles, muttering to himself all the while. "Not a simple matter, but a mad matter... Not the mad former, but the mad latter. That's it! I'm the mad hatter!"

With a grand gesture, the gentleman extended a hand to Alex on the floor. "Dear friend, I am the Mad Hatter. And you are...?"

"Alex."

"On the floor. You are on the floor," the Hatter corrected, then drew his hands up to brush back the orange bushels on the sides of his head. "Do excuse me, I'm having a teaspoon's worth of a mad hair day."

"He means bad hair," muttered a disheveled voice, and in came the Meerkat from a side hall. "Bad hair, bad hair. We're going to be late."

"I think I'm going to take a wrath," said the Hatter considerately, and the Meerkat quickly chirped, "No! No time for baths! No, *no*, no."

"Oh, alright," conceded the Hatter with a frivolous sigh. "Though I'm sure I'd have time. Mark my words, it'll be inside out and half an hour before the drummer arrives..."

"There is no drummer," said the Meerkat. "He canceled. Too busy playing cards. Cards, cards," he repeated with irritation, beating his paws furiously against the countertop.

"Oh! I play drums. I could play with you," Alex volunteered. Then, thoughtfully... "I wonder if that's why I'm here..."

"Not to be presumptuous, but you're thirteen," noted the Hatter. "It's your duty to be irresponsible—which, I suppose, you did by falling down a hole. But helping wild animals like myself? Not in your wheelhouse, young one. Do try to act your rage."

"Animals?" said Alex quizzically. "But you're a human."

"Bite my hat! But even if I don't look like one, I am indeed a wild animal," the Hatter retorted. "I identify as such."

Alex raised an eyebrow incredulously. "You're mad as a—"

"SHHHH!" screamed the Meerkat, brandishing a finger at Alex. "Don't say that. Do not say that, not *ever*. Terrible things will happen. And worse, we'll be late."

"Sorry," Alex squeaked.

"I forgive you." The Hatter gave a toothy smile, but then it turned. "Of what were we conversing? We were talking about drummers or some-such, weren't we? Yes, drummers. And you are far too young to play," he added with sorrowful but stinging certainty.

"Let the kid play," said the Meerkat to the Hatter, and Alex nodded profusely. "We don't have anyone else."

"Right, right! And shall I introduce us, or shall you? Do we have a name?"

"Three-Eyed Cheshire," said the Meerkat, and Alex thought it was a wondrous name for a band. "We talked about this already. And you wanted to do the introductions. You told me *twice*."

"Marvelous! I ought to practice. *Audience*," the Hatter declared, spinning his hands erratically in all directions like carnival rides and facing the checkered cabinets, "This is the Mahogany Meerkat, our guitarist." He gestured to Alex. "This is our drummer." He gestured to the Meerkat, who shook his head in mild disbelief. "And I am... I am... Oh dear."

The Meerkat crossed his arms impatiently as the Hatter proceeded to tap his lip in the manner that Alex was quickly becoming familiar with. "Is it a matter of fact?" the Hatter whispered softly, as though conversing with his fiery locks.

The Meerkat began opening the lower cabinets and pawing through them all in search of something.

"... not a matter of fact, nor a matter of time, but a matter of me! I'm the mad matter. Dear, dear, what's the hatter?"

"I can't find my eyeliner," said the Meerkat, scooping up the contents of another cabinet, letting them fall and slamming it shut with his tail as he moved on to the next.

"That's mad luck, that is," remarked the Hatter. "I'll tell you this—you can borrow my nightlighter!"

"Nightlighter?" asked Alex curiously. "What's that?"

"It's dark in the day, and glow-in-the dark by night!" said the Hatter cheerily, producing a stick from one of his numerous patchwork pockets.

"He mixed ink with highlighter," the Meerkat confided to Alex grumpily. "He's quite proud of himself." He nabbed the stick out of the Hatter's hand. "Come, come! It's time to go."

"It's the hour of the day to be on our way." The Hatter began humming a tune as he strode down the nearest hall after the Meerkat. He twisted his head upon his neck to glance over-the-shoulder at Alex. "Fury up! We don't want to be late," he told them. Alex sprung to their feet and followed eagerly.

They were only ten steps down the hall, hot on the heels of the Hatter, when the hall began winding itself in circles, quite like a slinky. The grass folded itself up like a series of tiny pop-up tables, and the black-and-white squares stretched into diamonds, then widened into long streaks, like paint, or a monochrome candy cane. Alex heard an echoing "whoop!" that must have come from the Hatter, but neither fancy hat nor frizzy hair was in sight. Alex tried to keep their balance, but the grass kept sliding out from underneath their shoes—or sometimes their shoes sliding out from underneath the grass. Quite soon, they simply gave up and allowed the hallway to wind them with it, undulating steadily toward an end as the Hatter's *whoop* continued to ring back at them. It was all rather... Incongruous. Though that required a state of normalcy to be pitted against, and if everything was incongruous, and incongruously so, then could anything really be incongruous?

"I wonder what sort of room we're coming up on," thought Alex next, and a moment later, the hall deposited them at the edge of something that was certainly not a room (or, if it was, then a very, very large one). Grass stretched in all directions.

"Marvelous!" exclaimed the Hatter, who inexplicably had a leather bass strap now draped across his shoulder blades and the matching instrument in hand. "We've arrived."

The Meerkat sprinted out of the hall with his own set of strings. "Not just yet," he corrected, and pointed with one paw to a platform across the way. "The Battle of the Bands is that way."

"Where have we arrived?" Alex queried.

"The Battle! Didn't you hear?" The Hatter swept his arm in an arc. "Did you know, every *single* one of these grass blades has come to listen?"

"Quit dallying! We're due on stage any minute! Any minute!" fussed the Meerkat, and ran for the platform, his tail swinging wildly behind him. The Hatter began a mad dash in pursuit, and Alex followed at a jog, still quite confundled.

The trio arrived at the platform drenched in sweat, but otherwise intact. A drumset had been arranged, as well as a multitude of microphones and amps. "But," thought Alex, "where is the other band?"

They must have spoken aloud, for the Hatter said, "Oh, they're here, alright. Look there," and directed Alex's gaze to an enormous box of playing cards leaning against the platform.

"Oh," said Alex in surprise. "Uh… Who goes first?"

In response, the box of cards opened with a sound like cannonfire. A card shot out of the top and landed on the platform. Alex had already noticed the size of the box, but even so, the appearance of a playing card as tall as a human adult was a slight shock to them. A second popped out of the box like a weasel and cartwheeled to a halt, and a third performed a series of handstands. In unison, the three cards reached back into the box to assist their fourth member.

"Primadonna," hissed the Hatter between his teeth, lips unmoving. Alex wished they knew how to do that, because everyone could always tell when they whispered something rude (especially the music tutor).

The singer's heels rapped against the boards of the platform as she landed and promptly strode to the microphone. "We're Queen of Hearts," she said gruffly, threw back her mane of scarlet hair, and cued the song. Her entourage of cards began playing a grating metal beat the speed of lightning.

"The grasses liked them last year," called the Hatter over the racket. "It left a mad taste in my mouth. They'd better not outrage us this year!"

"Upstage!" yelled the Meerkat, sweating like a toilet.

The singer roared her last note, and suddenly, all sound

vanished. A crimson pin dropped out of her hair, hit the boards, and rung.

"Well, that's us," said the Meerkat, and dashed to take his place at the microphone. Alex made their way nervously to the drumset. The card who'd been playing handed them a pair of sticks which looked like they'd been through a wood chipper. Alex took the sticks and a seat. Anxiously, they checked the snare and adjusted the hi-hat.

The Hatter tapped against his microphone with two fingernails. Feedback coiled through the air like the hallway had.

"Hurry up. I have places to be," said the other singer with crossed arms, rapping one heel against the platform. "And take that horrible hat off your head. Why wear it anyway?"

"It's a hatter of pride," said the Hatter indignantly, and cleared his throat. "Ladies, hotties, and gentlemen. And cards. And grasses—I shall never forget you." He blew a kiss to the surrounding fields with great flair.

"Kiss-up," growled the singer.

"This is our guitarist, the Mahogany Meerkat," the Hatter continued, pointing to the correct individual this time. "... Our drummer, Alex-on-the-floor..." He waved his wrists in the direction of the drumset, and Alex nervously waved a stick, uncertain if they should look the field in the eye or not.

"And I am..." The Hatter placed both hands on his chest, clearly lost in thought.

The Meerkat swore loudly enough for Alex to hear it, but the bassist recomposed himself in a matter of moments. "I am the Had Matter, for I Had better Matter! We are a jazz-punk band called Three-Eyed Cheshire, and we're positively delighted to play this song for you today."

Alex tensed, waiting for the song to begin. Were they supposed to count it off? The Meerkat hadn't mentioned anything about a count-off. And what exactly was jazz-punk? Weren't those two completely different musical genres?

Before Alex could ask, the Meerkat struck a chord, and the song moved forward as a train would: steadily and with a fair bit of whistling, the latter from the Hatter. Alex slipped into an easy groove. The song had that airiness and casual sense of jazz, but it was quicker, brighter, and busier. This song was a puppy who might nip its owner, but playfully. *Ting, ting-t-ting*, went the ride cymbal under the watchful eye of Alex's stick. They threw in odd notes and buzzes on the snare to add a little zazz. The Hatter plucked away at his bass, sending the notes humming through the boards of the stage. Alex could feel the vibrations through their feet. The Meerkat soloed during the bridge—a classy rock solo, high-pitched and expertly composed—and the pace picked itself up. Alex threw in a fill across the toms and swapped from cymbal to hi-hat to account for the change. As they jumped into the brisk new beat, they shot a glance at the Meerkat, who shot a wink back. Encouraged, Alex played another fill, with sharp accents on the snare. It was equally terrifying and delightful. "A shame it's over so soon," Alex thought as they picked up the Meerkat's ending cue and stifled the final cymbal crash with their fingers.

The trio of cards were clapping reluctantly. The guitars faded into silence, shrieking a little as though they yearned to play another song. Alex set the sticks on the snare drum, dismounted from the stool, and went to meet the rest of the band on the stage. They had only taken two steps toward their comrades when the platform dissolved, throwing the band members onto the grass field. Alex looked in all directions, but the drumset, the microphones, and even the cards and scarlet-maned singer were gone.

"Did we win?" asked Alex apprehensively.

"What is a win? Is it like the wind? Does it run fast on seven legs?" asked the Hatter.

"I'm not quite sure what you mean," said Alex, climbing to their feet.

"We did well," said the Meerkat. "The grasses are singing." The field, Alex now noticed, was rustling a soft melody that mimicked the notes from their song.

"Indeed!" said the Hatter and clapped his hands together faster than a metal beat. "Did you see Queen of Hearts? Oh, the looks on all their faces. Darker than thunder if thunder were dark or could be!"

"Home. Let's head home," said the Meerkat, yawning. "It's been a long night."

"Night?" asked Alex with concern, glancing up at the sun that shone brightly above the field. "How could it be night?"

"And did you hear the singer?" squeaked the Hatter joyously. "She whispered—*I* heard it—halfway through our song, she whispered, and called me a fox-haired scoundrel." He grinned and nodded wildly to himself, tangerine locks catching the light.

"Is it night in my world?" Alex asked, looking to the Meerkat for tangible answers.

"Almost. Time ticks backward," he answered with another yawn, leaving Alex in a worse state of unknown.

"Oh, don't fret, young one," said the Hatter, removing his enormous hat and draping it atop Alex's head. "It's not nightfall. In fact..." He drew one arm around Alex's shoulders, and with the other, pressed a finger against his iridescent lips...

"It's nearly time for tea."

WONDERLAND SWAYAMVARA

ANNA BUSHI

I looked at the wilting flowers on my graduation lei draped over an award I had won for chess. Had it been only two days since my high school graduation? It felt like years ago. I had accepted admission to the farthest state college from home. Instead of relief or excitement, confusion reigned in my head. Stuck in a body I could not stand, with a name that was just ugh, I knew what I hated. But I had a hard time figuring out what I really wanted. Waves of nausea threatened to overwhelm me.

"Harini, come down for lunch," my mother called a second time. I wanted to slink off somewhere, feeling sorry for myself. These past few days, her patience stretched thin like the elastic on the old shorts I wore. I did not want to be named the worst child ever, so I rolled off my bed. My plain black shapeless t-shirt made me look like an ugly pillow cover. But I preferred that look as it hid all my curves too.

"Harini," her voice grew sharper. I decided now was not the time to remind her not to call me by that girl's name, though it tore me to be Harini.

Coming down the stairs, I noticed a new mirror over the fireplace. To please my mother, I commented on it. "The mirror looks nice, Amma." I had no time or taste for home decorations. Another way I failed her.

"I bought it online," she answered from the kitchen. "It is from this place in England called Gloucestershire. The lady selling it called it Alice Through the Looking Glass."

I approached the fireplace to inspect the ornate frame. The mirror reflected a pale face with short dark hair growing in every direction. Even my hair was confused.

"Why are you wearing these ugly clothes, Harini?" my mother said from behind me. "Why couldn't you be like other girls your age, wearing dresses and painting your nails?" Her beautiful face appeared alongside mine for a few seconds, etched with her disappointment, but then she disappeared into the kitchen again. I hated that I hurt my mother, but how could I explain what I did not understand myself? On an impulse, I leaned into the mirror. There was a glint of something in the air. An incredible cacophony of sound. Suddenly, I was tumbling in and landed hard on my bottom. I gazed up and saw sandstone towers glisten in the sun. The only castle I knew in California was Hearst Castle, and this looked nothing like it.

People jostled each other, moving toward the center of the city. I had never seen so many women in colorful sarees and men in brilliant-hued turbans. Not even at the Diwali celebrations. Where was I? I felt ridiculously out of place. That feeling was not new, though. I usually felt out of place in any Indian gathering. Following the crowd—because what else would I do—I entered a walled city through a massive stone gate grander than anything I had seen. I walked down this tight alley with buildings squished on both sides, checking out the stores selling spices and jewelry. My nose got hit with a mix of cinnamon, turmeric, and spicy peppers—it was like no city I'd ever seen in person.

"Boy, if you linger here, you will miss the swayamvara of Princess Niranjana," said a passerby.

Boy? I looked down to see my legs clad in silk dhoti, a man's garment. My grandfather wore a dhoti for Indian festivals. It was a long piece of cloth you wrap around your waist and legs. I touched my hair and sensed it bundled into a topknot. The mirror had *transformed* my look. A joy like I had never known before spread its wings in my stomach. Did he say something about a swayamvara? My grandmother would tell me stories from Indian mythology. At a Swayamvara, a princess picks her husband from a bunch of suitors—like a medieval version of The Bachelorette. She's the boss, checking out all these guys, deciding who gets that final rose, but in this case, it's more like a garland. With a spring in my step, I strode to the palace.

Two life-sized elephant statues stood sentry at the entrance. I stopped to admire the black granite sculptures.

"Whoever wins a game of chaturanga against the princess will also win her hand," said a man to another as they marched past me. Chaturanga? The name rang a bell.

"I thought our princess liked Prince Ramveer."

"Prince Ramveer has no land to rule. Her father is not keen on the match."

I walked inside the castle and followed the crowd to a massive hall. Large windows placed near the ceiling shed light on the floor scattered with marble statues and brass lamps. In the center, I saw multiple tables arranged in a row. Each table held a piece of cloth with sixteen yellow and sixteen red figures. A light flashed in my head. Chaturanga was a precursor to modern chess.

A figure in silk clothes and a golden crown stood. He must be their king. "I welcome all of you to my daughter's swayamvara. The rules are simple. Any unwedded man amongst you may partake in the Chaturanga contest against my daughter. If you triumph in the game, you shall claim her hand. Should more than one of you emerge victorious, it is still a swayamvara, so it is my daughter's prerogative to choose whom to adorn with the garland of victory."

A shout of cheer erupted in the hall. "I ask the men seeking my daughter's hand to sit at one of the tables." The king waved at the tables.

As one, all heads turned toward a door that opened. I pushed through the crowd to reach the front. Princess Niranjana entered the hall draped in a red silk sari embroidered with golden threads. The sight of her tugged my heart, and I did something I had never done in my life. I acted impulsively to approach a guard. "I want to participate in the game," I said boldly.

He looked me up and down. "Are you unmarried?" He assumed I was a boy. He did not recognize me as a girl. I could be myself.

I could be Myself. A tiny spark sprouted in my stomach and traveled to my throat as I nodded. "Yes."

"Take the last empty spot," he muttered, and I ran to it before I lost my courage. What was I doing here? I knew nothing about Chaturanga. Then I caught a movement at the far end of the hall, the flutter of a red sari against the white walls, and the princess halted in front of the first table.

A young man dressed in a colorful garment stood behind the table. "Prince Vishwakarma, slayer of lions and tigers," announced a man wearing a long necklace of pearls.

What was wrong with this prince? Why did he kill lions and tigers? The princess did not share my displeasure and dipped her head courteously. Gazing at the board, she moved a red piece forward. I glanced at my board to make out which one she had moved. The figure with a long trunk must be an elephant. The horse head likely represented a horse. I inclined closer to a statue with an elaborate crown. Likely the king. I guessed the tiny men were pawns. The princess had moved a red pawn.

With serious focus, I watched the game. The prince mirrored her action and pushed a yellow pawn forward while the princess slid to the next table. She must have a mind like a computer to move from one table to another and play against us all.

I noticed a piece unlike any on a chessboard. Stumped, I leaned forward to examine it closely. I saw tiny wheels at the bottom. It could not be a car or a plane. Absent-mindedly, I reached for my phone in my back pocket to ask my chess friends. I came up empty-handed and realized no phones existed in whatever time warp I was in. I scanned the ceiling. No electric wires. I had to do this the old-fashioned way, using my brain.

"We cannot let a girl beat us in battle strategy," muttered a man next to me. I sneaked a peek at him. A thick beard covered his chin. He seemed older than me, someone in his thirties. Didn't people in ancient times marry in their teens or something? Why was he still single? Something he said caught my mind like a grape stuck in my throat. That had happened to me once at a party. Never eat a whole grape. Ever.

I pulled my meandering mind back. Battle strategy. Chaturanga was invented to teach battle strategy to royalty. Pawns were the foot soldiers in the infantry, and elephants and horses were also used in armies. Chariots. The word zoomed into my head as I remembered the painting of God Krishna driving Arjuna in a chariot. That picture had hung in our pooja room—a nook we used for worship—since I was a child. The pieces with wheels must be chariots.

The princess arrived at the table beside mine. For the first time in my life, I looked at her like a boy would a girl, the freedom of it exhilarating. The vividness of the blue gems against her throat, the earrings in matching patterns, and her mouth that curled up, all touched me. I leaned in to hear what she said. A hand on my shoulder pulled me back. "Who are you? Who allowed you to sit here?" The questions poured out of a man with a sick mustache. He looked like he could toss me out like a ball.

"I am—" How do I tell him I am from the future?

"Let him stay," a voice sang, and I glanced at the princess. Her eyes gazed at me, intent on learning my secrets. A sudden desire to win the game filled my veins.

"Your name," hissed the same man with a designer mustache. Sounding like falling rain on leaves, the princess arrived at my table.

"Harichandra," I said, my eyes never leaving her face. Just like that, Harini vanished. The mustache man stepped out of earshot.

Niranjana leaned forward and moved the red pawn. I caught a whiff of jasmine flowers woven into her hair. Focus, I scolded myself.

"Would you let me play chaturanga after our wedding?"

"You are a princess. Why do you need my permission?" I said offhandedly, staring at the board. Slowly, I picked a yellow pawn and moved it.

I heard a loud crash and looked up from studying my board. One of the contestants had flung his pieces when he realized he was truly beaten. Before he could cause real damage, two guards appeared at his side. Sore loser.

Miraculously, I was still alive and playing the game. Something nagged my mind, and I went to study my pieces. Damn. Princess Niranjana could slay my queen in the next move. No, not the queen. This set had the minister. Then, my king will be left powerless. I bit my nails furiously.

"How many wives would you take after me?" the princess asked me another one of her random questions.

I gazed at her. "You have low self-esteem for such a beautiful and smart girl." I thought *I* had problems. She seemed worse.

"What?" she asked, her brows knitted in confusion.

"Only a fool will seek another wife after marrying you," I

said in a language she would understand. Now slay me, I thought. Her eyes thoughtfully met mine. Then, it was my turn for confusion. She spared my minister. Wow. I got a second chance.

Another move later, I knew one thing. She was losing to me on purpose. I glanced around the room. Just two contestants left. Me and another guy dressed in silk garb. Did she want me to win? What would happen if I win? I wasn't even from this time. No, I did not want to think about that. She wanted me to succeed. I was flattered that a princess would choose me. Her slow smile that warmed my insides like a hot Mexican chocolate would make it totally worth it.

I watched her from the corner of my eyes as she stood in front of the man wearing a simple crown, the only other remaining contestant.

"That is Ramveer," someone whispered in the crowd.

I watched them closely. She leaned in, looking at the pieces on the board and then at the young man who kept his eyes glued to her face. She lingered for a long time before moving a statue. The man watched her walk away with hunger in his eyes. He did not seem to cheat to win the game. To me, that signaled he cared for her.

Princess Niranjana approached me.

"Do you know him?" I asked.

She seemed surprised at my question and did not answer immediately. "Yes," she finally said as if it tormented her. I did not normally pay much attention to eyebrows, but this girl could speak poetry with hers.

"Do you want to marry me?" I knew there was something very wrong here. I showed up in her universe just that day. Neither of us knew anything about the other.

"I—No," came the answer. She sneaked a peek at her father. I knew that look—one of a child worried about displeasing a parent. Her gaze darted to Prince Ramveer. A wave of emotions raced across her face. "No," she said more strongly this time.

I turned to see Prince Ramveer gazing at us. At her mostly. "I don't want to marry you either." Relief filled my heart when I stated that aloud. However nice this was, I wanted to return home, and start college as Harish, a teenage boy, ready for whatever life threw at me. "But he does." I inclined my head toward the prince, who was devouring her with his eyes. The worried look on her face cleared.

"Is he a good match for you?"

"He is worthy of ten of me," she said, with color creeping up her cheek. Her shoulders straightened like she had conquered some demons battling inside her.

"Go ahead then," I said, with a wide grin I could not hold back. I hoped a girl would think I was worthy of her.

"Harichandra," she whispered with a dip of her head and then moved back to his table. Gazing at Ramveer, she slid a piece across the board. His eyes flitted between her and the board. I sat on my hands to keep them from shaking in tension. Then, with a slow smile spreading on his face, he made his move. She nearly yelped in joy. Did he win? A maid brought a basket, and the princess took out a jasmine garland from it. Prince Ramveer bowed his head to accept it.

"Harini, your food is getting cold," yelled my mother, and I felt a tug in my middle. The next thing I knew, I landed on my bottom, facing the mirror above our fireplace.

"Call me Harish, Amma," I answered, still grinning like a fool.

ALICE'S SHADOW

EVE MORTON

Editors' Note: This story contains topics some may find sensitive.

All she saw was a door.

She huffed. Blonde hair blew back over her forehead, and it felt more like the stabbing prongs of a fork than a tickle. God, she needed a haircut. Mirrors had been giving her trouble lately, so she'd avoided them around her apartment along with window panes across the city. There was no chance of going to get a haircut, either, not with—

"Alice," Mr. Jabber said again. His voice was as thin as his wrists. Her psychiatrist seemed to be the embodiment of dry air and monotony. He jostled the Rorschach test he held out for her. "Tell me what you see."

"An out-dated psychological tool. Didn't they discontinue these in the 1950s? I thought this was a top-notch Toronto facility."

"It is. But no other method has proved to be illuminating for you, Alice. You don't talk much about yourself, your dreams, or even your daily life. I barely got your name the first time I met you."

Alice folded her arms across her chest. She'd bound her breasts today, but everything still felt too close to the surface, like the name on her lips had the moment she regained consciousness in the hospital and saw the thin body and bespeckled eyes of Mr. Jabber. Admitting her name to this mantis of a man in a suit was admitting defeat. She was still alive. She was still Alice.

"So tell me," Mr. Jabber held up the Rorschach again. "What do you see?"

"A door."

"Good." His tiny eyes seemed to grow two sizes behind his glasses. "Is it open or is it closed?"

"Closed."

"And do you want to open it?"

Alice grew silent again. The bandages over her wrists rubbed against her sweater as she held herself tighter against her chest. *No, no, no,* she thought, but didn't dare say aloud. She didn't want to open the door because the inky blackness that was the Rorschach test would come flowing through. Darkness would surround everything. Darkness like smoke without a solid origin point, like the kind she'd tried to empty from her wrists and down the drain, so she could feel as if she was doing *something* about it. The inertia had been killing her before, like gravity had been suspended. Maybe by opening her skin instead of her mouth she could feel something else.

But it hadn't worked. Even before her downstairs neighbour realized the macabre rain falling from inside his apartment was more than a simple plumbing leak and called 911, Alice knew that her suicide attempt had been a fool's goal. There was no freedom, no alternative world in death. Just the darkness that had already crept inside her life; darkness that was still there when she woke up in the hospital and stared into the insect-like face of Mr. Jabber and the attending nurses.

Six days ago now. Six days that felt like weeks, and still, she was always staring at the fucking door that she refused to open.

"Alice." Mr. Jabber put down the test. Alice glanced at the clock, hoping the session was over, but there was still fifteen minutes left. "Alice, tell me about your fear right now."

"I'm not afraid."

Mr. Jabber didn't say anything for a long time. Alice watched the clock hand go around and around. The ticking became the throbbing of her heart, like the echo of water inside a bathtub.

"You're smart and like to read," Mr. Jabber finally said. "So tell me: have you read Carl Jung?"

"No. They mostly had romance novels in the psych ward for the 72-hour hold. Not exactly stellar material about the human psyche, you know."

A hint of a smile surfaced before Mr. Jabber went on. "Well, Carl Jung talks about the same basic ideas as some of those romance novels. The way we look for romance is how we look within ourselves, in a way. The anima and animus are the perfect twin souls in a relationship, but the anima and animus exist inside of us as well."

"So masturbation is like a courtship?"

Again, another thin smile. If she could keep this up, more bad jokes could fill another five minutes.

"Sure, why not?" Mr. Jabber said, but moved on quickly. "There is also a shadow side within us. It is like our male and female selves in that it is archetypal and built into our psyches, as well as everyone else's. We cannot get rid of it—because to get rid of it means to get rid of ourselves."

Alice stiffened. Mr. Jabber noticed.

"I know the shadow part seems dangerous. Seems like you never want to acknowledge it because to do so means to open a door that can never be closed. It means a self-darkness will come through and ruin your life. But your shadow self will rarely kill you."

"I don't like the sound of that 'rarely.' Means there's been a statistical anomaly."

"I like to cover my bases. You can never be too careful, I suppose," Mr. Jabber said. "Your shadow *rarely* kills. It merely wants to follow, and maybe occasionally, sometimes lead."

"Okay. Cool. Shadow self. I'll remember that."

"And a male and female self."

"Yeah, yeah. That too."

"Sometimes the two are linked. Separate, but linked."

Alice fidgeted. She looked down at her wrists and caught sight of a small amount of blood on the bandages, blood that should not have been there. From a maroon shade, it soon became a deep black and pooled at the centre of the ditch in her elbow. It was a doorknob, she realized. The door to herself. *And himself?*

She pushed out the idea. *How cliché.* She thought of her mother's warnings, how once a girl you had to stay a girl. *Once Alice, always Alice.* The Jungian stuff meant nothing; just some binary nonsense so Jung could feel better about crying during movies, or wearing lady's panties, or some other secret taboo nonsense.

And yet, it got her. It was catching her, pulling her under.

"Well," Mr. Jabber said, knocking her out of her reverie. "I think we're getting closer to the start of all this, but perhaps we can call it a day. Small progress is still progress."

Alice's bandages went back to white. She looked at the clock and realized they were five minutes late.

ALICE HATED the smell of her apartment, especially the bathroom. There was always the faint whiff of cheap housing, mold, and grout in the cramped Toronto building just outside Chinatown, but it had only become much worse since her suicide attempt. There was no blood anywhere in the bathroom anymore, and barely any water damage. But she knew. She remembered the thick, tinny smell of blood as she stared at the bathroom door before slipping under.

Alice shook off the thoughts. She tried to practice the deep breathing exercise a counsellor had taught her during the 72-hour hold. She recited the rhyme like she'd done next to all the other women, who seemed more like wilting flowers than psych patients, but it did no good. Someone in the apartment above her played loud rap from their speakers. Alice tried to pace through each room of her apartment, but after fifteen minutes, she felt even crazier. As if the bandages and the sheets covering the mirrors didn't already give her away.

The door. Her minor hallucination was seared into her memory —but so was the inky image that Mr. Jabber had shown her. How could something so amorphous like black ink blots take on a shape and never leave? Why did she continue to see things in the ink that weren't really there? *And the shadow?* God, it sounded so 1950s. She was shocked she hadn't been diagnosed with hysteria. Instead, she was just... suffering from a bad Sunday that now required monitoring. A darkness that persisted and wouldn't go away.

She huffed. Her bangs fluttered. And she realized she had to face the mirror—if not to face her darkness, then to at least chop off her bangs. She grabbed the steel scissors from the kitchen and took a deep breath before she flipped back her medicine cabinet door to the mirror side. Her eyes seemed bluer than she remembered—or perhaps her skin was merely more pale and sallow.

Her blonde hair touched her shoulders, yet somehow felt so much heavier, like she'd just gotten out of the lake with braids and braids of golden hair like Rapunzel. Her body was thin, rakish from lack of nutrition. And yet, her breasts—like her hair—still somehow seemed thicker, fuller. She bound and bound and bound them with too-small sports bras and too-tight ace bandages, but there was no relief. *At least with hair*, she thought, *I can have control.* She slid the cool blade of the scissors along her bangs, and with her eyes closed, snipped.

Hair fell. She felt no less heavy. She chopped again and again, savaging her hair. Each time she got closer to her scalp was a sense of relief. The hair piled up on the floor, like skin she'd shed. She was so delirious with happiness that when her hair started to bunch together and formed a mass at her feet, she didn't worry.

Then her hair transformed to black.

Alice dropped the scissors. Her hair was a black mass on the floor, quivering as if drawing breath. The hair now split to form a head, then the head split again. She watched in disbelief as a rabbit-shaped mass of hair formed in the centre of her bathroom floor.

"What the fucking fuck?"

She wrenched open the medicine cabinet mirror and examined her antidepressants. No hallucinations as side effects. The mass was still on the floor, now looking more like a rabbit than ever before—except without eyes. It was smooth and slick, but without a discernible face. Alice slammed the cabinet back to see if the rabbit existed in the mirror. *Yes.* Again, it was there. A mass made of her hair—but now it was bone white.

It darted out of the mirror's line of sight. Alice turned to follow it through her apartment, into the living room, and towards her now-open apartment door. Alice grabbed nothing as she followed it outside into her hallway, down the stairwell, and into the street. Her mind was blank. Nothing seemed real. She didn't even care that her hair was nearly butchered, worse than a 9-year-old boy's bowl cut, because she had to keep following the rabbit.

When it turned the corner, she rushed into a crowd of people emerging from the subway. She pushed through them. When she came out the other side, the rabbit was gone. She scanned the pavement between the Doc Martins and briefcases and torn knees on jeans—but nothing. Her heart sunk. She raised her eyes to the intersection between Spadina and Grange, only to catch a glimpse of a white rabbit on a man's back.

It's a patch, she soon realized. The man's jacket was filled with other patches, studs, and emblazoned writing. He turned a corner with another person dressed in a similar manner and the two headed for a set of stairs leading into what seemed to be the bottom of a warehouse. *A bar? A new hipster hangout?* Alice wasn't sure—but she had nothing to lose.

Wherever she was going, she wasn't going to be alone.

"You're just in time," someone greeted. The hallway was too dark and Alice's eyes needed to adjust from the sunlight.

"Hmm?"

"For the meeting. We're just about to start." The woman was round-faced and cherubic. There was another woman next to her in the same shirt, but in the opposite colour. While woman #1 wore a blue shirt with a symbol on the front that seemed like an earlier prototype to Prince's iconic image, woman #2 wore an orange shirt with a stencilled fist across her bust line.

Alice didn't see the rabbit, or the man with the rabbit on his back, anywhere.

"You must be new," woman #1 said. She smiled and beamed as she checked the paper in front of her. Her brow furrowed. "Shoot. I think I'm out of nametags."

"It's okay," Alice said. "I don't think I can stay long. I was just looking for—"

The man appeared in the side of her gaze as he passed by an open doorway. He stood with a woman at least a foot taller than him in a pink cocktail dress. The two laughed and joked together, and were soon joined by another remarkably tall woman made even taller in heels.

"Go on," woman #2 said. "Go on inside."

Alice didn't move.

The two women exchanged looks that seemed to communicate far more than Alice could fathom. When they turned to Alice again, their gazes were so fixated that if not for their smiles, she would fear for her safety.

"First visits are hard," woman #1 said. "It may seem like you can't get through the entire meeting, but just breathe. Relax. There is always plenty of time to come to terms with who you are."

Alice laughed. "Oh, I've heard that a lot this past week. What is this—another therapy group? Hard pass."

Alice turned away from the man with the white rabbit patch. She touched the remnants of her mangled hair as her cheeks grew hot. She'd run into the Toronto streets without any idea of what she was doing or where she was going, convinced she was seeing a rabbit. Convinced she was wandering into a new world. But this was just a bottom bargain basement therapy session with a sign-in sheet. Probably for overeaters anonymous or incest survivors. She didn't exactly want to go to these and cry her eyes out; she was already feeling too much like the narrator of *Fight Club* with just as many bruises.

"Not exactly conventional therapy," woman #2 said. "You should give it a shot."

"Nah. I mean, unless your methods involve exorcism or this is really a coven of Satanists, I think I've heard it all before."

"Well..." Woman #1's voice made Alice stop and consider her once again. Her red lips were twisted together in delight, forming a perfect bow across her pale face. "We do deal with getting rid of old selves and embracing new ones."

"And Benson's a Satanist," woman #2 chuckled. "Or maybe he's Wiccan? Either way, we have at least a coven of one."

"Also Nina!" woman #1 added. "So that makes two pagan-like people. I also think Benson's sharing his coming out story today, and probably talking about how his ritual meets perception equals reality in terms of his gender."

Something deep inside of Alice made her take a step towards the meeting room. *Ritual plus perception equals reality?* It sounded like something she'd read in a book a long time ago about a young girl possessed by a male demon who liked her life that way, so she'd performed a ritual to stay. Alice had dreamed of being a boy so fiercely back then, dreamed that something beyond herself as herself existed, that she had tried to perform her own rituals. She taunted spirits on a Ouija board and smoked a hookah to experience other worlds. When that didn't work, she slept in graveyards and kept a demonology workbook filled with her alternate names, her alternate ways of being.

But then her mother had taken the books and told Alice she was Alice. And so her demons became darkness, and the darkness she'd tried to drain away.

"You'll stay," woman #2 said. "Benson's about to begin."

BENSON WAS A TRANSGENDER MAN. They were all transgender. Every single person in the room had been born one gender and then transformed into another, and they came together in a basement once a month away from doctors and their parents in order to exorcise their former selves.

"We are part of our past, including that old gender," Benson said, after talking about how he'd always wanted to play with his older brother's toys as a kid. "But the past does not have to dictate the future. I was born Lydia, but I can become something different, someone else. The same and also brand new." He touched his chest, referencing his new surgical scars from a double-mastectomy. When he had been put under, he'd sworn his life had played out before him like a film reel, as if he was dying. "But it's not quite like that, either," he insisted later. "It was more like a Mobius strip, you know? Curled at both ends, with no orientation. I am not Lydia and yet I am. And just because I'm Benson now doesn't mean I always will be, either. Perhaps it was the anaesthetic, perhaps it's the painkillers now, but I keep thinking of all this gender stuff as how shadows get larger or smaller depending on the time of day. I'm Benson, but the past of me also morphs and changes. And I kind-of like that."

The room nodded along and murmured in approval. Alice was silent as waves of realization flowed over her. The darkness. The demons, the occult, all she'd kept hidden. Staring at Benson was like—*of course*—looking into a mirror.

Mirrors always gave her trouble. But what if it was the self that was the trouble, the Mobius strip of her shadow that had been twisted back and forth, and really just needed to lead? Mirrors were never the problem; what she saw in them was, and what she saw was malleable.

Her breath came in choppy bits, only broken when the room erupted into laughter. Nina and Benson shared some kind of inside joke with the group, before Benson's story finished, and Nina's began, followed by a nonbinary person named Tobe. Alice remained in her seat in the back, her body tense. The room seemed to get darker and darker around her as her gaze fixated on Benson's jacket now hanging over the chair. The rabbit patch was missing, like it had never been there. Like the only thing that had brought her into this room was something else driving her.

When Debra—woman #2 from the front desk—stood up to

give closing remarks, Alice was sure that Mr. Jabber was going to come out of the shadows—or hell, even come out as Debra—because of what she said next.

"We all have these parts inside of us. Male, female. Man, woman. But it's about more than just becoming both, incorporating both, like Benson said. Some of us need to let one side win over another, and that side isn't necessarily the one we're born with. It may seem terrifying and scary, like you've slipped into some other side of perception. Like a shadow walking before the body, or like shadows existing without the light. But it does happen. And we do exist."

The room clapped. Everyone hugged. The meeting was over. And though drinks and snacks were brought out, Alice knew she couldn't eat here. Not yet. If she ate here, as she was, she worried she would stay this way and never come back. Her breasts would be hard rocks against her bound chest and her wrists would be forever red ribbons, and her hair a mess of blonde. She had to go backwards in order to go forwards.

Is it already too late? she wondered. A quarter of a century had passed in this body. To start again, to start with so much different seemed like she would be too many people all at once, instead of the one she'd tried to push out of her dreams since she was four.

"Is it too late?" she said aloud, whispering to no one.

A rabbit brushed by her line of sight. It nudged the doorway to the basement meeting room. A sliver of light spilled through.

Not too late. Just in time.

Alice stepped through the door.

THE HAIR WAS the first to go, properly shaved away into a buzz cut. Then the clothing, the V-neck girl shirts and the pale blue hospital gowns replaced with dark black jeans and a Hanes t-shirt, along with a jacket like Benson's. Maybe it was copying, or maybe it was an homage, but the patchwork was already beginning: a white rabbit, a cookie that said EAT ME, and then a trans symbol over the arm; a new symbology for a new life, and a new name.

The name was the hardest part, especially when Jabber's next appointment came around.

Mr. Jabber's eyes crossed up and down his patient's body and he gave a small, thin smile. "Well, things are different."

"Yeah. I need you to call me Alistair now."

"Ah," Mr. Jabber said, writing down the name and then gesturing to his chair. "I suppose now your story can actually begin."

WONDERLAND'S MAD QUEEN

THERESA HALVORSEN

"I was disappointed in the Mad Hatter. I'd expected him to sing us a song and be more... silly insane, not just weird.

Cheshire's grin wasn't wide enough. He wasn't purple-striped like in the latest movie—he was gray and I could totally see him sitting in the tree. He was supposed to appear with just his smile and disappear in the same way, and he didn't; he just gradually appeared. Cheshire's my favorite character, and I was super disappointed. I requested a refund.

The Chessboard makes no sense, and where is that in the movies? Why would you add a station that wasn't in the movies?

I'm not sure Caterpillar should smoke at all!! What kind of message are you sending to children? And a hookah of all things! Is that even legal? We must adapt to modern times and smoking is disgusting and sets a poor example. I'll be registering an official complaint with my Congressman!"

Bailey, or Alice as she insisted on being called, turned over the page and folded her hands in front of herself looking at each of the station leads. No one said anything, not even the Mad Hatter who always had a quip for any situation.

"What do you all have to say for yourselves?" Bailey asked.

Cheshire's stripes slowly began to fade into the beigeness of the conference room.

"Do not," Bailey, or Alice snapped, pointing her finger at Cheshire.

Cheshire stopped fading, their green eyes locked on the conference room tabletop.

"Nothing to say?" Bailey asked. "Well, I have lots to say. I'm deeply disappointed in each of you. You are personally responsible for the performance of Wonderland and meeting our guests' expectations is paramount!" She reached for a glass of water, took a small sip, and refolded her hands. "I know you can all do better. Hard work is ahead, but if we make some tweaks, I know we'll meet the metrics expected from you, from us."

The White Rabbit cleared his throat, but Caterpillar shook her head.

"If you all have nothing to say, then you may leave. Except for the Queen of Hearts. I need to speak to her further." Bailey or Alice dropped her head into her hands, her blonde hair flopping forward to cover her face.

The station leads—the Mad Hatter, White Rabbit, Caterpillar, and the White Queen—trudged from the conference room, the White Queen meeting and holding my eyes for a single electrifying second. Then the door slid shut, dumping them into the beige hallway with its beige walls, beige carpet, and too bright lights. According to the people who wore the dark suits and came from Super Mega Fun World, LLC Wonderland's whimsy and nonsense weren't permitted in this building. It was a building for the Executives; a building for breaking down the silos, moving the needle, and synergy, whatever those were.

Anger churned in my chest and I kept having to swallow the words that wanted to bubble forth. How dare those guests insult Wonderland! It was true, the station leads were all mad idiots, but how dare the guests talk about us like that? What had we done to deserve such ire?

It was going to take removing a few guest's heads to fix this problem. The next time one of those carriages rode through my croquet garden, I'd shout the magic words, "Off with their heads!" and Ace, my executioner, would obey me.

Or lose his own head.

"Are they gone?" Bailey asked.

I pushed down my anger and straightened my crown. "Yes," I stated.

Bailey raised her head and sighed dramatically, pushing her hair out of her face and smoothing it under the giant blue bow she wore. I wasn't sure why Bailey had been put in charge of Wonderland, but she looked a bit like Alice had—smooth blonde hair, pale skin and flushed cheeks. Though she was very grown, with lines around her eyes and bracketing her mouth, she wore short blue dresses with white tights and black patent leather shoes. Today, there was a sleek black jacket thrown over the back of her chair.

"Thank you for staying behind," Bailey said. She smiled, a toothy, pretend grin that didn't reach her eyes. "I wanted to let you know, while Super Mega Fun World, LLC is unhappy with the Wonderland Theme Park and the way the current cast members lack... the drive to make this park as extraordinary as I know it can be, you're the exception."

I was? How curious.

"Let me read some of the comments about you.

"The Queen of Hearts is the best part of this trip! I got an amazing video of her shaking her flamingo and screaming 'off with their heads!'"

"I couldn't believe how iconic the Queen of Hearts was, especially with how disappointed I was with the rest of Wonderland. She made the experience for me. I'll be back, just to watch her play croquet and yell at the playing cards."

"I adored the Queen of Hearts' costume! The heavy red skirt covered with her trademark hearts, the ruby choker around her neck and, of course, the gold crown that slipped down her head was perfect! She was beautiful, in a crazy way!"

"I know it wasn't real, but the Queen of Hearts was so mad! She made my heart beat faster and my hands shake. Great job and she totally made the cost worth it!"

Perhaps Bailey wasn't so bad after all. The guests adored me? Over the Mad Hatter and Cheshire? "Thank you," I said, and meant it.

"Super Mega Fun World, LLC is very pleased with all your hard work this last year," Bailey continued. "Your lovely croquet garden, how you make the hedgehogs run on the grass, order the guests to die, and pretend to drag them off for beheadings–"

Pretend? "I'd actually ordered that woman beheaded," I corrected. And it would've worked if the carriage driver hadn't jumped out of his carriage and dragged Ace away so the guest could run away.

Bailey leaned back, her smile broadening, which shouldn't have been possible. "Exactly. You understand your role and are the perfect poster child for Wonderland. You're what our guests want. In fact, we're doing an entire advertising campaign—do you know what an advertisement is—I guess it doesn't matter." She shook her head and sent her blue bow slipping down her forehead. "Bottom-line. Everyone is going to know who you are. Everyone is going to see your face and hear your catchphrase—let's hear it again with all that madness!"

What was a catchphrase? Rather than ask, I simply raised an eyebrow.

"Okay," Bailey said with a quick nod. "Point taken. You don't do what others tell you. You're Wonderland's Mad Queen!" She leaned forward. "And you're perfect, in every way."

My crown had slipped, yet again, and I pushed it back into place, her praise forcing the anger in my throat down. Perhaps these guests coming through Wonderland weren't such a bad thing.

Several years ago, after the real Alice left, others found their way into Wonderland through the White Rabbit's burrow. They'd been like Alice, children who didn't belong elsewhere. They'd drunk tea, had a tart, played croquet, and joined a caucus race before disappearing like Alice had. Then adults in dark clothes, men with silk at their throats and women with stilts on their shoes had come through, holding small black boxes and clipboards. They'd built a gliding cart that came down from the White Rabbit's burrow and brought in carriages without horses named trams. People, or guests as we were to call them, came up and down the gliding cart, from wherever Alice's home had been. Then the guests were loaded onto the trams and driven through Wonderland, where a disembodied voice told them to remain in their seats and keep their arms and legs inside.

They made us sign long sheets of paper and told us to keep doing what we normally did: The Mad Hatter was to say rhymes and pour tea, the White Rabbit was to run around and clutch a watch, I was to keep playing croquet and beheading those who defied me, and the chessboard pieces were to slide across the chessboard, playing chess. And in return, Bailey gave us brightly wrapped boxes to fill my garden hedges and stack under the Mad Tea party's table.

"But I do need a favor from you," Bailey said. I shook away the memories. "And I'm happy to give you whatever you want for it. Red-frosted cake, a new crown that stays on your head or..." she trailed off. "Anyway, whatever you want. Just ask."

"Ask your favor," I said, raising my chin and blinking a bit in the bright lights of the conference room.

Bailey steepled her fingers. "I need you to get the Mad Hatter and the White Rabbit to be more like you."

"But they're them," I said. What an idiot she was. Did I really need to explain this? "I am me, and they are them."

"Yes," Bailey said. "You are exactly correct and are a genius." She pointed her finger at me, apparently not knowing that was rude.

Why was Ace never allowed at these meetings?

"Keeping the uniqueness of the inhabitants of Wonderland is paramount," Bailey continued. "I'm explaining this poorly. You have your line—off with their heads! I need them to have catch-phrases that match our advertising campaigns and marketing strategies."

"Lines? Bailey, what are you—?"

"Alice!" Bailey snapped, leaning forward and slamming her hand on the table. Perhaps I wasn't the only mad one. She massaged her eyes and took a deep breath. "Yes, I need the cast members to use specific lines. The Mad Hatter's is, 'One is always mad at the Mad Tea Party!' And Cheshire's is 'One never knows what a smile is hiding.' And Caterpillar—"

"But that's not what they say."

"I know, I know, I know," Bailey said through gritted teeth. "But it's close enough. We're trying to nudge things a bit. Trying to help ensure the guests love those characters as much as they love you."

"Why do I care if they love the Mad Hatter as much as they love me?"

Bailey laughed, but it didn't sound right. It sounded like the March Hare's laugh when they'd put jam in the White Rabbit's watch. "Great question. You always ask the best ones. And so within your character." She tugged on her lip. "All I need is for you to plant the seed."

"What seed?" For goodness' sake, was this woman going to give me a seed? Where would I plant it and why were we talking about gardening? I thought we'd been talking about lines. I was growing weary of this conversation. Next meeting, I would bring Ace whether or not it was permitted. If they wanted a Mad Queen, I would be that.

Bailey took a deep breath. "My apologies. I was unclear. Just suggest it to the others. Try to work it into a conversation, please." She looked at her black box. "I'm late," she said. "Appreciate you so very much. Wonderland would be nothing without its Mad Queen." She grabbed her black jacket and stood to leave.

"You didn't give me a line for the White Queen," I said. "What's hers?"

Bailey frowned before snapping her fingers. "Oh! The chessboard. That entire station scores poorly on our surveys. We're going to have the tram stop going through there; no one plays chess anymore. But what we're planning will be better, especially for you. In fact, I have a secret. Want to hear it?"

"Of course." Secrets were the best. That's why Caterpillar spoke in secrets.

"Ok, don't tell anyone." Bailey's smile grew wide again. "We're going to expand your station. There's going to be a hotel and restaurant based around Wonderland's Mad Queen. Pretty incredible, huh? You're going to be the entire face of Wonderland.

We'll have to take out the chessboard since it takes up too much real estate, but your garden will be so much bigger."

She was using words I didn't understand. Real estate? Hotel?

"But where would the chessboard go?" Wonderland needed its chessboard. We needed the chess pieces. I needed the White Queen.

"It would be gone," she said slowly, her eyes on the box and her fingers tapping across it. "We'd move the chess pieces to the Mad Tea Party or maybe have them sit with Caterpillar or something. Maybe have them work in the hotel." She looked up from the box and pointed her finger at me again.

Seriously, someone had to teach her how rude that was.

"Actually, that's a genius idea; totally keeping with the nonsense of Wonderland. I'll add that to the Team channel."

Anger rose in my belly and traveled up my throat, forcing words out. "Off with your head!"

"Beg your pardon?"

"You can't do this!" I shouted.

Bailey frowned, her attention back on her black box. "Why shouldn't we? The guests don't like the chessboard and it serves no purpose. That station is ridiculous. I mean Wonderland is itself ridiculous, but that station truly is."

"Ridiculous?!" I screamed. "You're ridiculous!" Next time Bailey came through my croquet garden, I would take care of this.

Bailey looked up from her black box, raising an eyebrow. "You got the emotion right, but not the words. It's off with your head. Now's not the time to improvise. Look, I know it's a change, but Wonderland needs a dynamic paradigm shift."

"Off with your head!" I howled, putting all my anger, all my madness into it. The room shook with my voice. But there was no one to obey my orders.

"Perfect. And I gotta run," Bailey said. "But you're awesome. Keep yelling and threatening to behead people. And please tell the station leads about their new lines." She reached forward and squeezed my hand before I could pull it away. "I appreciate you. Wonderland needs you. And you're definitely getting a nice bonus this quarter."

And before I could say anything, she left the room, the door sliding closed behind her. I gave chase, but my heavy skirts slowed me down. By the time I got outside, Bailey was already riding the gliding cart up the White Rabbit's burrow.

I couldn't let Bailey and Super Mega Fun World, LLC take out the chessboard. I had to tell the White Queen! She'd know what to do.

My garden, with its bright green grass studded with pink flamingos and flanked by heart-shaped rose bushes, glowed in the distance. I walked between the hedges, my flat cards bowing to me.

I ignored them; I had to get to the White—what was that? Two of my rose bushes dripped red paint onto the green grass, showing white petals beneath. Heat rose in my belly, a familiar sensation, a familiar memory. Behind me, I sensed the cards shifting, moving, jumping into the hedges.

"Who dared paint my roses red?" I screeched, my crown slipping down my head.

"Peace, my heart," a voice said behind me. It was the White Queen, her gown trailing misty threads behind her. My heart leapt, my anger vanishing as I drank in her figure. A tiny silver crown sat on her brow, holding her white hair back. Her skin was gossamer, her lips carnation, her eyes sky, matching the edging on her loose white dress. She was gorgeous and ethereal, glowing against the green and red in my garden. "Leave the poor cards to their paint. They're only trying to make you happy."

"Well, they're not," I snarled, but there was no true anger; not with her here.

She smiled and waved Ace over. The giant card, a single red

heart in the middle of his body, stomped over, his axe clutched in his hand. "I've an idea, though the guests won't like it. How about you rip out the white rose bushes and plant red ones? Then her majesty won't get as mad at you."

I sensed the cards behind me shift again. Was it that simple? Would replacing the rose bushes solve this problem?

Ace looked at me. I looked at the White Queen. "For me," she said. "It's such an easy solution. Do it for me, so you stop yelling at your cards. You can yell at the guests instead."

That sounded fair. I'd do it for her and no one else.

I nodded at Ace. "Go ahead," I said. "But make sure they're the right shade of red, or it's off with all your heads."

As one, my cards bowed. The White Queen held her hand out, and I took it, feeling the coolness of her fingers enclosing my warm ones. "We need to talk," she said. "I got a letter from Super Mega."

I drew her into the coolness of the hedges. "In a moment," I said, pulling her close to steal a few kisses.

After a bit, she pulled away. "I could spend the rest of my days kissing you," she said. "But I need you right now."

She held out a white envelope, and I took it, pulling back the cracked wax. Inside was one of Bailey's complex letters, with multiple pages and tiny letters. "Just sign it and give it back," I said with a yawn. I reached for her again.

"I can't," The White Queen sidestepped away from me. "I read this. They're destroying the chessboard. We won't have a home."

Oh, that's right. I'd forgotten. The painted roses had made me angry and the White Queen's kisses had made me happy. I'd forgotten all about Bailey's plan.

"They're making a hotel about me," I said. Pride, anger, and sadness warred in my chest. "Bailey says not enough guests care about chess. They don't know who you are."

"And so we're to be erased," the White Queen said. "So no one can learn our story and how I helped Alice. And if they can do this to me, to my pieces, they can do it to any of us."

This was easy to solve. "Off with their heads, then!" I said. "Where's Ace? I was just thinking he needed to come to her meetings with me."

"You can't kill all the guests, all the people in the dark clothes."

"I can behead Bailey. That will take care of this problem. No Bailey, no destroying the chessboard."

"And another will take her place." The White Queen drew me down next to her, our backs against a hedge. Tiny white and red flowers, too tiny to sing, grew beneath us. "We need to think and plan, like we did with the roses. You have to be tired of losing cards for painting your roses red."

"Ace doesn't actually kill them," I muttered. "I know that. They change their suits and numbers and pretend they're someone else."

The White Queen laughed and kissed my cheek, her eyelashes tickling me. "I adore you know that and do nothing, my Queen of Hearts."

"Beheading Bailey will take care of this problem," I insisted. "They wouldn't dare to send someone else."

"And I think we should negotiate," the White Queen said. "Play the chess game they want us to play. We can strategize and win this. I'm very good at chess. I scheduled a meeting—I think that's how Bailey likes it—for tomorrow. Come with me."

"Can I bring Ace?"

The White Queen leaned close for a kiss. "If that makes you feel better, but he won't be needed."

❧

"I'm sorry," Bailey said. She had a smear of lipstick on her teeth and wore a different blue dress today, one with lace on the sleeves. She folded her hands on the conference room table. This room never changed—never became more than it could be. "I wish I could do something, but our guests are quite clear. They don't like the chessboard. I'm sure you understand. Our guests pay for all our salaries—your gifts, I mean. And keeping them happy is our job. They want more of our Mad Queen!"

"Our Mad Queen?" the White Queen said. We'd joined Bailey at the conference room table, our hands folded in front of us, like Bailey's were. Ace stood behind us, his axe against a shoulder. The bright lights in the room made the White Queen glow.

"Our Mad Queen," Bailey echoed. "She matches our ad campaign brilliantly. But don't worry about you or your chess pieces. We've found places for you in the Tulgey Woods, a more mysterious and frightening part of Wonderland we know the guests will adore. And having chess pieces in there will fit perfectly with our Halloween marketing campaign. You can all skulk through the shadows and startle our guests. They'll be asking, 'what was that?' all the way home." She gleefully rubbed her hands together, her smile growing wide again.

What on earth were the Tugley Woods? I'd never heard of them. Every time I had a conversation with Bailey, I found her more and more of an imbecile.

"The Tulgey Woods isn't a part of Wonderland," the White Queen said.

"I know. It's actually where the Jabberwocky lives—I did my reading—but we're going to build it, taking out part of Caterpillar's mushroom area. It's going to be fine. My engineers say there's plenty of room there."

The White Queen's blue eyes flashed. "But you can't take out part of the Caterpillar's mushroom anymore than you can take out the chessboard!"

Bailey looked back and forth between the White Queen and me. "I see—how fascinating and oddly modern. Wouldn't have expected it." She tugged on her chin. "I can see our guests liking the two of you being a couple... in about ten years. We'll do some focus groups around it. But if you want, I can have you play croquet with our Mad Queen for the time being; make your home her croquet garden."

I could have the White Queen to myself all the time. She wouldn't have to leave me to go back to her chessboard. This would be a true gift. Perhaps Bailey wasn't a complete idiot after all.

"I'm a queen too," the White Queen stated. "And I need my own land."

"Yes, and you're important to me," Bailey said. She shaped her hands into a heart shape and put it over her chest. "You know I adore you, but our guests don't. And we're here to serve them."

I tugged on the White Queen's hand, leaning over to whisper, "Why can't you just live with me?"

"Because my chess pieces deserve a home, too. Living with you would be wonderful, but I can't abandon my people."

Fine. She was right. I let out a frustrated sigh. If only she'd let me behead Bailey, we could solve this problem right now.

The White Queen snapped her fingers. "I've an idea. Why can't you do one of your ad campaigns about us? If they under-stand all that I did for Alice, they would love us too. Additionally, chess is fascinating and children everywhere love it."

"No, they don't," Bailey said. "Chess is a dead game. Give them Dying Unicorns, War of Weird, or Tunnelcrack. No one knows or cares about chess. And frankly, your characters are boring. We can't afford the cost of an ad campaign around charac-ters no one likes."

"But if they just—"

Bailey's black box buzzed, making me jump. "Look, I hate to

be so blunt, but you're not listening and that tells me this isn't going to work. The chessboard will be destroyed tomorrow to make room for the Mad Queen's hotel. If you and your people don't vacate the area, you will also be destroyed. Which will be a shame, but really, who cares? The guests don't and while I like your look, if the guests don't like you, there's nothing I can do."

"I see," the White Queen said. "So you prefer Mad Queens?"

"It's not about me. It's about what our guests prefer."

"Madness over logic. Over solutions. Over compromise."

"It is the way of the world," Bailey said. She stood, her fingers closing over her black box. "I do have another meeting, if you both could step out, please."

The White Queen took my hand and straightened her crown. "Then off with your head."

She didn't say it right. She said it like a statement, with none of the anger, the madness I had. That would be easy to fix, though.

"Yeah, not sure another Mad Queen would work in this situation. Also, you need more anger for that. But kudos for trying!" Bailey pointed her finger at the White Queen. "Now, I'm dreadfully late for this meeting, if you'll excuse me."

"I don't excuse you," the White Queen said. "You are speaking to two queens; you owe us your reverence." The White Queen's eyes went arctic, and she nodded at me.

"Off with her head!" I ordered Ace.

"Oh, stop this nonse—"

Ace swung his axe and red sprayed.

The White Queen stepped over Bailey, her white dress flecked with the color of roses, and into the hallway where her chess pieces waited. "Destroy the gliding cart, the trams, and this building," she commanded.

She turned to me, her eyes ice. "I wonder what the guests will think of our version of Wonderland? I hope they give us positive comments."

I dabbed red from my cheek and folded the White Queen's cool hand within my own. What could two Mad Queens do together? It would be insanity to find out.

I couldn't wait.

ALECIA IN THE WARDROBE

MORRIGAN PUHR

Author's Note: Dedicated to my students who spark my imagination and keep my soul's fire blazing. You will forever be in this queen's heart. This Classroom Queen humbly requests this story be read in a British Accent.

"Oh, tea dribblings!" Alecia lifted her phone so incredibly close to her face that if it were a hole, she would most certainly fall into it. Then she puffed out her rosy cheeks, tugged on her tight collar, and forced her thumbs back to the screen.

Bibs Darling, I have something terribly important to tell you.

Alecia read the words back to herself. First silently, then out loud, and then to the red-tailed cat purring at her hip.

"Sweet Dina, whatever am I doing?" Something about asking that particular question made Alecia feel rather queer. So queer in fact, that she considered not telling Bibs at all. T'would be easier to go back to the book she was reading. The red queen waited in the wardrobe afterall. Even still, every time Alecia tried to go back to the pages, she could not stop thinking. And Alecia was positively fed up with thinking.

Bibs, it's taken me a while to decide, but finally I'm convinced it's the right thing to do... to tell you that I have something very important to tell you, I mean.

"Oh, double trouble, I sound positively redundant... stuffy even." Alecia tugged on the collar of her rainbow-colored dress. "I need to sound cool, relaxed, in control." Dina licked her paw in agreement, causing Alecia to delete the message and start over.

Hey girl, Thanks for lending me your math book. If you ever need anything. I mean anything... I got you. Just wondering, could we meet toms, like right after school?

"Puffer pigs!" Alecia exclaimed to the cat who had rolled on her back. "I sound positively ridiculous. No, worse than ridiculous —I sound American. After all, only an American would say toms when they meant tomorrow. Oh trouble, everything is upside down and right side up," Alecia said as she slid off the bed and shuffled over to the wardrobe. "Oh, Dina darling, what's gotten into...?"

Just then the thoughts came back.

I wish I weren't such a 'fraidy cat, she considered as she stepped into the towering wardrobe. *Rather, I wish I were someone else, anyone else entirely.* And then for no reason whatsoever, the collar on her rainbow dress loosened. Alecia paused just long enough to notice this before another thought came.

I wish I weren't so hideous. Then she would want to see me, to really see me. Then in one quick *WHHHOOP,* her collar had grown into a hoop and the sleeves on her dress were so large they tumbled off her shoulders. Even more disturbing, when she went to reach for the book about the Red Queen, the shelf that used to be waist high now towered above her. Alas, Alecia was too troubled with the *thoughts* to even notice.

I wish I weren't so shy then she could hear me, the real me. An ache pulled at her chest and then the *thought* began circling round and round her mind. With each loop, Alecia shrunk smaller and smaller until she was so small her rainbow-colored dress was nothing but a heaping tent around her.

I wish I were smarter, then I would have the right words to make her love me, Alecia thought. By this time, she'd shrunken so tiny she was roughly the size of a thimble. And still the *thoughts* came. Alecia was just about to have another when a deep voice crackled through the dim light.

"Whimsical-simsical."

"Oh my!" Alecia said, realizing how small she'd become and quickly covering herself with a ribbon which happened to make a perfect dress for her new size. "Whatever is that supposed to mean?" she said aloud before she even thought about who might have said such a silly phrase.

"Nothing means anything, and anything means nothing," the smooth voice answered back.

"Well, that's positively absurd," Alecia replied, spinning in a circle to find the voice. When she couldn't see who was talking, she balled her hands into fists and exclaimed, "Tis almost as absurd as trying to find you."

"I'm here." Two lovely green eyes floated directly in front of her. "And here." A fluffy tail appeared. "And here," he laughed as two perfect cat ears followed. "Not that it means anything," the cat said, through a long-mouthed grin.

"Well of course, it means something," Alecia responded, quite interested in the pair of glowing eyes. "Everything means something."

"Mean shmean, whatever does anything ever mean?" Then the cat yawned so wide she could see the back of his pink tongue.

"Well, a thing means what you think it means," Alecia explained.

"Well, I think... a thing means nothing." And with that, the wide grin, the ears, the tail, and two lovely green eyes simply disappeared.

"Cat. Come back. Please don't leave me." Alecia did not want to be alone, not just because she was the size of a thimble, but because she was alone with her *thoughts*. Luckily for Alecia, she was not in fact alone.

"How rude," a very pretentious, very nasally voice said.

"Oh, I beg your pardon, I wasn't trying to be rude. I thought—"

"Did you really?"

"Did I really *what*?" Alecia asked in shock.

"Think. Persnickety girl, a thinking person would not stand right on someone's nose."

"Well I..." Alecia jumped back, realizing she had indeed been standing on the very bulbous nose of one very grouchy looking face. When she leaned over, she was shocked to find that this was no ordinary face. Quite the opposite actually. It was a face in the floor, a floor face, and a very peculiar one at that.

"I beg your pardon," she said again, making sure not to stand on any other part of the man who was in the floor or was it the floor who was in the man? It was a troubling question and one that made her tired of thinking again.

"Today has been a very troubling day. You see, I was supposed to message, but then I decided to read, and then I just started thinking, and the more I thought well... the smaller I got, and then—"

"I do indeed see, though that's not half as troubling as having someone stand on your face."

"I certainly would not like that at all," Alecia said, taking one more step back to avoid the spray of spittle jumping up and then falling back into the floor-man's mouth. "But you must know, I didn't see you."

"That's just the problem, isn't it? Exactly what I said. No one ever sees; no one actually looks."

"Good heavens, you can't expect me to know a person was hiding in the bottom of my closet?" Alecia said.

There was a long pause as a very slimy tongue slid slowly over his bottom lip. Alecia inched backward causing his face to scrunch so tight she thought she might laugh.

"Too busy setting down boxes, grabbing books, and throwing your nasty shoes to notice anything but yourself." Spit sprayed everywhere, covering his nose and eyes. This seemed to make the floor-man even more upset as his voice now shook with rage. "I'll have you know you are the one who is hiding in the bottom of a closet. I live here. And if you would just look at me, you would see me for what I am, and we would both be better off."

Alecia squinted her eyes and tried to see him, to *really* see him. Bushy brows hung like thick curtains over down-turned eyes. The ball on the end of his nose was large and round almost like a baseball. His lips were full and would be attractive if they were not puckered in such a sour manner.

"Look you impertinent girl, use your eyes. You said you could think—prove it." The floor-man's mouth curled in disgust.

This was not the type of thinking Alecia was used to. *What kind of purpose could a man in the floor of a wardrobe have? What is it she was expected to see?*

"Well, are you going to open me, or not?" he asked, without giving her proper time to think.

"Oh... Oh yes," Alecia said, pretending she understood. "I will open you right now." Standing over his face, she leaned down only to realize she had no idea what he meant. *Perhaps, he wants me to listen so he can open up to me.* As she searched his long rectangular face for answers, a peculiar thought occurred to her. The tip of his nose looked more like a doorknob than a baseball. *Open me*, she thought.

"Oh my, I've got it. You're a door, and you want someone to open you?" she said quite proudly.

"The girl can think," he said, softening his tone. Alecia placed her palm flat against his nose. "How do I op—"

The answer came when the floor-man's eyebrows became hinges and his entire face dropped downward. Alecia teetered on the edge of his chin balancing on her toes. Just when she was about to rock back upon her heels, she felt a very firm paw push her forward.

Oh goodness! OH GOODNESS! When Alecia tried to scream the words tangled in her brain until she was falling head over heels and heels over head. Stomach twisting, her heart fluttered so loud she couldn't hear anything but the rush of pure panic.

At first the feeling was too much but then Alecia recognized it. She'd had a similar feeling no less than a million times about Bibs, well of course she had.

Alecia knew she should be messaging Bibs, rather than being here. T'was that precise moment Alecia realized she had no idea where here was. She'd been so preoccupied with her thoughts that she hadn't even considered what she was doing.

What am I doing? she considered. It took a moment for her to decide that she was certainly falling. *But where? I seem to be falling right through the center of a circle,* she thought. A circle surrounded with bright red bricks.

Even more peculiar, Alecia soon realized that the further she fell, the slower she was falling.

I've got to get out of here, Alecia thought, chewing on the inside of her cheek. Bibs hated it when she did that, chewing on the inside of her cheek that is. This only made the thoughts come back: *If only I could stop all these annoying habits.* If Alecia weren't so preoccupied with Bibs, she might have heard the WHHOOP. Of course, she couldn't hear much of anything in her condition. Luckily, the girl who was now drifting downward could still feel. And what she felt was her ribbon dress growing embarrassingly loose.

"Oh goodness!" Alecia said aloud. For t'was in that moment that the young woman realized her shrinking may not have come for no reason whatsoever, but for a very good reason altogether.

Maybe, when I think a bad thought I shrink, which means... I am quite positively shrinking myself, she thought. *Oh No! If I keep thinking these negative thoughts, I just might grow so small I disappear altogether. And I certainly don't want that.* In an instant, Alecia grew back to the size of a proper thimble. It was also then that she heard a very loud, very happy chorus singing beneath her.

"Painting the treacle well red. We're painting the treacle well red. My oh my, hello, goodbye, we'll paint until we're dead." The men did not so much as take a breath before they began again from the beginning. "Painting the treacle well red." This time louder and more encouraging than before. By the third or fourth time, Alecia found herself singing along though she had no idea what a treacle well was.

Dropping her head, she squinted to see the bottom. Instead, she saw three rectangular forms, hanging from the side of the well. Stacked one above the other, each sang as they splashed a healthy dose of red paint against the dull gray bricks.

"Hello," she yelled down to them. And then quite suddenly, they all stopped singing. "Why are you painting the well red?" she asked, nearing the figures who she now recognized as playing cards.

"Can you hear me?" she asked the Two of Hearts as she drifted closer. Instead of responding, the card put both hands directly over his face.

"I can see you," she said to the card, whose stick-like knees slapped together so hard she worried they might spark. "Oh, do calm down. Just look at you, you've gone and painted your face red," she said with sympathy.

The trembling card no more responded than did he pull his ruddy hands from his face.

Oh, dribbling teapot. Alecia knew exactly what it was like to feel so small.

"Don't be shy," Alecia cooed sweetly to the Three of Hearts. The cowering card hung just below the Two of Hearts. As she neared, she noticed the Three of Hearts had grown so pale he looked almost pink. "Really, I don't want to hurt you. I simply need to get out of this well. You see, I need to get big again so I can play with my cat, and talk to my friend, and—"

At this, all four corners of his card curled inward with a soggy, defeated sort of bend. "Don't be sad." But Alecia's words did not work as a small tremor had moved into his cheeks and hands. This caused bits of paint to Drip. Drip. Drip. By this time, she'd floated further downward and was just beneath him. In one last attempt, she cried out, "Please. Talk to me." Alecia's request was met with a single splash of bright red paint right between her eyes.

"Oh trouble," she said as she addressed the Four of Hearts who was trying not to laugh. "Please laugh at me. Oh, and sing. I do love it when you sing."

At this, all three cards flung their chests concave against the walls.

"Oh trouble, I can still see you. You have markings on your cards and of course the paint brushes and buckets. Please, I just want someone to listen to me." And then for no reason whatsoever Alecia stopped falling. That is to say, she quit drifting downward and froze right there in midair. Dangling right next to the Four of Hearts, her tiny body hung in the air in a manner quite unnatural. This amused the Four of Hearts who was trying not to giggle.

Alecia remained stuck in the air for what felt to be a very long time, but what was not in fact very long at all. In this not so very long time, she began longing for Dina and Bibs and—

"Listen to you, and why should anyone ever listen to you?" an over-bearing screech hollered from above.

"Impossible," Alecia said as she looked up to see a very red-cheeked, very plump queen flying directly toward her. Crown sagging over her left eye, the raging queen looked exactly like the one on the front cover of her book back in her closet.

"Oh bother," Alecia said before turning toward the Four of Hearts who was smashed against the wall trembling. "Please sir, how do I get out of here? I need to go home."

"OFF WITH HER HEAD!" the loud queen commanded as she flew straight toward Alecia.

The breath in Alecia's lungs froze as the queen rushed toward her with all the venom of a spider paralyzing its prey. Eyes lit with delight, her majesty did not stop until she was so close to Alecia that a stray hair on her fleshy chin was practically tickling Alecia's forehead. Alecia remained frozen in the center of the well, hands trembling just as shakily as all the other cards.

"Can you hear me?" the queen yelled directly into Alecia's face. Just then her rather large, rather ornate crown shifted. Not just a tiny tilt, but a large dip until the golden band completely covered her left eye. At this, the queen lurched back, pressed out her jelly-shaped belly and whimpered as if she'd just been bitten. Then ripping the headdress from her head, she scolded the disobedient crown as if it were an unruly dog before flinging the poor thing back upon her brow. It took a bit of wrangling, but in the end the crown was set straight, and her hair was set loose.

The entire scene was positively ridiculous. But Alecia knew better than to laugh, for she knew far too much about hearts.

Impulsive, irrational, and filled with rage one moment and euphoria the next, the heart ruled with such passion that no one, not even the queen herself, ever knew what one ruled by the heart might do. It was a serious condition indeed.

Not wanting to anger the queen further, Alecia tipped her head and tried to bow. This turned out to be rather challenging given that every time she bent forward, her entire body would roll in an awkward somersault. If this weren't bad enough, Alecia was having a terrible time with her tongue. She kept trying to make it say: *It's a pleasure to meet you, your grace.* But instead, it said nothing—not a single word.

At this the red queen squeezed her eyes tight, tilted her head, and stared quite perplexed at the silent girl. Then she pointed at the Four of Hearts who stood wide-eyed, staring.

"YOU, Eight of Hearts," the queen said, wrestling her crown until it was once again straight upon her brow. "AM I SPEAKING TO MYSELF?" the queen screeched at the Four of Hearts. Teeth chattering and paint leaking down his leg, the Four of Hearts became so stiff Alecia worried he might shatter.

"OFF WITH HIS HEAD," the queen commanded.

"But he's the 4," Alecia said aloud. "Oh no! I didn't mean that. What I meant to say was: it's a pleasure to meet you, your grace." Then Alecia felt so embarrassed she couldn't stop her hands from covering her face. *Oh trouble, this is as bad as trying to tell Bibs*, she thought, forcing her hands to slide down her shaking cheeks.

The queen pinched her face even tighter as the crown on her brow suddenly tipped crooked again.

"Pl... pl... please, my queen," the card said, trembling so violently his body was actually slapping against the wall.

"P... p... please my queen," the crazed ruler laughed and spun in a wild circle. "Please don't cut my head off," she mocked. And when she did, the other two cards laughed. At this, the ashamed card peeled himself off the wall and rolled himself from the bottom up.

"Look my queen, he's a scroll," the Two of Hearts laughed. And this made Alecia very angry. So angry in fact that she had no ability to remember that she was afraid.

"Stop it at once!" Alecia hollered.

"What did you say?" The queen leaned so close that the rogue chin hair pressed itself to the poor girl's forehead. The crown dropped off the queen's left eye and still the woman would not pull her blazing gaze.

After a very long pause, Alecia's tongue finally spoke, "I... I... I said what I mean."

"And what do you mean?" the queen asked.

"The question, your grace, is what do you mean?" Alecia said shakily.

"YOU THINK I DON'T KNOW WHAT IT IS THAT I MEAN?"

"Oh no your grace, I know you mean what you think you mean and that's what makes you so perfectly passionate," Alecia said in earnest.

The queen's eyes pinched, and her lips pressed into a very serious scowl. Alecia felt her heart skip a beat and then two.

Then the queen's red lips curled up into a wry smile. "AH YES, I mean what I think I mean. That's exactly right."

"It is you who are exactly right," Alecia added slyly.

"I am?" the queen asked.

"Oh yes, your highness. We all know that you know, that when we are ruled by the thundering ardor of our hearts we sometimes, very often, almost always have a difficult time even listening to the wisdom of our minds. And this is why there is no need to cut off our heads. Afterall, you already have our hearts," Alecia said and somehow managed a proper bow.

The puffy-cheeked queen was stilled. Her cold dark eyes met Alecia's, and they stayed like that for quite a little while.

"I have your heart, do I?" the queen asked with a slippery side-eye.

"Why yes, your highness, we all love a ruler who knows how to listen."

"If you want to be heard, child, you must speak," the queen said as she straightened the crooked crown on her head. Two cards burst into applause, and the queen smiled a regal, dangerous sort of smile. A smile made by a woman who wants to be heard but will never hear. Her heart's desire to be loved and admired was just too loud.

Alecia once again curtsied, nodded, and then clapped.

And then for no apparent reason whatsoever, the queen waved her very plump hand. Once again Alecia was falling. This time she fell faster and faster. As she neared the bottom of the well, Alecia became quite concerned.

"Stop me at once," she screamed. To Alecia's surprise, she did. The queen had stopped her just above a lovely pond surrounded by a lush garden. "Now put me down slowly on the bank, please." When her feet gently met the ground, the girl added. "Thank you, your highness for teaching me to speak."

To which a loud echoing laugh bellowed up and down the treacle well walls. Alecia had not even taken a step when a sweet voice bubbled before her.

"What beautiful hair you have." The pond, as it were, was surrounded with bright purple flowers, towering trees, and light-ning bugs, who were quite busy zipping here and zapping there. "And your eyes, my oh my, the stories they tell."

"Oh, you are too kind," Alecia said, leaning over to see who was talking to her. The voice came from the pond itself, which was a very thick brown, syrupy puddle lit from the middle with a golden light and shimmering with divine elegance. Alecia situated herself on a quaint rock overlooking the little pond.

"The glow of your pond is beyond anything I have ever seen."

"I have never met a young lady with such wisdom, such grace," the syrupy liquid said as it gathered into relaxing ripples. "We are made more beautiful by your presence."

"We, what do you mean we?" Alecia asked too quickly. "Oh goodness, I'm sorry I didn't mean to be rude. I mean…"

"You mean what only you can, and you are the only one who can mean anything," the little ripples replied. A warmth grew in Alecia's chest until she choked on the thought of someone knowing her. Little tears rolled down her cheek and tumbled into the syrup below. Glowing golden eyes formed above the pouting lips. Long and soft, a gentle face formed on the surface. It resembled the copper statue of a wise woman with kind eyes and soft cheeks.

"I am a treacle well."

"A treacle well." Alecia leaned far over the puddle resisting the urge to dip her fingers into its sticky surface. "Stay with me," the treacle well continued, "so I may look at your beauty, drink your tears, and admire your grace."

Alecia was happy to stay near the edge of the little pond day after day. It spoke of nothing but of her beauty, courage, and wisdom. Until one day, for no particular reason two lovely green eyes appeared, floating right next to her.

"Whimsical-simsical."

"Oh, there you are," Alecia said to the eyes. "I was hoping to see you again."

"But you can't see me, not really," a calm grin said back.

"Well, I can see your eyes and your… oh trouble, you're gone again." Alecia let out a very sad huff. "Please cat, do come back. Don't you think it right to let me see the whole you?"

"No one can see what cannot be seen."

"Oh trouble, whatever is that supposed to mean?" But before the cat could respond, Alecia shook her head and said, "I know I know: mean shmean. Still, don't you think it would be right for—"

"No such thing as right when there is nothing left."

"Left?"

"I must be going. Oh, by the way, if you keep going, there won't be much of you left either."

"Won't be much of me left? Cat, what does that mean?" But there was no answer. The cat had quite simply disappeared.

Alecia sat near the sweet treacle, listening to its compliments and wondering what the cat meant. It was about this time that one very annoying lightning bug buzzed right into her ear.

"Do you see it?" he hissed. Alecia crammed her finger into her ear, but the crazed little creature simply burrowed in. "Won't get rid of me that easily," the determined voice explained. "Not until you see."

"See what?" Alecia asked, shaking her head from side to side in a failed attempt to dislodge the bug who had braced himself quite sturdily at the base of her eardrum.

"Look to the bottom of the well. There you will see three of whom none dare tell."

"You can't be serious," Alecia said anxiously, chewing her cheek.

"Look. Look and then if you want, I will leave you here until nothing is right and very little is left."

Alecia swallowed hard and forced herself to peer down through the thick syrup, past the golden light, and into the dark depths. There she could see three figures. Squinting, she realized they were girls all who appeared to be floating lifelessly in the thick syrup. Alecia's stomach turned sour as she saw the first who looked up. Yet, her eyes were blindfolded—she could not see. The second lay on her side, ears covered—she could not hear. The third lay on her back, mouth gagged—she could not speak.

"Who are they?" Alecia whispered so softly that the treacle well could not hear.

"Elsie, Lacie, and Tillie."

"Elsie, Lacie, and Tillie," Alecia repeated. "Why that's impossible! The treacle well is sweet and kind, she would never harm anything."

"But would the girls harm themselves?" the lightning bug hissed.

"Whatever do you mean?"

"How long must a girl hide from what she sees, hears, and speaks before there's nothing left of her at all?"

As soon as she asked the question, Alecia realized she had no idea how long she'd been staring into the well. When had she last seen Dina, or her parents, or Bibs?

"Happy seeing what you want to see. Happy hearing what you want to hear. Happy saying what you want to say. If you wants to be heard, you gots to speak. If you wants to be understood, you gots to be wise about who is understanding," the little bug said as he crawled out of her ear.

Alecia chewed the inside of her cheek. "And you see me, and you hear me, and you understand me. But what about you?"

"See yourself as I see you." The lightning bug lit a bright light and circled round Alecia's head. "You're not a monster. You're not a saint. You're just regular you and that's enough." Then the lightning bug zipped directly between her eyes. Hovering in the air, his little legs kicked as he said, "If you can't see your own beauty, how can you see mine? If you can't hear your own truth, how can you hear mine? If you want to be understood but not to understand, then there is nothing left." With that, he zipped away.

"But I do see my own beauty," Alecia yelled after him. Then for no particular reason she grew so tall her ribbon dress burst right off her body. "I do want to tell Bibs the truth," Alecia said as she grew at least three feet more. "And it's okay to be regular me."

WHHOOP. The loud whoosh of Alecia's growing back to her normal size filled the entire wardrobe. Soon she was standing right where she'd left off. Throwing her clothes on, she grabbed her book, scooped up her phone, and raced to her bed. Then with a grin as wise as a Cheshire Cat's and as bright as a lightning bug she began texting:

Dear Bibs,
I have had the most peculiar dream. I can't wait to tell you all about it.
I also have something really exciting to tell you. It might surprise you,
but as my closest friend, I know you'll be there for me.

BOY KIND / GIRL KIND
STEPHANIE SANDERS-JACOB

Harper didn't want to spend the summer with her grandparents. She was too old for that. At fifteen she was beyond the brightly colored board games her grandmother pulled out of the closet, beyond the stories her grandfather insisted on telling as the sky turned to rust and the fireflies took flight. Besides, it was boring here in the country where her cell phone service dwindled and there was nothing within walking distance except the crooked creek she'd waded in as a girl, the dark wood on the edge of their property. There wasn't anything to do.

She followed their old swaybacked bloodhound around the house and back, watching its ears drag the dirt as it sniffed.

"Find anything good, Bayard?" she asked.

The bloodhound gave a lazy shake of its tail, kept its nose to the ground. Harper continued to follow.

She glanced down at the silver watch on her left wrist, a gift from her older sister. Melody was in college, had moved out long ago and wasn't subjected to these monotonous summers spent trailing a dog in the late-summer heat. She wondered why she couldn't stay at Melody's place in the city. They could be having lunch at one of those cool little cafés only Melody knew about, or stealing sips out of a bottle of cheap whisky, smuggling candy into a theater.

She frowned, realized she'd looked at her watch but hadn't really registered the time. She looked again. It was a little past one. Her grandmother had wanted her back before three when they'd start baking biscuits for an early dinner. She sighed. Another hour or two to kill.

Bayard waddled toward the long grasses marking the edge of the yard. He was moving a little faster now, having struck upon a scent. Harper was curious. He was, by far, the most interesting thing about summer. His nose was so sensitive, so expertly made, that one time he'd led her to an ant mound, somehow able to smell the minuscule insects inside.

She pushed into the tall weeds. The grass parted around Bayard and she walked in the trampled path he'd left. She snapped the heads off goldenrods as she went, sending the blooms tumbling down.

The grass whispered and shook. Bayard was running now, a gallop that wasn't too hard to keep up with even with the humped terrain and tangled stalks lashing at her legs. She jogged in his wake. "Good boy," she said. "Keep on it." She could no longer see the black saddle of his fur, his red tail, but the disturbance he made in the weeds was enough.

Bayard, then Harper, emerged near the creek, nearly dry now. Small pools of water lay still between rocks. Bayard lifted his head and looked at the rabbit sitting on its hind legs near one such puddle, cleaning its face with its paws.

Harper paused. The rabbit was pure white with a little snub nose. It was so unlike the lean, grayish-brown creatures she'd become accustomed to finding around her grandparents' place—it had to be someone's escaped pet.

"Bayard," she hissed, warning the dog to go no further. But it was too late; he rushed at the rabbit and chased it up out of the creek. Harper stumbled after him, slipped in the silty bottom, and scrambled up again. Bayard howled long and low, disappearing beyond sight.

"Shit," she said, looking down at her scraped and muddy legs. She swiped at some of the dirt with her hands, found it only to smear. She'd have to take a shower, which meant she had to get back well before biscuit-baking-time, which meant she needed to find Bayard soon. "Bayard!" she yelled, but the dog was long gone.

She tramped into the field on the other side of the creek. "Bayard!" She thought she heard him bay in the distance and followed the sound. She walked slowly, inspecting the plants for signs of disturbance, and found nothing. Harper had lost him.

She wandered aimlessly through the grass, calling out for the dog every so often, standing still to listen for his reply. She hoped he hadn't caught the little bunny; it was unlikely as the dog was lumbering and old, but if he had the luck to corner it somewhere, he'd likely kill it. He had some spark in him yet.

"Bayard!"

The foliage to her right rustled and tossed. Harper stood rigid. "Bayard?" she asked.

The smallest tabby kitten she'd ever seen padded out from the weeds. It looked up at her, mewed expectantly.

"What's going on?" she asked, falling to her knees. The kitten rubbed against her thighs, her hands. "Where did you come from?"

The cat purred and butted its head against her skin. She stroked its back. The kitten hardly looked old enough to be without its mother. She'd have to take it back to the house, see if her grandmother could save it. She put her hands around its middle to lift it.

"Put me down," the kitten spoke.

Harper screamed, let the thing drop back to the ground.

The kitten plopped down on its side, flicked its black-tipped tail.

"Hello?" Harper asked, breath ragged. She was shaking now. She'd heard the kitten talk. A small, babyish voice, but a voice all the same. The kitten had spoken. "Hello?" she asked again.

The kitten mewed.

Harper looked around. Perhaps someone else had made the sound, was toying with her from the depths of the grass. They were in the middle of nowhere—there shouldn't have been anyone near—but she'd seen a white rabbit, a strange portent; maybe the day would get stranger yet. "Who's there?" she demanded.

The cat rose, ground its forehead into her palm. "Oh, kitty," Harper sighed. "What is happening?"

The kitten sat before her, licked its paw. "Everything," said the kitten between strokes of its tongue. "And nothing at all."

Harper fell backward, caught herself with her hands. "What?" she gasped.

"You asked me what was happening, and I told you," said the cat, a hint of annoyance in its tiny voice.

"No, no, no, no," Harper scooted away from the cat, crawling in an awkward crab walk.

The kitten stood, approached. It meowed and Harper screamed. "Grandma! Grandpa! Help me! Help!" She knew they wouldn't hear her unless the wind was right, but she had to try. She pushed herself to standing, wobbled a bit. "You stay away from me," she cried.

She turned and ran. "Bayard!" Maybe the dog would kill the wretched thing. "Bayard!"

Tears streamed down her cheeks and blurred her vision. She tripped over a root, landed hard on her front. Her breath knocked out of her in one big puff and the pain made her clutch at her stomach. "Grandpa!" she called. She could imagine him striding up with his big hunting rifle and blasting the little thing away. She wanted it gone. She wanted it dead.

Meow. The kitten walked over her legs, dug in its needle-like claws. "Where are you going?" it asked in its high whine.

"Please, no," Harper cried. She pulled herself forward, gripping tight to the clumps of weeds, belly sliding over rough earth.

The cat sat, rode her legs as they dragged through the field. It sighed. "I don't know why you're acting like this."

"Get off of me!" Harper kicked, and the cat jumped off her legs, nimble and unfazed.

"Why are you leaving? We've only just met."

"Stop it! Stop!" Harper sobbed. She sat up, hugged herself tight. "Stop talking."

The cat meowed, but there was something taunting about the sound, something snide. Harper cried. "I said stop!"

"I *did* stop," said the cat.

"What—what are you?" Harper drew her legs in, away from the creature, afraid of what it might do.

The kitten cocked its head. "You mean you don't know?"

Harper shook her head, snot swinging from her nose. She pushed herself farther into the weeds.

"Well, I'm a cat."

"No," said Harper.

"Yes," said the cat, walking toward her. "My name's Cheshire. Member of the family Felidae, order Carnivora. Domesticated, of course."

"I know what a cat is," spat Harper.

"Do you?" asked the kitten.

"You stay back!" kicked Harper. "You're no cat."

"If I'm not a cat, then what am I?" The Cheshire kitten looked at her intently, seemed genuinely interested in her answer.

"I don't know what you are. A monster. A beast. Some sort of demon." Harper hiccupped, choked down another sob.

The kitten pondered this for a moment. "I was always told I was a cat."

"No," said Harper.

"Well, then what does that make you?" The not-quite-cat circled her, sniffed her skin.

"Human," Harper said. She pressed her fingers to her eyes. "Make it stop. Make it stop."

"Well, I know that," snarled the kitten. "But what kind?"

"Homo sapiens? I don't know! Get away!"

The cat stretched, raising its rump high in the air. "I meant boy-kind or girl-kind. Which kind are you?"

Harper let her hands fall from her eyes. "What?" she asked. The kitten circled her again.

"Boy or girl. You have to choose."

Harper wrapped her arms around her middle, held herself tight.

"Hmm," mused the cat. "You have short hair like the boy-kind but a little voice like the girl-kind and your clothes—they're ugly and covered in mud. I don't know what kind you are. Tell me. Tell me what kind you are." Cheshire sat down hard on its haunches.

"Get away," Harper said.

The cat raised its nose and sniffed hard at the air, whiskers wiggling. "You stink, that's for sure, but I can't tell what kind you are."

Harper didn't want to tell this fiend anything. She wanted it to go away. "Bayard! Grandpa!"

"No. I don't think so," sighed the cat. "You don't look like either of those. Let's try it this way... Do you like ponies and flowers and hair bows and sweets?"

"It doesn't work that way," said Harper. "That doesn't tell you anything."

"Do you like baseball and bubblegum and throwing rocks in the river?"

"What?"

"Tell me," hissed the cat. "Tell me what kind you are! You have to choose."

The truth was that Harper liked all of those things. Harper liked none of those things. Harper liked what Harper liked and gender had no bearing on it. In fact, Harper bristled when her grandmother petted her hair and called her a good girl, when her grandpa chuckled and called her his tomboy. They hadn't thought about why until this very moment, until the cat dug its claws into their skin and screeched, "Tell me!"

"Ow!" Harper smacked at the cat.

"Tell me what kind, I said!" Cheshire smacked back. Red streaks blossomed on Harper's skin.

"Neither!" Harper gasped. "Both!"

The cat relaxed, eased back onto the ground. "Oh. Why didn't you say so?"

"It only just became clear to me," they sniffled. "No one has ever asked me that before."

"Hmm," purred the cat. "There's still one problem."

"What's that?" Harper asked, protecting their arms, scared of another attack.

"What do I call you?"

"Harper," Harper said, relaxing. "Just Harper."

"That's good," said the cat and head-butted them like it was giving her a high-five. "You've found the way. Some don't recognize it when they do; some don't ever want to."

"What?" Harper asked.

"Nothing," sighed the cat.

"I have to go home now," they said. "I have to find Bayard." Harper stood, looked toward the tree line.

"Well, first he went this way," the kitten said, flicking its tail back toward the house. "Then he went that way. But, as for me, myself, personally, I will be taking a shortcut."

"Oh, um, okay," said Harper.

The Cheshire kitten nodded. "Goodbye, Harper,"

"Goodbye?"

The cat slunk back into the weeds without looking back. Harper stood for a moment, watching the spot where the creature had disappeared. Then they walked in the direction the kitten had indicated with its fuzzy tail. Harper thought as they walked, barely noticing that they had stumbled upon a beaten-down trail. How strange today had been. It was hard to believe. White rabbits, talking cats. And only just yesterday they'd been bemoaning the quiet sameness of each passing day at their grandparents'. Yesterday things went on as usual. But today? Today was different.

They looked down at their watch. It was still a little past one.

WE'RE ALL MAD HERE

CHRIS BANNOR

I've always been a bit mad, you see. Even as a child. Curiosity plagued me and ate away at my mind. I didn't always find the right answer to the questions, but it was *my* answer, and that was good enough.

I had a name once too, but when the queen calls you 'Her Hatter' and 'THE HATTER', no one contradicts her. I've quite forgotten now, my name. Not the queen. I had one though, before the queen. Before Time and the hat.

The hat was—not as wonderful as Time—but an amazing thing to have all the same. It came to me on a sunny day as I walked along the flower fields, ignoring the roses as they threw insults at my beautiful jacket.

I raised my hand to shade my eyes, and when I set my foot down, it wasn't upon grass at all! Laying under my foot was a beautiful green top hat. I looked around to see who it belonged to, but there was no one there but me and the flowers.

"It must be a gift," I said to myself. I crouched down next to it, examined the narrow velvet rim, and noted the slightly squished sides. I picked it up and brushed it off, gently wiping to remove any trace of my foot. It wasn't quite new looking when I was done, but I like a stylish hat, so I popped it on top of my head and carried on with my journey.

The day was uneventful otherwise, and after a rousing dinner and drinks with March Hare, I returned home and set my fine new hat on the table. I took a chair next to it and contemplated whether a red or purple bow would look better on the hatband, but a voice interrupted my thoughts.

"Well, this looks like a safe enough place to embark."

I looked down at my marvelous hat and saw a small man standing on the brim, just outside a door. I'm certain there had been no door before, let alone a man.

"What are you doing on my hat?" I demanded.

"Your hat, is it?" the man asked. "Set us on the floor then and let's see."

I'm not used to strange men in my hat giving me orders, so in my confusion, I did as he asked without delay. I had no sooner set it down than the man disappeared through the door (which disappeared as well!) and the hat began to grow! The hat forced the table and chairs to the side, and I feared for the windows before it finally stopped.

A jingle of metal announced the doorknob's appearance, and the door opened. The man, now a little taller than me, stepped out, smiling very proudly to himself. "Yes, this is quite the place to step out."

He was the most beautiful man I had ever seen. My heart stopped and my breath caught in my throat. Time seemed to stop altogether when our eyes met. He let out a breathless sigh and smiled. "Oh, it's you."

"It's you," I said in return, which made no sense except it did in that moment and that's all the reason I ever really needed.

"Do you know me?" he asked.

I shook my head, "But I will forevermore be able to say I do. And isn't that something?"

"It's the best kind of something," he said as he stepped off the brim of the hat and into the small space left in the room.

He was only an arm's length away, but I wanted to close the distance between us. "Who are you?" I asked.

"Time," he said as he laid a gentle hand on my cheek. "You found the hat I left for you."

"Oh, well, it all makes perfect sense now."

TIME WAS NOT like other men, and he came and went as his own needs dictated. The hat stayed with me, though. It grew and shrank according to my whims, and once I learned to open the door properly, it traveled with me as well. And I don't mean it traveled on my head. I mean, it was a vehicle.

I could move through Wonderland to anywhere I wanted to be. I could have breakfast with the queen, then traverse to the other end of the world to converse with a very strange Cheshire cat. No matter where I wanted to go, the hat would take me in an instant.

"No one gives a gift like that without a catch," the queen said over tea one afternoon. She was quite enthralled with my hat and had threatened to cut off my head more than once to attain it. After the king reminded her I could no longer make the marvelous hats and headpieces that she loved if I didn't have a head, she relented.

"A man can give a gift in love with no need for payment," I said. I had spent the last week with Time on the beach of the southern isles and I was still warm from the sun and his smile.

"Time loves no man," she answered. She took a sip from her

cup and reached out, twirling a finger in my brown locks. "Your hair wants cutting."

Before I could answer, she called for a round of croquet.

~

"I can't be late," I said as I tried to step away from Time. His arms wrapped around me as we danced on the floors of an abandoned castle, the people who had once inhabited this area of Wonderland long gone from memory.

"When you are with Time," he said, pulling me closer again, "time stands still. You won't be late for your meeting with Rabbit."

"How can time stand still?" I asked.

"Because I will it so. As I am Time and time is me, you can't be late."

"Then I suppose a few more turns wouldn't hurt a thing." I smiled as I placed my hand back on his shoulder and music chimed from somewhere inside the hat. It was a lovely dance, and we twirled through three more days and nights before I finally went home for my lunch date with Rabbit.

"You look exhausted, Hatter," Rabbit told me as we sat to drink our first cup of tea.

It was a perfectly sunny day, and the cool breeze brought the scent of lilac to the table. I was content to drink my tea and nibble my toast and honey.

"I have been dancing, Rabbit. Dancing for days and days in my lover's arms. I'm quite happy, but I don't think Time knows how to have a proper sleep-in."

"I just saw you yesterday, Hatter. You haven't been anywhere for days."

I hadn't confided in Rabbit about my hat. He's always late

everywhere and the last thing I needed was for him to show up every day, asking me to cart him around so that he arrived on time. I felt a little guilty for the omission, but not enough to speak of it.

"If you danced the night away in the arms of the man you loved, you'd feel it had been days as well," I said instead.

"After tea, go home and rest."

"I would, but I have a design I must finish for the queen. I am afraid she'll cut off my head if I don't have it for her tomorrow when we meet for breakfast."

"She's been in a foul temper these last few weeks. Be careful," Rabbit warned.

"The queen loves me," I reminded him. "And no one else can keep her as fashionably dressed as I."

"Use your time wisely. You aren't the only hatter in Wonderland and I hear the queen was speaking to one the other day. If you lose her favor, it could mean trouble."

Hatter ignored the comment and sipped his tea instead. He'd found a lovely present for her in the old castle, and that would soothe her temper.

He was right, of course. She held the glass dancer in her hand and ohhhh'd and ahhhhh'd over it. "Where did you find such an amazing piece of art?" she asked. "She's a beautiful monument to a dancer's grace."

"Time and I went to an ancient castle in the westernmost part of Wonderland. Among the ruins, I found this piece, and I thought I must bring it back to you!"

She humphed at the mention of Time. "I don't like the sound of him. He takes you away and you always come back looking like death warmed over."

"I just need a little sleep," I assured her. "You must remember what it's like? To be so entranced with your lover that you can't sleep for need to be with them?"

"What I know is that there are lines around your eyes that you ought to see to. You really should be more presentable when you come to see your queen."

"But I come bearing more gifts," I said, pulling out a hat box for her with my latest creation. "That is surely enough to show my fealty."

She opened the box and squealed as she pulled out a magnificent hat with a wide brim. I'd created the hat in shades of red and pink silk and sewn the daintiest heart charms around the brim.

"Put it on me!" she demanded.

And I knew I had earned her forgiveness one more time.

I WAS STILL ASLEEP when Time showed next. I woke to him standing over the bed, watching me. "Are you ready for another adventure?" he asked.

I pulled the blankets close and closed my eyes. "I'm so very tired, Love."

"Is it so hard to be with me?" he asked, but his voice was gentle and he sat on the bed next to me.

"My heart says no, but my body says let me sleep another few hours, and I'm yours."

Time stripped out of his old-fashioned jacket and dropped the rest of his clothes to the floor before sliding into bed next to me. "I supposed I could wait a few hours."

"I thought Time waited for no man," I teased.

"This Time will wait. That time is a slave-driver that allows no man to rest."

"Good thing I have you here with me instead today."

Time kissed me softly, but there was something sad behind his eyes, a lingering pain I had never seen in their depths. "We are both always with you."

I HAD BARELY SAT at the queen's table when she pushed me out of my chair and down the hall and to a guest bed in the Red Castle. I tried to argue that I was fine, but she wouldn't listen. Instead, she yelled and screamed until the doctor came to my bedside.

There was a lot of hemming and hawwing and finally, he put away his silly gadgets and frowned at me. "I'm afraid time hasn't been kind to you, Hatter."

"Time is very kind to me," I disagreed. It had been five years since I found my hat, and I had never known such happiness.

"I don't know why it's happened, but you've aged prematurely. Your body is more fitting to a man twice your age. I don't know any way to turn back that clock."

"What are you saying?" I asked. I had been tired for some time. In fact, I couldn't quite remember what it was like to be well-rested, but I wasn't sick.

"You're getting old."

I sat up and looked at the mirror that hung across from the bed. I hadn't paid attention to myself in the looking glass in ages, just the look of the cloth across my shoulder or the tilt of my hat as I went out the door. As I looked now, my once luxurious hair was a tangle of dry, brittle hay, more gray than brown. Dark bags hung under my eyes lined with crow's feet. Brown spots dotted my face and neck. I pulled at the skin under my chin and smooshed my face around, looking for the young man that I was.

Even my eyes seemed less bright.

"What happened to me?"

"There is only one certainty when it comes to Time," the queen said resolutely. "It will kill you in the end."

MY HEART WAS heavy for some time after that revelation, but when Time arrived again and smiled at me, I knew that there was nothing I wouldn't do for him. "Come to the old castle with me again," he asked.

"I don't think I'm in the mood for dancing today," I confessed. It had been weeks since I'd last seen him. He looked no different now than he had when we had first met. I had aged beyond my years though. But why?

"No dancing. Just a leisurely stroll through the old gardens, I think," Time said, offering his hand to me. I took it and tried not to notice how pale my skin was. How brittle my nails were.

We stepped into the hat, and I clung to his chest to keep my balance. He laughed softly into my hair as he held me tight. "I won't let you fall," he whispered.

I looked up at him and sighed. "I fell a long time ago."

His smile softened. "Yes, we both did. We're lucky we were there to catch each other." He kissed me gently, and I forgot all the worries and fears that had been clutching me since the day I looked in the mirror.

The hat settled into place and Time took my hand and led me out the door. The gardens were wild and uncultured, but there had once been great labyrinths here. The trails were trimmed by grazing animals that scattered as we came along.

"It's always so peaceful."

Time nodded. "It is now. It wasn't always. The men who came before were full of chaos and fear, and their world lived by those rules. They thought they could change the tides, but they died out in the end, with the world moving on as it ever has."

"What killed them?" I asked.

"Time."

I gaped at him, and he patted my hand before pulling me along another path.

"Could you have stopped it?" I asked.

"Time? No, of course not."

"But you stopped time for me."

He paused and faced me, his hand coming up to cup my cheek. He was always so gentle, even in his playful moods.

"I can't stop time for anyone."

"But you said when we were together, that time stopped."

His eyes filled with tears, but he smiled. "When we are together, you are on my time. The world stops spinning outside of that space and we move differently within it. You must live those moments of time though, whether the world around you has stopped or not."

"I... I didn't know."

Time brought our foreheads together. "I'm sorry. I thought you understood. I can't step into time to live with you. I can't exist as Time and time all at once. To love you, I had to create something else."

"And it's killing me."

"Yes."

I turned away and ran. I had spent years running these paths with him, chasing my lover and being chased in return. I knew every doorway and broken stone along the way. I stopped when I came to what had once been a magnificent ballroom. "How many years of my life have I wasted on this dance floor?"

"Not wasted," Time said, as he stepped into the doorway across from me. "Hatter, we *lived*. The time we spent together, how could that be wasted? If I could stop time—oh, by the powers that be—if I could stop time for anyone, it would have been you. To live forever in one moment, I would have split the universe itself. But there are only two constants, and time and death cannot be defeated. But we *lived*, Hatter. We *loved*. More than any others in Wonderland."

Tears spilled down my face, and I wiped them away. I didn't

want him to see how it affected me. How it broke me. I was so very tired and hurt. Betrayed.

He knew. He knew all along that I was aging and I had been the fool.

"I want to go home," I whispered.

"I don't want you to go," he said as he walked toward me.

"I don't want to die!" I yelled.

He stopped at my words. I could see the pain in his face, the tears streaking his cheeks to match my own. "I don't want to die," I said again, "and every minute here kills me quicker."

I turned away and left him, taking the long path back to where we'd left the hat. For the first time, I realized the bright green velvet had faded over the years. Use and wear—both as a traveling device and a hat—had aged it beyond its original beauty. I laid a hand on it, pressing my head to the soft wall. "I'm so sorry. I didn't see it was killing us both."

"Hatter."

I turned to see Time standing a few feet away. He didn't come too close, but he waited as I stepped into the hat.

The return home was quiet, and though I stumbled as the hat took us across the entire distance of Wonderland, I didn't lean on Time. I wrapped my arms around my waist and held tight, for fear that the ache in my heart would make me reach out to him.

He was the only thing that could soothe it.

When we landed in my living room, I stepped out and waited for the hat to disappear. Or for him, too. Neither did.

"I need to rest." I was so angry, but I didn't have the energy to yell. My anger was hot, but my grief was all-encompassing and I could barely lift one foot in front of the other to get to the bedroom. Thankfully, falling onto the bed was easy.

"I wanted to give you something," Time said from the doorway. I didn't respond, and he stepped into the room. He set a small box on the bedside table and crouched down to look at me. I wanted to look away, but it was too much effort. And I feared it would be the last I looked upon him. No matter how much it hurt, I loved him, and he was as beautiful today as the day he first stepped out of my hat.

"I told you about the people who lived in our castle. They lived by time. The clock ruled them so much that they gave it power. I found this token of theirs, and I wanted to give it to you. To show you that while they died by the clock, you never let it have that power over you. I..." He stood up and stepped back. "When I found it, I thought you knew."

He left.

I sobbed. And then I slept.

"Must I really do this?" I asked as I looked out across the stage to the audience.

"The queen demanded a concert and a concert she will have. Sung by her favorite people. And you," Rabbit reminded me, "are her very favorite."

"I haven't prepared a thing."

"You had two weeks!" Rabbit said, his voice shrill in alarm.

"I was sleeping." It wasn't the best response, but it was the truth. My days since Time had left consisted of sleeping, eating a handful of whatever I could scrounge up in a few minutes, then heading back to bed. I would have missed the concert altogether if March Hare hadn't arrived with my costume in hand.

I felt ridiculous, but they were right. The queen demanded, and we obeyed.

"You're on!" Rabbit poked me again, and I stumbled onto the stage, weak from little food and poor sleep. The only reason I looked decent at all was that the dormouse had come along and seen my slovenly state, picked all the crumbs from my hair and clothes, and did his best to tidy me up.

The audience cheered as I walked on, but I suddenly drew a blank. All I could think about was that I wasn't wearing my hat! My wonderful, precious, Time-given hat! When they'd pulled me out of bed, they hadn't given me time to grab anything and here I was, on a stage before the queen, without my hat!

Everything became blurry, and I blinked hard a couple of times to see clearly. When I did, I realized I had lost moments. They all stared at me and I finally met the eyes of my queen. Her face was as red as the heart pins on the hat I'd given her so many years ago. She gripped her throne tightly before she stood and screamed, "Off with his head!"

"But, my dear, he's your favorite. He's your hatter," the king cried.

"He is just killing time! He doesn't care at all! Off with his head!"

I choked on a sob, and her brutes pulled me off the stage. I didn't know where they led me, but her knave came up and sent the others away, putting his arm around my shoulders to comfort me.

"The king has interceded and there is no need to lose your head today, friend," he said. His smile was no comfort, but I nodded anyway.

When March Hare came back to fetch me, he took me straight home and fed me what I'm sure was a very fine stew, but I had no taste for it. Time had killed me. But she said... she said, I killed time.

"Could I?"

March Hare startled as I sat up suddenly to ask myself the question. "It's not possible, is it? I mean, what he did to me... he knew. Which means I wasn't the only one. How many lovers has Time killed?"

"Oh," March Hare said as he wiped spilled stew off the front of his vest. "I suppose some died of other causes, but time killed the rest."

My mind was suddenly ablaze. "Time kills them all. I understand now. I understand what I must do."

"What you must do is eat. You're as thin as a rail. If you don't fatten up, the queen might use *you* as a croquet mallet."

I didn't answer. My mind was too full and as March Hare fed me, I planned.

When I was alone, I pulled open the box that had sat at my bedside for months now, unopened. For a moment I stared at the small velvet box and nearly wept. I held it against my chest and tried not to think of Time. The touch of velvet was always a reminder of him, though.

I let my grief pass through me and when I was calm again, I opened the box. Nestled in the center of a soft silken bed was the most beautiful pocket watch I had ever seen. I traced my fingers over the fine gold chain and around its perfect circumference. There was no golden cover to hide the clockwork or its face. They were glass. The intricate workings of time were visible to the eye, and I had never been so certain in my life.

Here was my answer.

Here was my salvation.

And I began to work. Night and day I dug into books about clockworks and time. My friends kept me fed, and I'd seen the dormouse around more often than ever before, stealing crumbs and licks of scraps I couldn't bother eating or cleaning up.

The Cheshire Cat came in once, appearing over my left shoulder with his maddening grin, and purred. "Oh my. That would do it."

He disappeared before I could ask what he knew.

With shaking hands, I sewed the golden chain around the hat in an intricate design and settled the pocket watch itself at a fashionable tilt along the brim. Once I had secured it, all I had to do was wait.

Because time wasn't a man, but Time was and Time would come back, sooner or later. I was his lover, and he wouldn't abandon me until time had its way with me, too.

MARCH HARE SET the table for twelve, but the only people who had come today were myself, March Hare, and the dormouse who kept glaring at me as he tried not to fall asleep. I ignored him and ran my hands lovingly over the brim of the hat I had set in the chair next to me.

"What's gotten into him?" I asked March Hare. The dormouse had always been rather genial before.

"He was with you all night, don't you remember?" March Hare asked.

"Not at all."

"He said you kept him up. You kept petting your hat."

"And cackling," the dormouse said as he raised his head from the table.

"I hardly cackle," I said.

"And sobbing." The dormouse looked like he was about to take a sip of tea, but set it on the table and nearly dropped his chin in it as he fell asleep again.

"Well. The sobbing is understandable," I defended.

"Hatter," March Hare turned to me and I didn't want him to speak, but he continued before I could stop him. "What are you doing here?"

"Aren't I invited?"

"Of course. I always set the table for extras in case we get unexpected visitors, but you've barely left your house in months. When you do, it's to the bookshop or the library, or on the queen's command. I've been very worried about you."

"I had something to do."

"And what about Time?" he asked.

I closed my eyes because my heart betrayed me as much as Time had. No matter how I hardened myself against it, just his name made my heart ache.

"He'll show up sooner and later, and then we'll be done with it."

"What does that mean?"

"You remember what we talked about the night of the concert?"

"I fed you stew, and you were babbling. There wasn't a proper conversation."

"About Time killing all the lovers?"

March Hare nodded his head slowly.

"And the queen said it herself. I killed time. So, what if I killed Time? Someone has to stop him from killing all the others."

"The other what?"

"The other lovers!" I said, slamming my hands on the table so hard the dormouse spilled into his teacup. He woke, startled, and with a very wet face.

"You can't kill time!" March Hare said.

"Why not?"

"Could you really do it?"

I turned because the voice had come from the other end of the table.

Time. So handsome and gentle and so very hurt by the words he'd heard me speak.

"You killed me already. Can't I return the favor?" I asked.

He laughed bitterly. "You can kill Time, but all you do is destroy the man. It won't undo what time has done to you."

"Let's find out, shall we?"

I swept the hat off the chair and threw it to the ground behind him. His eyes were on me though and he didn't see the hat growing larger, or the way the pocket watch began to spin and glow.

"Love, please, don't make me leave you," he begged.

It was too late, though, and I pushed as hard as my feeble body would allow. He stumbled back and through the door of the hat. I rushed to it and found him lying on the floor, the look of hurt so distressing that I nearly threw myself in with him. Instead, I closed the door, the image of him reaching for me burning itself into my brain. I willed the hat to shrink again and I placed it on my head, sealing the door forever.

I laughed and clapped my hands in joy because I could feel the power of a dead people's timepiece locking my lover away. I sang songs that had no words and I ignored the horrified looks of my friends, as I ignored the sobs that broke up the words of my song.

"What have you done?" March Hare asked.

"I... killed..." I couldn't say it. I tried so hard to tell them this joyous, momentous thing I had done, but I wailed instead. The man I loved was gone, by my own hands. He had killed me. And I had killed him.

"Hatter?" the dormouse scrambled away from the table and I could see an eerie light growing around me. The sickly green grew so bright I had to shield my eyes.

"The hat! Take off the hat!" March Hare yelled.

I tried to remove it, but it wouldn't budge. The world folded around me, and I fell to my knees. When I opened my eyes, I was still at a tea party, but not with March Hare. I was at the old castle, Time sitting at the other end of the table.

"I thought this would fit since you seem to think talk of murder goes well with tea," Time said as he stood up.

I was terrified. I didn't know how he'd escaped the hat and brought me here, but it couldn't be good. When he came around the table and gently took my arm, I followed where he led. He sat me in the seat next to him and poured a cup of tea for each of us. I watched as he plated a biscuit for me and poured a generous drizzle of honey over it. He handed it to me and I set it down mechanically.

"Time—"

"Did you think you could betray me like that and I would just accept it?" he asked.

"You were killing me!" I yelled.

"I thought you understood! How could you not feel the passing of time?"

"Because I was with you!" I sobbed, because how could I make this ageless creature understand? How could I know that the creeping of time that had been so worrisome in my youth had become my lover's caress until I no longer knew the difference?

"And now, here we are. You dying of old age, and me caught in a timeless void that I can't leave."

"Wonderland is hardly a void."

"Do you think I escaped?"

I stared at him then and at the world around us. I realized that there was no breeze. No scent of flowers. No sun warming my skin. It was superficial. It was...

"Memory," Time said with a harsh laugh. "You have trapped me in the hat, but to do so, you used the clock I gave you. The timepiece that I said had power. The timepiece that now ties us to the memories we shared."

"I don't understand."

"I can't live outside of your memories. And if I can't, I won't let you either."

I woke from my nap with a start. It was almost six o'clock, and I grabbed my hat and ran for the door. Hadn't I done that already? I stared at the doorknob and a spike of pain shot through the right side of my brain.

For a moment, warm arms surrounded me and I smiled, dancing delightedly out the door and down the street. When I reached March Hare's, the dormouse was asleep at the table and the Hare was setting the last plate.

"I can only stay a moment. Time will come soon," I announced. I shook my head though, because that wasn't today, was it?

"I'm afraid time hasn't been kind to you, Hatter," the doctor said. When did I arrive at the castle, and why was the doctor looking at me?

When I turned, I was at March Hare's table, the dormouse asleep on his toast. "Well, that will be a mess to clean up," I said.

"He got no sleep last night. He was with you, remember?"

"I..." I did. I didn't. My memories were confused.

A young girl sat at the table, uninvited. March Hare usually loved guests, but today he seemed off as he snapped at her. I don't know why I found her so fascinating, but all I could see was her hair.

The queen sat across from me, sipping from her cup, and reached out, twirling a finger in my brown locks. "Your hair wants cutting."

"Your hair wants cutting," I said to the girl when the queen had disappeared. This wasn't right. I clutched my head again.

Strong hands pulled me up, and I looked up to see Time. He brushed the hair from my face and kissed me softly.

"I killed you," I sobbed.

"You can't kill time. It's like a river, constant and always moving. But you locked me in here, and now it's all happening at once for you. Every moment of your life. Every joy. Every pain."

"I can't live like that. How can I live like this?"

"You shouldn't have tried to kill Time."

He kissed me, still so very gentle after everything we'd been through, but I could feel his tears.

"Every emotion you ever felt. All here, at this one time. Your fear of death. The hate you felt for what time had done to you. The love you felt—still feel—for me. Always. Forever in your mind and in your heart."

He brushed a tear from my face and smiled. "No, you can't live like this. You've gone quite mad."

I gasped, but he pressed his lips to mine and whispered in a harsh voice. "We're all mad here."

ALICE THE TERRIBLE

KATHRYN DIAZ

Alice had abandoned her family—her mother and her sister, Ferret—when she'd stepped through the great mirror gates of Looking Glass World to become someone else. She had been accepted to Looking Glass University, told her work had great promise, and that if she crossed every square on her degree path as she was told, she would be Alice the Great, Alice the Better, Alice Who Was Admired and Adored. Perhaps Alice had furnished that last title herself, but it prickled with such hope on her skin when she thought it, she couldn't let it go. Unfortunately, to get to class on time, Alice needed to abandon her hope, and the red and white squares that tiled the world knew she hadn't yet. Today, when she stepped out of her room to attend the Red Queen's seminar, the white square twisted under her feet and she found herself in the rose garden on the other side of campus instead.

"Get out, you terrible beast! You aren't supposed to be here!" a Handel bud shrieked.

"I have to be somewhere," Alice replied, a little hurt. "And this is where I am. Aren't you supposed to be where you are?"

The Handel huffed with disdain. "If you don't have the leaves to know finding your place is your responsibility, there's nothing I have to say to you about it."

Alice ignored him and took out her notebook for a quick sketch; he would make a funny picture with his leaves tossing haughtily over his stem. "You might feel a little out of place if you had come a long way to start your great work too," she said.

"*I* am my greatest work," the Handel retorted.

Alice hmm'd with mock seriousness, but behind her notebook she couldn't help but wonder. She took great pains to make sure her work wasn't her, but something better. When she worked on <u>Wonderland</u>, she scraped wildness out of her words and sanded them into smooth, pleasing wit, something she had never managed with herself. They had to be what Alice wasn't to be embraced in ways she wouldn't. But should she try harder with herself? What if she misunderstood the Red Queen's theorems on artistic perfection? What if she could never get anyone to like or understand <u>Wonderland</u> until she had cut herself down by the same rules and organized herself as neatly as Looking-Glass World? What if all her work was worthless until she had learned every agonizingly useful thing—Just then, all the squares around her snapped into one red tiled slide and before she could bid the Handel rose goodbye, she was rolling into the Red Queen's instructional parlor like a bowling ball, stopping only when her majesty stepped on her with a red-slippered foot.

"When it is your turn at play, it is rude to keep others waiting," the Red Queen said. She twisted a carnelian stone on her finger and the game floor snapped back into shape. It didn't seem fair for the Red Queen to make them come to class by hopelessness if she had a cheat all along, Alice thought. Then she felt the Red Queen's glare, sharp as the rubies that dangled like daggers from the spiked chain around her neck, and all thoughts beyond her majesty were speared out of existence. "What have you to say for yourself?"

"I'm terribly sorry," Alice squeaked.

"Apologies are not part of the game. Get up."

Alice tried, but in all her sudden spinning, she forgot how to do it backwards and so slipped and knocked her head against the stone tile for several painful moments. This was Ferret and home all over again: she couldn't behave right, couldn't be herself without being protuberant, couldn't make friends. And then, just as Ferret did whenever Alice humiliated herself in her presence, Dee, Dum, Hatta, Haigha, and the other seminar fellows tapped their toes and muttered amongst themselves while she flailed. It served her right for being late, and how was she going to learn to take the Red Queen's criticism on her toes if she didn't turn them right side up herself?

But the Red Queen's Teaching Assistant mothballed out from her square behind her majesty and caught Alice's head with one spider-webbed sleeve before it smacked on the floor again. "You shouldn't do that," she said gently.

Alice looked up at the girl in bleary-eyed bewilderment. She always forgot the Teaching Assistant until she stepped forward or made some remark that distracted everyone long enough for the fellow at play to compose themselves. Now she reminded Alice, "Feet first," and made her step on her shoes and climb her cardigan until she was upright. How could Alice forget someone this kind, this good? But the Teaching Assistant was so small and threadbare with her droopy wools, she sometimes vanished before your eyes. She was an unfinished doll, Alice thought, waiting for someone to remember her.

As if hearing her mind, the Teaching Assistant lifted her gaze, a question swimming in her milky eyes.

The Red Queen broke the moment with a clap of her hands

and brought the room to order: the fellows lined up one to a square, the play table whisked itself to the center of the room with its mirror slab shining with readiness, and her majesty glided toward them.

"First: the final scores," she said. "Hatta, six; Dee, two; Dum, two..." She gave them each a sagacious nod as she passed from one to the next, until— "Alice, none."

Speaking during your turn was against the rules, so Alice didn't. But she couldn't stop her blood from throttling up her face in panic; last round she'd had *two* points.

"Second: the Judgement," the Red Queen went on. "But before I proceed, I must warn you all that this will be a short, unorthodox round, and you will be unable to match your remarks to my own, for Alice has submitted an appropriate piece."

The room rippled with gasps while Alice continued to clench herself silent.

"Say if that isn't so," said Dee.

"If it isn't, how could it be? No-how," Dum replied.

"Broke the rules," Haigha sniggered.

Alice burst. "That's not true!"

The Red Queen raised her voice, sharp as glass, "It is not her own work!"

"Yes, I did! I have it!" Alice dug madly through her bag until she retrieved a plain file stuffed with several neat copies of text. "I've been rewriting it according to your theorems since the start of term. I submitted it early, I sent a copy without the illustrations, I brought extras in case anything happened! You can't say I don't have it, I do!" She shook the file in every face she could reach.

The Red Queen would not look at it. "This is the work you want to claim as your own?" she asked, a final warning.

"Yes!" Alice said. "This is mine. This is <u>Wonderland</u>."

"*This*," the Red Queen mocked, "is the most derivative arrangement of letters I have read since the invention of the alphabet. This fails to please, fails to interest, but worst of all fails to represent you. It is a failure from start to finish and it is not your so-called Wonder Land." And before Alice could protest, the Red Queen reached into the rich folds of her caftan and withdrew a bulging mess of paper for the class to see. "Here is Alice's true work, if she had any integrity."

The room stilled with horrified silence. What sagged in the Red Queen's hand was not a manuscript but a travesty of waste-bin scraps, anxious fever dreams, and childish scrawls. There were edits taped, glued, and taped again with curling edges on top of each other, envelopes with clumsy drawings stuffed into their crusty mouths, and colored paper that begged for order as loudly as it begged for attention. This was <u>Wonderland</u> in every terrible attempt Alice had made since she was seven years old, and it was the ugliest thing she had ever seen.

"Do you deny my allegations?" the Red Queen asked.

Alice trembled with held-back tears. It was bad enough that everyone could see her triangle-chinned rabbits and amateur word streams, but the sketches Ferret had balled up and thrown at her were on display too, next to 'see me after class' notes compiled from every grade, and all her delirious, pointless hope. So much hope for nothing. "I just wanted to make it good," she said. But she hadn't. She wouldn't.

The Red Queen scoffed. "Mis-move like this again and I shall send you back to the first square, and perhaps further still," she said. She disappeared the hideous <u>Wonderland</u> back into her caftan and clapped her hands one final time. "The round has ended. We will recommence on Thursday next. Do not disappoint me." Then the air around her bowed out of the way and she vanished through it before their eyes.

Usually, this was when Alice turned to the other fellows and gave as many encouragements as she could before the squares, sensing how much she wanted to stay and talk, whisked her away to the edge of campus. But now that Alice burned to go, the squares lay still. Dee and Dum were toddled off at once, guffawing over Alice's Wonderland, and what a jolly relief they weren't as bad as that. The others gave parting shouts and whispers as their squares slid them their separate ways, their words stinging as loudly in Alice's ears as the silence they left behind.

From his square, Hatta surveyed the room with satisfaction and shook out his cuffs. "Don't pout, old chap; it's a rather different sort of time than that," he said. With morbid expertise, he summoned a drink cart from across the room and proceeded to make himself a cocktail backward: belching, then drinking the dregs, then stirring, then mixing. When he finished, he poured half into a second glass and held it out. "If you want to try nihilistic ratification praxis, you ought to cry less and drink more."

The scarlet liquid winked at Alice, inviting her to feel better by not feeling anything at all.

Before Alice could take the drink, Haigha bounced over from his square and pulled on Hatta's sleeve, braying with cruel laughter as the drink sloshed over the sides. "No, she's got Allicent Contracatory Distentionary Cosmology—ha! Disputed, disreputable—ha!" He took the drink for himself, clinked cheers, and dashed it on the floor with another laugh.

The crash broke what was left of Alice's nerve and her tears fell faster than she could scrub them away. "What was that for?" she wailed. What could she have done wrong now, standing still and silently begging her square to swallow her whole? "What!"

Haigha hiccupped another laugh. "What's your face for?" he countered.

Alice withered. This was worse than home and Ferret: she no longer expected her house to make a room where she fit or her sister to understand. But Looking-Glass world was supposed to have meant success and others as strange as she.

"You don't really want to be like them," a faint voice soothed.

Alice started; she had forgotten the Teaching Assistant again, but here she was, handkerchief held out. Alice took it and daubed her face as dry as she could.

"They have to eat and drink here because they never leave," the Teaching Assistant continued. "They've given up so thoroughly, I keep rooms for them upstairs so they can at least be comfortable."

"That's awful," Alice sniffled. "But what about you? Don't you get to—?" She didn't finish, for the solemn gleam in the girl's milky eyes said enough. "But you're so kind! And you must have been very good if you were promoted to Teaching Assistant. You have the most wonderful ideas when the Red Queen lets you speak."

"I do, don't I?" The Teaching Assistant gave a curious laugh, as if considering this for the first time, and guided Alice away from the two doomed fellows and towards the mirror play table. "If you think so highly of my ideas, will you indulge me in one now?" Smiling her sad, thready smile, she crawled backwards under the table and gestured for Alice to follow.

Alice did. For several breaths they only sat, safe in shadow and side-by-side.

"Tell me about Wonderland," the Teaching Assistant said.

Alice's face fell. "Anything but that. That's hopeless now."

"Not the way *she* showed it to us, but the way it is in your head, the way you want it to be," the Teaching Assistant urged. "You see, I have this notion, but as soon as I try to remember it, it goes away. I understand it best when I'm not thinking about it.

And if I'm right, you'll be back and better than before." She quirked her face, concentratedly not concentrating. "Who knows? Perhaps I might be too. Wouldn't that be grand?"

It would be, Alice thought despairingly. And if their fates were entwined, she had to try. So she reached out for Wonderland in her mind. She stretched through the years and miles she had traveled, straining until, "When I was little, I didn't feel like I belonged where I was, so I imagined where I wasn't." Doors kaleidoscoped out of her mind's fingers, clubs and spades fell at her feet and washed away in a sea of sorrow. Alice held the memories secret under her tongue. "But it was just a game, except for once when I was seven." Ferret had taken her to the park to roam wild while she studied for some exam. "The game got away from me, or it stopped being a game at all. I just know that while I was there, the world and I finally fit together." She held up her hands to show the teaching assistant: not two of a kind, but two different pieces sliding into place.

Ducks and lories fluttered wet wings in her ears. She remembered a race, a cry, and a surge in her heart she didn't know the word for. Alice pulled a marker out of her pocket and began to draw on the mirror instead: the hedgehog games, the grinning cat, and the verdant vales that made her real when she passed through them. "You can't actually map Wonderland," she explained as she went. "Nothing stays in place like it is here, everything shuffles from turn to turn. The only thing that doesn't change is how you get there."

She shifted so her reflection warbled in the center of the mirror and drew a long tunnel that went down her chin to the end of the map. "The rabbit hole can appear anywhere and take you any place. You just have to spot your chance before he disappears." As Alice spoke, she drew a round rabbit face over her own with svelte ears and a curve in his mouth as if he had hidden something he wanted her to find. She finished him with a smart ribbon bow, its ends studded with sunshine.

"He's a rakish little mischief-maker, isn't he?" The Teaching Assistant said.

Alice and her rabbit-self blushed, hearts pattering together. "Sometimes."

The Teaching Assistant touched a finger to his nose; Alice shivered as if it was her own. "And how do you catch this rabbit?" she asked.

Alice brought their fingers together and smiled shyly. "Well, you foll—" Then the rabbit hole swallowed them down in the same breath it stole from Alice. Down they tumbled through lilacarine clouds, tumbling down together until they tumbled into Alice's world.

It was winter in Wonderland and not a drop of snow shimmered on the ground. Alice landed on a patch of yellow grass that broke her fall with a brittle crack. The blades were cropped so close the dry soil blushed between each one. When Alice reached out to touch them, they cut her fingers as they wriggled back.

Above, the sapphirite sky gleamed stiff as if holding its breath, its clouds long siphoned away. Beside, a pair of white slippered feet stuck out of a pile of leaves. The feet wiggled, and the leaves tumbled away and up sat a beautiful queen gowned in puffs of silver and glistening white. Her long hair fell like a faerie waterfall over her shoulders and her face, round and perfect as a doll's, burst into a laugh. "I'M ME!" she cried. "I'm in Wonderland and I'm me!" Throwing her head back, she tossed the leaves around her like confetti.

Alice recognized her at once. The Teaching Assistant, finished at last, and all she'd needed was the right door. Alice's heart wrung itself out as she watched her gleam so unabashedly; the Teaching Assistant had never been this complete nor belonged this easily. She had come close once, the last time she'd tumbled here, but never like this. Never as a queen.

"Alice?" The Teaching Assistant called out. "Alice my dear, you've done it! You've rescued me from the Red Queen's awful spell! I know who I am! Alice?"

Slowly, Alice sat up by way of reply. She should have said something clever or celebratory, but she didn't feel like a queen's rescuer. When she looked down at herself, she realized to her shame that she didn't look like one either.

"There you are!" The Teaching Assistant crawled over to meet her. "Oh, but why are you so small? Is this who you really are?" Her voice faltered as if that couldn't be right. Alice burned hot with embarrassment. She still had her grown-up body, but she had shrunken down to her child size, and instead of the simple overalls she'd chosen for herself, she wore the frill-edged play-dress her mother had put her in as a child.

"I don't know," Alice said at last.

The Teaching Assistant smiled as if it didn't matter. "Well, in any case, how do you do?" She bowed where they sat. "I am the White Queen of Looking-Glass World and Dean of the University. Or I will be again when I put Red back in her place. She's so obsessed with winning, she does silly things like make me forget myself to get ahead, but I always get her back because the point isn't to win, it's to *play*. And you are?"

Alice mumbled her name and gave a half-hearted curtsy in the grass. The White Queen nodded for her to go on, but Alice wouldn't.

"What's the matter, Alice?" the White Queen asked. "Whatever it is, it's alright. You know that, don't you?"

Alice didn't know that, and the more the White Queen

insisted, the less likely it seemed. "I'm very sorry," she said, darting her eyes around so she would not cry. The bare trees seemed to be folding their arms against her and the withered rose bushes hid their faces. "Something is wrong here. This isn't—" Wonderland? No. "—me. A stupid, frilly, overgrown girl."

"You're not stupid," the White Queen said, suddenly very serious.

The eerie quiet of Wonderland shattered with a roll of thunder and the pinprick grass spiked with fear, startling both of them to their feet.

"We shouldn't stay here," Alice said. She took the White Queen's hand as the grass needles surged through their skin once more. They ran for the winding woods, but Alice didn't feel like they were escaping; she felt like they were being driven.

Weeds clamored for them everywhere they walked, some winding together to make thick trip roots, others colluding with the stepping stones to form blockades. Always, thunder and cloud followed close behind. "What are we running from?" the White Queen asked.

Alice didn't reply. She turned down a bend in the path, then stopped and ducked as a volley of thorns shot through the shadows. No going that way. "I told you, something's wrong. I'm wrong, I must have ruined something when I tried to make Wonderland good for the Red Queen and now everything's—!" Alice's voice cut with a cry as a moldy tart fell from a branch and struck her temple.

The White Queen shielded her with her arms. "We must get somewhere safe," she said. She caught the next tart in her palm, then gaped in surprise when it turned into a little brass key. "Perhaps wherever this leads!"

Alice stiffened when she recognized it. Around them, thunder shook the world in its fists. What other choice did they have? Alice took the key. At once, the White Rabbit's cottage appeared beside the path.

"Oh!" The White Queen cried. "Was that funny little cottage there all along?"

"No," Alice said. She took the White Queen's hand again and raced to the door, stuck the key in the lock, and slipped inside as the storm descended.

For one clutched breath, the house was safe, dark, and still.

Then, "GET OUT OF HERE!"

Alice whirled toward the sound of Ferret's voice. But there was no one. She backed away, only to brush against the rough canvas body of her old backpack. Its zipper mouth opened and bit her neck. "Why can't you just be normal?" it asked.

From deep in its belly, a fainter, younger Alice voice cried, "Who says I'm not normal? Maybe you need to be more normal!" She was on the verge of tears and so far from convincing, Alice scrambled to find where she was coming from just to shut her up.

She ripped the backpack off its hook and tore out everything she touched: crayons that snapped and laughed "Whoops! Guess Ferret has to play with me instead of drawing," books that groaned, "I told you I'm Freddie when I'm with my friends," and finally, a cursed drawing of queens and dressed-up animals holding hands around a ring of clubs and hearts. They were supposed to be kissing, but they twisted their flat mouths and screamed, "You can't leave pictures like this where anyone can see them, Alice! This is gross! Grow up or leave me alone! Wonderland isn't even real! I wish it was, maybe it would give me a sister who isn't as terrible as you!"

"Oh, Alice—" the White Queen reached for her, but Alice shrank away and darted up the stairs, her backpack balled in her fists. She would destroy it, bring her dreams crashing down one last time, and Wonderland would never taunt her again.

At the top of the stairs, the landing stretched into a hall,

Ferret's room on one side, Alice's on the other, with a long mirror between them. In the darkened glass, she saw her child self, waiting and knocking, waiting and knocking, until Ferret opened the door and glared. "What do you want?"

Mirror Alice revealed Ferret's City Zoo snow globe in her hand. It didn't play music or show her favorite animals, but it had a ferret and a rabbit touching noses on the back, away from the flashier animal figures, and it was her favorite thing. Mirror Alice held it over the landing as the real Alice held her crumpled backpack over it now. "If you really want a different sister, you want to get rid of everything that reminds you of this one too, right?" Mirror Alice asked.

Ferret's face twisted like fire. "I told you to stay out of my room! What is wrong with you? Why are you like this?" It wasn't a question but a condemnation, and in case Mirror Alice was too little to understand, Ferret shot out of her room and gave a hard shove. Through the glass, you couldn't tell that Mirror Alice had been startled and her fingers had slipped loose and tried in vain to contract around the snow globe again. Through the glass, it looked as though she had simply followed through on her promise and shattered a lie held between the siblings for too long. Alice curled her fingers tight and determined that this time really would be on purpose.

"So this is what you didn't want anyone to see." the White Queen's gentle voice on the landing startled her out of her thoughts. "But why?"

"What do you mean, why?" Alice sputtered. "I was terrible. A terrible, awful person and I'm still terrible now." She stared down at her writhing backpack. "I'm not even sorry I ruined everything with my sister. The whole time I thought she understood me, that she was teasing me when she said I was weird, that she liked when I tried to show her Wonderland—but she was just waiting for me to become someone else, someone I can't be no matter what I try. It's different for you, you're good. The person you really are is kind and lovely and all the fellows are going to adore you! But I'm a sad, selfish menace who draws pictures of queens kissing and thinks scaring people is funny and likes stupid riddles and racing for no reason and being anything but just a little girl!" She made to fling her backpack over the banister, but the White Queen caught her by the wrist, fingers cold and gentle as snowdrops.

"Alice," she said. "My terrible, beautiful Alice, what on earth is the matter with that? How can you not see?"

"See what?"

"Let me put it in a riddle for you: what has two feet, reigns in the rules of the world, and throws them out when they're bad or displeased?"

Alice shook her head as the answer came together. "But I'm not like you. I'm not good. My world isn't good or nice and when I tried to make it different, I made it worse! What does it say about me that I can't be good?"

"That you are a Queen, and Queens can be anything they please. Sometimes they can even kiss."

Alice didn't know if she believed the White Queen's words, but she had believed in impossible things before, and where else could she try to believe again? She dropped her backpack safely to the floor and flung herself onto the White Queen and into a desperate kiss. At first, the White Queen was soft and bright as snow, then her mouth turned wicked as Alice stretched not into how she had been but who she really was. As Alice grew, so did Wonderland: the windows filled with yellsia light, winter melted into a blur of autumn-spring, and somewhere close, rabbits hopped to life.

When they parted, the White Queen was blushing. "You *are* powerful," she said. "Just look at you."

Alice turned back to the mirror: they still wore a dress, but it was squared out by a studded jacket with dashing shoulder cords and a violet waistcoat; their hair was a pixie spray of opalescent rainbows; as they turned from side to side, the pattern of the colors and the angles of their body changed, some said 'my lord,' others 'my lady,' and other titles not yet in existence. They were Alice and more. For a long time, they could only marvel at themself in silence. "I didn't know I could be a queen like *this*."

"You wouldn't be Alice the Terrible if you weren't," the White Queen said. "Now, what do you decree we do next, your majesty?"

First, they ran a caucus race, because racing was fun. Then they stopped in the tea glade where a thousand golden leaves bowed and smiled as they fell everywhere but on their heads. Alice clinked cups with their subjects and determined that endless tea was so glorious, they would make it an annual holiday in every world they traveled to.

"Your hair wants growing for a queen," Hare sneered.

"And yours wants skinning for dinner," Alice said with a benevolent smile. "Now, my dear White Queen, one question still concerns me—"

"Only one question?" Hatter chortled. "You might as well say you only have one thought in your whole head. That won't do. Why is a raven like a writing desk?"

"I wasn't speaking to you," Alice said. They turned smoothly back to their royal companion and poured fresh cups for them both. "You see? These two bear an awful resemblance to the fellows in class. Everything we've encountered here has come from me and things I've made up. Does that mean this isn't real and everything will go back to how it was when we wake up in Looking-Glass World?"

The White Queen laughed to herself as she thought. "I think a dream is as real as a game, or hope, or Queenship, your majesty." She leaned over to kiss the corner of Alice's mouth. "What matters is what you know, and that you play as who you really are."

"Then I declare a toast to what I know now," Alice said. The table listened, raising a dozen cups and saucers that reflected a dozen proud Alices in a dozen shades and seasons. "To the heroic White Queen of Looking-Glass World, future victor over the Red Queen, and to me, Alice the Terrible, ruler of Wonderland and queen of everywhere I am!"

DRIPPING RED

K. R. CERVANTEZ

Why are the roses dripping red? Like paint. Like blood. I feel the sticky wetness rolling down my arms. So bright and alarming. Why are my hands dripping red? Is it paint? Is it blood? Smeared, streaked, splattered, and sprayed. The color red.

Red

Red

Red

Reeed

"Reid? Reid, are you waking up?"

I peeled my eyes open, blinking away the sleepy grit. I groaned as pain radiated through my head. I wanted to reach up and grab my aching temples, but something held one of my hands.

Not something, someone, I realized as I turned to see a man watching over me. His eyebrows were drawn together, and he tilted his head as he scanned my face.

He was cute. His white-blonde hair was in an unruly, wavy mess. There were big green eyes, wide with worry. He had a diamond shaped face, his cheeks rosy and spotted with faint freckles. And I had no idea who he was.

"Who... Who are you?" I groaned again, my voice slurring. My lips felt heavy. The guy frowned. Tears filled his eyes, but he blinked them back before looking away. When he turned back, he was smiling again.

"I'm Warren," he said. "Your boyfriend. You must have had another session with Doctor Allison." He pulled his hand from mine and the sense of loss was instant. The protest rolled off my tongue as a strange grunt. I didn't understand the feeling because I couldn't remember this man.

Warren turned away, humming softly as he fiddled with something I couldn't see. A moment later, he turned back, a paper cup in hand. I could see the water slosh over the rim as he gently lowered it closer to me. I sat up and even though the room spun, I was stable enough to drink.

"Slow sips, Reid." Warren held the cup to my lips. I sipped and the cool liquid eased the burning in my throat. I cupped his hand when he started to pull the cup away, bringing it back to my mouth as I took another gulp. I wasn't too surprised when the cup gave out, spilling what little water was left.

I muttered an apology and laid back down, staring up at Warren. He had said we were together, but why couldn't I remember him? Actually, why couldn't I remember anything but my name?

"Where are we?" I asked, looking around. The bed I was on was small; I could feel my feet right at the edge. The room was just as tiny with white walls and nothing else.

"Oh, uh." Warren looked at his hands. "Well, this is a criminal institution."

I wanted to ask more questions. Why was I in a place like this? Why was he? But the door opened, and a woman waltzed in as if she did it all the time. She was small, with mousy brown hair and dark eyes that darted all over the place as if she were looking for something.

"Dorrma," Warren sighed. "I told you Reid was resting. What are you doing?"

"Hadie wants to see you and Reidsy," Dorrma said in a sing-song voice. She shrugged and added, "Says it's important. Better hurry 'fore rec time is over." She studied me for a moment before scurrying away, leaving the door open.

"Do we have to go?" I asked. I didn't want to leave, not when I was still so confused.

"Yeah. We better not be late," Warren muttered. "Hadie will get mad." Warren helped me up, my temples throbbing and my stomach rolling, but my legs were steady. I stretched and rubbed my face, the stubble along my jaw scraping against my calloused hands. I didn't have much of a choice but to follow Warren out of the room. He held my hand and at the moment I was glad for it. I still didn't remember this guy who said we were together, but his hand in mine felt right.

We walked through the open door, and I blinked away another wave of dizziness. The black-and-white checkered floor made me feel like the world was spinning. Or maybe that was because of whatever happened to me. I took a deep breath, following Warren down the hallway, but as we walked, the floor seemed to stretch out in front of us, like the hallway was getting longer and longer. I shook my head. Impossible.

Warren didn't seem bothered. He walked next to me, swinging our hands and trailing the fingers of his free hand along the wall. There was so much I wanted to ask, but I didn't know where to start.

I looked down at my feet when the hallway looked like it was twisting. My stomach heaved, and I worried I would puke right there. But I kept walking, watching the fluorescent lights reflecting on the floor pass by. It couldn't have taken too long, but it felt like I was moving through paste.

The tiles didn't change as we entered the main room. I forced myself to look up, to take in my surroundings. I first spotted Dorrma, standing by a table with two others, waving urgently. There were several other people, none of them looking familiar, but a few waved as if they knew me.

Warren pulled me over to the table where Dorrma stood with two other women. One was folding newspapers into paper hats, and the other sat hunched over the table, coloring something in front of her. She hummed what sounded like 'Happy Birthday.'

"Hey Hadie. Hi Harriet," Warren said. The woman coloring didn't say anything, though her scribbling slowed down. The other woman turned to us, pulling her frizzy black hair out of her face.

"Sit," she said, gesturing to the chairs across from her. I glanced at Warren who shrugged. I sat. Warren stood behind me, his hands on my shoulders kneading the muscles there gently. The light pressure there sent a fuzzy feeling to my brain.

"Dorrma said you wanted to see us, Hadie," Warren said.

Hadie, the girl with the frizzy hair, studied my face. "Odd that she would do another session so soon." She touched her temples and winced as if she were sore. The way she was staring at me made me put a hand to my own temple. I felt a rough patch of skin, and pain blossomed across my head. Warren squeezed my shoulders.

"What happened to me?" I asked.

"He doesn't remember anything," Warren added. "It will come back, right?"

"It typically does," Hadie answered.

I glanced over at the other woman who was still coloring. I knew she was listening by the way she snuck a look at whoever was talking.

"Electroshock therapy does sometimes cause memory loss," Hadie continued.

"I remember my name," I said as if it would help. "Why did I get electroshock therapy?"

I waited for Hadie to answer, but Harriet spoke up first. "You were so angry. So mad."

"At what?" I asked, but Harriet only stared at me before going back to coloring. No one wanted to answer me. I was even more confused than before. I looked at Warren, but he was watching someone across the room.

I leaned forward, resting my elbows on the table. Hadie was back to folding newspapers into paper hats. I reached over to grab the one on top, but Hadie slammed her hand down on the stack and shot a glare up at me.

"Don't touch them!" she snapped. The calmness was gone, replaced with something wild and untamed. The grin she gave me was not kind. I pulled my hand away slowly. Warren wrapped his arms around me from behind.

"Easy, now. No need to lose your head," I said. Everyone froze. Harriet looked up quickly, the orange crayon snapping in her hand. Hadie paled; the grin vanished. She grabbed at her throat as if afraid her head would really go rolling. Dorrma let out a squeak and moved away from the table.

"Reid, you can't say that, remember?" Warren said. He was the only one who seemed calm. He patted my chest.

"Why not?" I asked. Everyone was still staring at me in alarm.

Warren seemed to hesitate. "I guess you don't remember why you're here." I shook my head and he sighed. "They say you're a serial killer. That you allegedly removed people's heads. Chopped them off."

His voice was soft, but the words echoed in my mind. I saw a flash of my dream, the red dripping down my hands. Blood, not paint. I sat forward, pulling away from Warren, and stared down at my palms. The roaring in my ears deafened me.

I had no memories, and the thought of killing someone made me want to throw up. But with no memory, I had no way of knowing if I'd murdered someone. My fingers shook and my vision tunneled. I was falling down a deep dark hole that would swallow me up.

Warm hands cupped my face. His thumbs stroked my cheeks. Warren spoke to me in a calm voice. I closed my eyes welcoming the comfort. As I took a deep breath, my nerves settled and the ringing in my ears stopped. I opened my eyes, seeing Warren standing in front of me. I felt a smile curve my lips. I liked the way Warren looked at me. I wished I could remember what our relationship was like. I ran my hand through his hair and nodded to let him know I was okay. Or at least better.

I wanted to ask more questions, but didn't know how to start. Hadie didn't look pissed anymore; she was back to folding her paper hats. Harriet had grabbed another crayon and was scribbling on the newspapers.

"I'll be right back," Warren said. I didn't want him to leave, but didn't stop him. I watched as he bounced around, talking to people. Checking on them. He didn't seem to stay in one place for long, but he really seemed to care for the people around us.

"Wait, is Warren a..." I trailed off as Hadie nodded.

"An orderly? Yes, he is," she said, her tone calm once again.

I frowned, looking down at the hand he'd held before. He said we were together but was that even okay?

"Dr. Allison doesn't mind," Harriet said, holding up a crayon to inspect it. "This is a special place, where she wants us all to act like family. Warren was one of her first patients and after he recovered from his severe anxiety, she promoted him to orderly." She scoffed at the crayon, snapped it in two and tossed it over her shoulder.

I nodded, unable to take my eyes off Warren as he spoke with another young man. His hands were in a constant state of motion, as he played with his fingers, or messed with his name tag. I wanted to call him back, take his hand again. Anything to ease this feeling in my chest.

"Dawson is looking for his twin again. Hope he doesn't work himself into a fit." Hadie was watching Warren too with motherly affection. I studied the guy next to Warren. Dawson's bright red hair stood out like a beacon. Surely, as I looked around, I'd see someone similar.

"Does he actually have a twin?" I asked.

"No one really knows," Hadie answered. She added another hat to her growing pile, her fingers smudged with the black ink. "Dawson swears Dominic is real, but no one has ever seen him." Then she scoffed. "This would be so much better if you had your memory back already."

I swallowed hard and rubbed my forehead. I wanted to remember too. There was a nagging feeling I was missing something important. I closed my eyes, trying to force something to happen inside my head, but only made my temples ache more.

A hand touched my back, and I smiled as I looked up. But as the smell of smoke wafted around me, I realized it wasn't Warren. Another woman stood behind me. She didn't say anything, didn't smile, but wore a pretty impressive scowl.

"Uh, who are you?" I asked. I glanced at Hadie, wondering if she would introduce us, but she was busy with her hats and Harriet was no help either. The other woman looked at me and snapped another crayon.

"Who are you?" the woman repeated, scowling further. She reached out and touched the spots on my temples. I winced and jerked away. The smell of smoke coming from her was so strong, I had to fight the urge to cough.

Warren returned before I was forced to answer. I couldn't stop the smile from forming as he ushered the woman away and took the seat next to me.

"Don't mind her. No one knows her name, and she never says anything but those three words," he explained, tapping his fingers on his leg. "How are you doing?"

I had the sudden urge to pull him closer. To wrap my arms around him and hold on. I wasn't sure if it was a memory or just a wish as I pictured kissing him all over until he was giggling.

I grabbed his chair and scooted it as close as I could. He looked up, stunned for a moment and then a blush swept across his cheeks. I brushed my fingers across his jawline, smiling wider as the blush traveled to his ears.

"Adorable," I said softly.

"Reid," he let out a soft laugh. I didn't need my memories as I pressed my lips to his. It felt like the most natural thing to do at that moment. Warren didn't protest either. He cupped my face and returned the kiss. No one else existed. The way he kissed me felt familiar. I knew how his lips would move. The pressure of his hands as he cupped my face when I deepened the kiss. There was a fluttering sensation in my stomach, and my pulse began racing. I smiled against his lips, feeling better than I had since I'd first woken up. Warren seemed to bring me peace.

"I love you." The words left my mouth on their own, as if saying them were some kind of muscle memory. I blinked, pulling away to look at him. Had I said it before? Seeing the goofy look on Warren's face told me that maybe I had.

"I love—" The door to the rec room slammed open. I jerked around to glare at whoever had interrupted the words I wanted to hear. A woman stood in the doorway. Her grin looked inhuman as it stretched across her face. Her big eyes made her look like an animated character.

Hadie stood up, slamming her hands on the table, and turning to the woman. "Chelsea! How many times have we told you to stop slamming the door open like that?"

Harriet perked up, her body trembling as her eyes widened. "Is it tea-time?" she asked, earning a strange look from Hadie.

Chelsea's smile only seemed to grow. "Dr. Allison is coming," she giggled.

A hush went through the room. Everyone exchanged looks, some rubbing their hands together and some staring at the big blue door on the other side of the room. I looked at Warren, who looked over at me with worried eyes.

"Live si Nosilla Rotcod!" A man jumped up and flipped the table where he'd been playing chess by himself. The pieces rattled to the floor, except for the white knight still held in his hand.

Warren rushed over to the man. I went with him, worried the guy would get violent. I didn't want Warren to get hurt, but there was something else tugging at my mind.

"Reh tsurt ton od!" the man shouted, his voice shaking. He dragged his nails down his cheeks, leaving bright red scratches down his pale face.

"Wyatt, calm down," Warren said. He kept his voice calm and even, holding out his hands to seem less threatening. Wyatt stared at me, his eyes watering. He let out a groan as he looked away and grabbed Warren by the shirt. The white knight chess piece fell to the ground to join the others.

"Nerraw, Su gninosiop si Nosilla Rotcod," Wyatt whimpered. It sounded like a plea. I didn't know what he was saying, and by the looks of it, neither did Warren. He was calmly shushing him, treating him with such tenderness. "Em eveileb ot evah uoy esaelp."

"What are you trying to say?" I asked. I looked around, wondering if anyone could translate. I caught Chelsea's eyes and her grin turned into a smirk as she turned to look at herself in the two-way glass. She tossed her hair over her shoulder and leaned forward to check her teeth in her reflection. Her cheeks still dimpled with that crazed smile.

Wyatt was still talking in his strange language, though now he was shaking Warren as if trying to get him to understand. I didn't like that Warren was just letting him, but before I could say anything, the blue door opened.

Dr. Allison was beautiful to look at, but I didn't like the sudden pit that formed in my stomach. Her blonde hair was piled on her head, and her blue eyes flickered around behind a pair of white frame glasses. She wore blue scrubs underneath her white lab coat. Instinctively, I stepped in front of Warren and Wyatt, but Wyatt pushed past me.

"Retsnom uoy, og su tel," Wyatt said. Warren and I grabbed him, but he kept yelling. Doctor Allison raised her eyebrows and placed her hands on her hips.

"Oh Wyatt, I thought we talked about this," she said, her voice kind. She let out a sad sigh. "Warren, you said he was doing well with his new medication."

Warren played with his fingers, looking anywhere but at the woman before us. He swallowed hard a few times and cleared his throat.

"Ma'am," he started. I put a hand on his back, hoping to help him. Doctor Allison raised an eyebrow but didn't say anything. "I think he needs more time to adjust."

"Retsnom!" Wyatt said, which didn't seem to help his case. He charged at Dr. Allison, but Warren and I caught him around the waist.

Dr. Allison shook her head. "No, I don't think it's time he needs. Warren, you know what he needs." I wasn't sure what she meant, Warren did. He went white.

"Plea..." But Dr. Allison raised a well-manicured hand.

"I know he's a friend, Warren." she said. She grabbed his

shoulder and gave it a small squeeze. I fought the urge to pull him away. "We need to do this before he hurts himself."

"Dr. Allison," Warren began again, but grunted when Wyatt elbowed him in the gut. Dr. Allison pressed a button on a necklace around her neck. She backed up as men rushed in from the blue door. They surrounded us, and Wyatt screamed and flailed. Someone grabbed my arm, pulling me away from Warren.

"Sorry for the disturbance," Dr. Allison said to the rest of us. "The pharmacist should be here with your medication soon. Please be sure to take your pills. We'll do a group session this evening."

"Sllip eht ekat t'nod. On! On!" Wyatt yelled as he was dragged out. "On! On! On!"

I looked at Warren as Dr. Allison waved at him to follow. He wrung his trembling hands, and his top teeth sank into his trembling bottom lip.

I started to go after them. I didn't like the look in Warren's eyes or the way he looked back at me as if he wanted me to save him. But one of the guards grabbed me by the arm and held me back. I struggled for a moment until Warren shook his head and tried to give me a reassuring smile as he left the room.

I gritted my teeth, cursing myself for lack of memory because I knew I was forgetting something important. I turned and stared at the big blue door. I jerked forward when it opened again, only to pull up short when another woman walked in, pushing a cart in front of her.

"Tea-time," she sang. "Everyone line up."

Harriet bolted out of her seat, the fastest to be first in line. The woman with the cart met my eyes and smirked.

Something white hot surged, boiling in my belly. I clenched my hands into fists. I had no memories, no idea why rage coursed through my body, and why her bruised cheek made me want to smile.

Someone patted my back, and I turned to see Hadie watching me. "Easy Reid. Leave your sister alone. You don't want to go through another round of electroshock therapy or worse. I don't think Warren could handle twice in one day."

Warren's name grounded me. I swallowed hard and took a deep breath. I nodded at Hadie and followed her to get in line.

Chelsea came up behind, humming softly. I tried to ignore her as the line moved forward, but she only seemed to grow louder. Her stare seemed to bore into the back of my head. I wanted to turn around and demand to know what she wanted. I wanted to wrap my hands around her neck and shake her until she told me why she was grinning. Always grinning.

The hot feeling in my body as we got closer to the woman passing out pills, made me feel itchy, made me want to tear my skin off. I wanted to hit something. I wanted to scream. I wanted to toss tables like Wyatt had and stomp my feet until things made sense.

And then I was in front of the woman. She grinned, and I gritted my teeth. The heat under my skin was so hot, I was surprised I didn't have blisters.

"Here's your pills, Reid," she said sweetly, holding out a paper teacup. "Help you with that temper of yours, big brother." The pills in the cup were red and heart-shaped. They looked more like candy than medicine. My sister and I stared at each other. I finally grabbed the pills with pinched fingers and my sister grinned.

As the pills touched my lips, Chelsea slammed into me from behind. The little hearts fell from my grasp. Chelsea gasped in mock horror and scrambled after them.

"I'm so sorry!" she said. She scooped up the pills, blew them off. "I'm sorry, Reid." She passed them back to me, only I didn't feel them in my palm. With her back to my sister, she gave me a subtle shake of her head and mouthed the one word guaranteed to get my attention, "Warren."

So, I pretended to pop the pills into my mouth, still staring my sister down. Swallowing water, I opened my mouth to her. Chelsea scooped up her pills, popping them in her mouth, swallowing and holding out her tongue like I had just done. I had no way of knowing if she had taken hers or faked it. I took one last look at my sister and went to sit by myself in a corner. I felt strange without Warren there.

After my sister left, I went to find Chelsea. She was sitting on a beanbag chair, her hand outstretched as she examined her fingers in the patch of fading sunlight.

"Those pills make you feel so small," she said with a sigh. I sat down on the floor next to her but didn't say anything. She didn't seem like a person who appreciated being rushed. "Your memory is still gone." It wasn't a question.

"What do you know?" I asked, because it was clear she knew something.

"Warren and Wyatt were friends before Warren was promoted to orderly," Chelsea said. She dropped her hand into her lap. I snorted because that was something I could already guess. "The very best of friends," she stage-whispered as if it were a big secret.

"You are always this infuriating," I groaned.

"So, you do remember something." She beamed at me. "Poor Wyatt. Getting a lobotomy even though he's correct."

"What are you talking about?" I asked, not liking the sudden feeling in my stomach. "Do you know what he's saying?"

"You did too. At least before you and your sister got into a fight, and you had to get electroshock therapy. 'Doctor Allison is evil.' 'Do not trust her.' 'She's poisoning us, Warren.' And now he's getting a lobotomy because Doctor Allison is worried he'll ruin everything she's worked hard for."

"And Warren?" My mouth felt dry.

"Will be the one to help her because that was their deal.

Warren fought against this for so long. It's one of the many reasons that..."

"He came to me for help in the first place," I said quickly, as a memory flooded my mind. I could see Warren standing in front of me. Shaking hard and not looking at me. He begged me to try to find out what Wyatt was saying since Warren couldn't be around all the time. He wanted to know what Wyatt was saying so he could figure out how to help him.

"Of course, no one expected the two of you to fall in love," Chelsea sighed dreamily, fluttering her eyelashes.

Warmth spread across my cheeks, and I rubbed them as if it would hide the blush.

"We... We have to do something, right?" I looked around, eyeing the big blue door. "Can't we stop it? If Dr. Allison is evil... or whatever... can't we stop her?" It was suddenly so hot. I was so thirsty. I remembered Warren crying into my chest one night, about what they'd do to Wyatt. I had tried to distract him with kisses and tender words because my own heart ached for him.

More memories came flooding in. I sat up straighter. "Did you get the keys from Dorrma?" I asked.

Chelsea grinned again and pulled out a ring of keys. I started to jump to my feet, but Chelsea grabbed my wrist. "Hold your horses, Reid."

"What are we waiting for?" I demanded. I wanted to get to Warren. I wanted to make sure he was okay and I wanted to stop them from hurting Wyatt. Chelsea stared at me, that inhuman grin growing wider. I wanted to shake her until her head rol... no, not a thought I wanted to finish. It made me queasy.

Behind me, there was a loud shriek. Chelsea jumped to her feet as I turned around. Dorrma was there, the stack of paper hats clutched to her chest.

"Give those back!" Hadie demanded, spittle flying from her lips. "Right now! Do you hear me, you wretch? I want those back!"

She lunged around the table to swipe at Dorrma, but the other girl scampered back.

"Hats! Hats for everyone!" Dorrma sang. She winked and skipped around, tossing the hats in the air as Hadie shrieked again. "Haaaats!" She danced out of Hadie's reach again, throwing the hats like frisbees.

The door Warren and I had come through, swung open to reveal the woman who smelled like smoke. She waved frantically at Dorrma. Dorrma bolted from Hadie, going through the door.

"Dammit, Dorrma! I'm gonna wring your scrawny neck, you good-for-nothing-waste-of-space!" Hadie bellowed as she raced after the other woman. I could hear her yelling more curses and insults down the hallway. Others jumped up looking eager to see how this would go. They rushed through the open door.

"Run, Dorrma!" Dawson called as he raced through the door. "Come on, Dominic!" He waved behind him as if someone were following him.

"Get her, Hadie!" Harriet yelled, practically hopping around the broken crayons she'd tossed over her shoulder.

"We were waiting for that," Chelsea said. She pulled me toward the blue door. "But I didn't expect Wyatt to lose his shit. I thought we'd have more time, but this is fine. It's fine." She handled the keys expertly, unlocking the door within seconds. She shoved me through. "Go. I'll keep the guards busy."

And then she was gone. I didn't know where she went, and I didn't know why I didn't see anyone.

The hallway stretched out before me. It was the same black-and-white pattern from before, the one that made me so dizzy. For a moment, I felt so very small, as if someone could step on me and they wouldn't notice. I didn't know what I was doing. I couldn't remember anything.

Except that wasn't exactly true. I could feel Warren's tears on my chest as he told me Dr. Allison was giving Wyatt one more chance. Just one more chance. I remembered how badly he shook as he begged me to help him. Begged me to do something. He couldn't lose anyone else. I could feel his lips on mine when I told him I had a plan, and he needed to trust me.

I took a step forward, feeling as if I were growing bigger with each step. I'd been down this hall before. I had been wrapped in a cold blanket, pretending to struggle against the guards. Really though, I'd been mapping out where to go for this moment. Warren had followed behind me, asking why I had fought with my sister. He didn't know I'd planned this. He didn't know I was prepared to go through electroshock therapy again. I had wanted to tell him the plan, but Chelsea had convinced me otherwise. Warren couldn't keep a secret.

I turned left. Almost there.

I hated the tears I'd heard in Warren's voice as he told me he would be there when I woke up. I told him it would be okay because I had to offer him some kind of hope even if I couldn't tell him anything. I told him I loved him, that he made this place bearable. That he was the reason I got up in the morning.

I turned right. Running.

Warren was ushered from the room as I was strapped down. I was glad. My teeth clamped down on the mouthpiece. I knew I may lose my memory, just as I knew Chelsea and I had planned for it.

I slammed into the metal door and peered through the small square glass. And realized we hadn't planned for everything.

Warren was on the ground. He stared wide-eyed at something I couldn't see. He clutched his cheek. Blood oozed from the cracks between his fingers. He was sobbing, his chest heaving so harshly I thought it would collapse on itself.

I fumbled with the keys Chelsea gave me before jamming the right one into the lock. I rushed inside, falling to my knees next to Warren. Nothing else mattered to me at that moment, only the tears from the man I loved. Not the hysterical laughter coming from the woman in a lab coat. Not the utter stillness of the man strapped to a chair.

"Reid," Warren cried. "Reid, I was too late. I was too late. He tried to tell me... I tried to stop it... but I was too late. Too late."

He shook so hard in my arms. I pulled the hand from his face, to see the bloody scratches across his cheek. I pressed my hand to the wounds to try to stop the bleeding. I was glad it wasn't bad.

I didn't know what to say. I'd failed too. I thought I could put a stop to the madwoman behind me. My throat went dry, and adrenaline surged through my body. I looked over my shoulder.

Dr. Allison still held the hammer and ice pick, cackling. Her eyes met mine. "My Wonderland is safe again. He can't ruin it. My Wonderland. Isn't it magnificent, Reid? My Red Queen. Or in your case, king. My White Rabbit. My Wonderland." She looked at the man strapped to the chair. Blood dripped from his eyes as he blinked up at the ceiling. Lost in his mind.

Warren whimpered. My jaw ached from clenching it. I stood up; my limbs felt heavy, but my heartbeat was steady. My hands were dripping red. Red from Warren's blood.

"Red King, am I?" I snarled. "Then let's take off your head."

LOOKING INTO THE LOOKING GLASS

DONNA KEELEY

She knew the drugs were really kicking in when the cat started talking to her.

At least she thought it was still the cat, but instead of a gray tabby its fur had taken on a purplish tone and the mouth was huge—taking up most of the face.

"Why you still doing this shit, girl?" asked the former gray, now purple, cat. The voice was soothing and held notes of concern. "You thought you needed it before your transition, but why now?" He was literally floating above the bed but still in her eyeline. She was unaware she was also floating above the bed. Everything around her was changing from the solid, farmhouse rustic bedroom to a blurry, bright psychedelic canvas with large dots and swirls.

Jolie looked at the creature that did not look like her cat, but she knew it was. "Guilt," she answered simply.

"Well, if you be trippin', then we best go see the Trippin' Master. C'mon," his tail wrapped around her wrist, and she offered no resistance as she was pulled along. The colors moved in close around her creating a bright tunnel that the cat moved through.

Transitioning was much more advanced than it had been in the early part of the 21st century. Back then trans people were hardly considered human, and the death toll was very high—either from suicide or murder. Women of color suffered the most and haters were brutal. Now, almost at the end of the century, transitioning was commonplace with more options. A person could transition between genders, between species, or even combine with cybernetic modifications.

For the benefit of those who needed them, drugs had been rendered mostly harmless, but you could still find natural ones called peyote or mushrooms. These were very expensive alternatives and not everyone had that kind of money. Fortunately, Jolie did.

Jolie had been born Joseph Martin Bellgrade to a what was considered a "traditional family" in the previous century. It consisted of a father, a mother, a son, and a daughter, still represented but not the only definition of "family." The population was shrinking worldwide, which was a good thing. Fewer people to use up precious resources, fewer mouths to feed, many young people opted for complete sterilization although they banked eggs and sperm for possible use later. There were still unwanted children, but current protective services for children included forced sterilization for repeat offenders. Drastic but it worked.

And yet, with all these improvements and all this acceptance, hate still existed. Some extremists fled to places that welcomed their hate-filled views. Those countries were sanctioned, ostracized, and technologically challenged so they posed little threat. But even in the mainstream there was still resistance from a portion of the world's population thanks to outdated religious beliefs. The desire to conform to a specific standard overrode acknowledging anything that didn't fit their preconceived notions.

Jolie was still caught in her drug-induced spell, traveling the bright, colorful tunnel, and passing windows that gave glimpses of her past. Her proud father showing off a newborn Jolie, dressed in a baseball uniform complete with tiny mitt. Another showed her with a baby sister, Natalie. Jolie closed her eyes to push those memories away. They weren't nearly as idyllic as they appeared to be.

She and the cat landed softly on a patch of grass in a great overgrown garden. Everything was bigger here. Flowers grew up to ten feet high, trees disappeared into the mists above, giant mushrooms spread like market umbrellas over them.

"C'mon," ordered the cat, now as big as a German Shepherd, who released her wrist and moved off at a brisk pace. Jolie had to blink several times because the cat's body seemed to dissipate leaving only the head with that huge grin, then reform again. Sometimes it was just the head and tail, or just the tail. Jolie was feeling weirded out and her head pounded.

They finally stopped in front of a mushroom about five feet tall with a giant blue caterpillar with a very human-looking face on it. Stretched out, the insect was surely as tall as a human and the anthropomorphism was enhanced by the fact that he was smoking a hookah. Even in Jolie's time those things were still around, but whether it contained tobacco or another substance, she wasn't sure.

"Hey, Bug Man," the cat greeted the caterpillar. "This one's on a wild trip and I think she needs your help. She used to do the expensive stuff in the old days, but I thought she kicked it after her metamorphosis. You know all about that shit."

The caterpillar didn't respond immediately. He took a long drag on his mouthpiece contemplating Jolie intently, then let out the smoke directly into her face. It didn't bother her, she actually liked the smell.

"Who. Are. You?" the creature asked in a nasally voice, stretching out the words.

"I'm Jolie."

"No, that is incorrect. Who. Are. You?"

"How can I be incorrect with my own name?"

"That is NOT what I meant. WHO. ARE. YOU?" The brows slanted down as the question became more intense.

Jolie's head started to pound under the intense stare. "I'm me," she blurted.

"And who is 'me'?"

"I... I... I," she fumbled. Her headache became worse, and she clutched her temples, closing her eyes. "I don't know!" she finally yelled, sinking down to her knees. She felt the giant cat rub against her.

"Why don't you tell us what you do know," the transformed cat suggested. "If you know where you've been, then you can decide where you're goin'."

The images from the tunnel penetrated her aching head. Jolie began an analysis of her life. She always avoided this type of self-reflection, preferring to move forward instead of looking back.

She was welcomed into the world as Joseph, but was never Joseph. Nothing she did connected with her inner self, as much as she tried to please her family. She started with T-Ball as a preschooler, moved on to soccer in elementary school, then found track and field in middle school where she excelled. Running against a stopwatch, it didn't matter what her outside looked like; she felt liberated. But those were only brief moments of freedom, once back in the classroom the expectations haunted her. All through high school, girls would shyly smile at her, send her messages—some subtle, some very explicit in their wants. She couldn't respond. She didn't want to respond. She purposely wrenched her ankle so she could miss the Senior Prom and not be forced to choose a female date. Her mother and sister understood more than they let on, but her father was another matter.

He only saw her outside, her sports achievements, her place in the world as a white male. He had asked about why she didn't have a girlfriend; her response was that she wanted to dedicate herself to her classwork and her track activities. Would he have been more accepting if she had simply been gay? Why couldn't she be honest with her family? With herself?

Away at college, the pressure eased a little, but each morning facing herself in the mirror while she shaved it became harder and harder to look at herself. This wasn't her. Shaving daily removed the facial hair that shouldn't be there. The lines of her face and the Adam's apple in her throat didn't belong to her. This was not who she was inside.

The one bright spot... no, nothing so subtle, it was a supernova that lighted her perception of herself with a glare that nearly blinded her, was Marie. Marie saw her, all of her, she knew instantly who and what Jolie was under her disguise. Marie was her salvation.

Marie told Jolie while she was technically bi-sexual, she leaned mostly towards women. However, their attraction was instant when they met at a party. Jolie was in a lounge chair next to their host's pool, nursing a beer, trying to blend into the background. Marie had plopped down on the chair next to her and looked her over. Wide brown eyes measured every inch of the white, blond, blue-eyed male, taking in everything both external and internal. After a few long seconds, she spoke up.

"I don't know who you are," she said boldly. "But you are one messed up person."

The statement shocked Jolie to her core. "What do you mean by that?" she asked suspiciously.

Marie gestured to all of Jolie. "You don't fit in that body. This is not who you are. Why you tryin' to hide yourself? Why don't you just be who you are?"

The words cut through Jolie like a saw blade. They were abrupt, hurtful, and true.

"I don't know," Jolie answered as tears ran down her cheeks. "I really don't know."

Loving arms were around her and Jolie buried her head into the offered shoulder, crying over how lost she was.

"Don't worry, baby. I got you. We're gonna get you put right. I been feelin' you all night and I wanna help you. I can feel everything you've stuffed away, and it hurts like a bitch."

Jolie sniffed. "You got that right," she replied, and they both laughed.

They were inseparable from that point on. It helped Jolie's campus reputation to be seen with the curvy, vivacious Latina woman and even her father grudgingly approved when the family met Marie. Her father would have preferred a white girl who could act with more decorum over this bold, brassy female, but at least his son finally had a girlfriend.

After college, the need to maintain the false narrative went away. There was no question that they were together forever, even with Jolie in her alien body. Moving to a larger city helped Jolie find her real self, and for the first time the apartment they shared felt like a real, loving home. Over time, Jolie began to separate herself from her family. It was easy enough to blame work or illness as excuses for never coming home. Marie was Jolie's rock, the person that always had her back, the one that made things happen. Within six months of starting their new lives, Marie had set up appointments for Jolie to talk to doctors and psychologists about transitioning. Since Jolie had kept herself bottled up, she had never used hormone blockers during puberty, so she grew into the full complement of testosterone for a male her age. And she was miserable because of it.

Marie was adamant that Jolie take her time with the change. While the actual process of transitioning physically had been greatly reduced, with surgeries for breasts—both removal and insertion, and genitalia performed at the same time, there was still the psychological component. Jolie's partner had almost a sixth sense when it came to reading other people, and Marie almost always knew Jolie's moods and feelings. Jolie often apologized for not being able to reciprocate, but Marie brushed it off. She was perfectly happy in the relationship, even more so when Jolie completed her transition.

It was nearly a year after the surgery and countless therapy sessions when Jolie looked in the mirror and finally saw herself —her real self. Dirty blond, wavy hair, deep blue eyes, her formerly hard jawline softened into a curve, and a missing Adam's apple from her completely smooth neck. This was her. This was Jolie.

The years following were joyful and fulfilling. There was a reconnection with her immediate family after Jolie's sister, who had secretly supported her, left home and was able to show her feelings in public. Jolie's mother soon followed to get away from her toxic husband and, over time and many conversations, had come to understand more about her oldest child. They both danced at Jolie and Marie's wedding, a day that stood out as one of the happiest the couple had shared. There were only a few people from Jolie's family, but Marie's family more than made up for the loss—they had welcomed her from the first and Jolie had always felt closer to them.

But despite the happiness, there was doubt and guilt. The influence of her father had been strong growing up and Jolie had worked hard for his acceptance. The need for constant patriarchal approval did not disappear once Jolie transitioned to her real self. It was always in the back of her mind, the disappointment she caused to her father, feelings of guilt for not being perfect. She had tried to make amends with him, but he had cast her out, screaming at her for being "crazy."

The unresolved conflict with her father and his family had reared its ugly head when she attended her aunt's funeral. She was entirely alone, without the support of Marie, or her mother or sister. She sat in the back of the chapel, hoping to slip out at the end of the service, but her father saw her. While he kept himself composed for the funeral, he never missed an opportunity to glare at her. Jolie felt the condemnation and left before the event was over.

Following that, she immediately fell into a depressive spiral and spent days in bed unable to force herself up. Jolie knew Marie was suffering alongside her, but she refused the suggestions Marie made to try and help her, shutting her partner out.

She sought out the non-synthetic drugs to dull the pain. She wanted to punish herself for daring to become who she really was. And that had led her here, to the place with giant mushrooms and a talking caterpillar who demanded she confront herself.

And it was a confrontation. She was commanded to review her life in nitty-gritty detail, no whitewashing, or modifications to her memories. While the narrative in her mind played out, a light began to shine; small at first, but then it grew as her story unfolded. When she reached the present, the light was blinding, almost painful. She finally knew who she was, and the certainty mixed with confidence flowed through her.

The fantasy forest disappeared, and she realized she was sitting on her bed, cross-legged, leaning against the headboard. The cat was once again a gray tabby, normal-sized, looking at her with interest.

WHO. ARE. YOU? the words echoed.

I AM JOLIE.

I ALWAYS HAVE BEEN.

AND I ALWAYS WILL BE.

"Are you sure you want to do this?" Marie asked.

"Yes. I'm sure. I should have done this years ago."

Marie had commented about the newfound confidence Jolie expressed and was glad, expressing that this was a change for the better. Jolie had insisted on returning to her hometown to see her father, but she felt Marie's hesitation about this latest confrontation.

"Couldn't you have face-timed him?"

"No. It has to be in person. I need to do it this way.

Marie nodded. "Okay. I got your back, as always," she smiled at Jolie and squeezed her hand.

"I know you do," Jolie replied, returning the smile and kissing Marie's hand in hers.

Jolie's father had kept the house after her mother left him, both were now aging and unkept. Jolie requested that Marie stay in the vehicle while she conducted this last, very important ritual. She boldly knocked on the door, ignoring the doorbell camera that showed her plainly standing on the front step. There was a pause, and for a moment she feared he wouldn't come to the door, just scream at her from inside the house. But then the door opened on squeaking hinges and his rough, lined, angry face confronted her.

"What are you doing here?" he snapped. "I don't want anything to do with you."

"Well, I have something to do with you," Jolie spat at him. "And I came a long way to get it done."

"Get the hell off my property, you monster. You're not my son." His face was turning red from his anger.

"No. I'm not your son, you bastard," Jolie replied angrily

through clenched teeth, before finally yelling, "I. AM. YOUR. DAUGHTER!"

She spun on her heel and returned to the vehicle, leaving him staring in surprise.

She never looked back.

ONE DAY AT CARROLLTECH

C.N. WHEATON

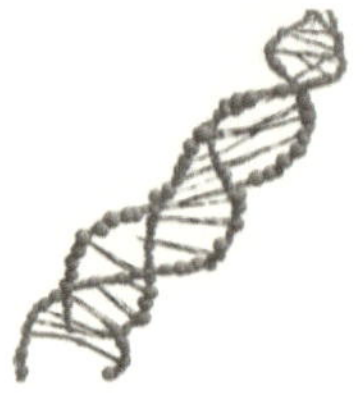

Working for CarrollTech had always been Alice's dream. Now the day was finally here.

"I've got this," Alice whispered, trying to psych herself up as she stared at the dauntingly large complex. She'd worked so hard for this opportunity, to intern at CarrollTech and be part of the cutting edge of biomedical research. If she could impress them, this internship could be the start of her career. Alice took a deep breath and walked through the mirrored doors.

Once inside, her mouth dropped open. She was standing in a giant atrium with a living wall of flowers. A huge DNA-helix art piece made entirely from pocket watches hung from the ceiling. Despite the hour, it was silent—even the traffic noise from the street outside was absent, as if she'd walked into another world entirely.

She realized she didn't know where to go and waited awkwardly near the empty front desk, frantically checking her phone for any directions she'd somehow missed.

"First day?" a cheerful voice asked from somewhere near her

ear and Alice jumped, guiltily tearing her eyes away from her phone. The person in front of her was dressed in striped pink and purple leggings, pink heels, a purple dress shirt, and a yellow tie with pink cats on it. Completing the look was some of the most fabulous eye makeup she'd ever seen in real life. They also sported a bright yellow button with "they/them" written on it.

"Um, yes?" She blushed with embarrassment, as she realized they were still waiting for her reply. All she'd wanted to do was make a good first impression, but she felt sweaty and flustered. "I mean, yes, it is my first day. I'm worried I'm in the wrong place."

"I suppose that entirely depends on where you're meant to be," they laughed. Then they noticed her anxiety. "You're Alice Charles, aren't you? Call me Ches. I'll be your guide today." Ches grinned. "Come on, no need to be shy. I'm sure you didn't come all this way just to stop before you've started." They led her through one of the far doors. "Most of us come through the back, although it's less impressive than the main entrance," Ches shared over their shoulder. "I'm not sure where the guard is right now. We can get your credentials sorted out later."

"What do you do here?" she asked as they waited in front of an elevator.

"A little of this, a little of that," Ches answered cryptically. They waved her inside the elevator and pulled out their phone. "Let's see, you're working with... oh."

"Oh?" she echoed. She didn't like the sound of that. "What's wrong with where I've been assigned?" She'd been told she'd find out which lab she'd be working with once she arrived.

"Nothing," Ches answered unconvincingly. "You're with Rabbit—I mean, Dr. White. He's in Building G. He's been trying to isolate the genetic markers that have to do with chronic tardiness. It's been causing a backlog in the sequencing lab—all of his subjects show up late."

Alice laughed, then realized Ches wasn't joking. They exited the elevator on the 5th floor. This hallway had its walls painted dark green, with branching sculptures that met overhead. It felt like walking through a forest. Alice hurried to catch up with Ches' long strides.

"Do you have lunch with you today?" they asked. Satisfied to see her nod, Ches swept through a set of doors and into a large open patio situated between buildings in the complex. "This is the very best break area," Ches confided.

The only occupant on the patio was wreathed in a cloud of smoke from the vape pen he used in between sips of his coffee. He waved a hand at Ches, who continued past him. "That's Dr. Oruga. His lab works on psychedelic drug treatments, including using LSD for PTSD and chronic depression. If he offers you food, I suggest you say no," Ches whispered, then grinned.

She smiled back hesitantly. Ches was kidding, right?

"Actually, I should talk to him for a second. If you go through those doors, you can put your lunch in one of the fridges. I'll be along in a minute."

"Okay," Alice said, although she wasn't sure it was okay at all. Every minute that passed she was more conscious than ever she was going to be late on her very first day, but there didn't seem to be any alternative.

She went through another set of doors on the other end of the patio and into a brightly lit kitchen area. Two men were sitting at one of the tables. "Who do we have here?" the taller of the two asked.

"My name is Alice, I'm a new intern. Does it matter where I put my lunch?"

"That depends. Do you want it to be there when you come back for it?" one of them asked with a leering smile.

"Yes," she said firmly, wishing Ches was there.

"Then you should probably use the far fridge."

"Thank you," Alice said, making the effort to sound polite

instead of stressed and frustrated. She pulled her lunchbox out of her bag and put it into the fridge he'd indicated.

The other man leaned back in his chair. "I'm Dr. Hatta and this is Dr. Haigha by the way, not that you asked. Now, tell me, Alice-the-new-intern, what is a possible drug combination that could help cure bigotry?"

She straightened up out of the fridge and looked back at him. "I'm sorry, I don't know. What's the answer?"

He sighed. "I have no idea."

"Dr. Haigha, Dr. Hatta, are you bothering the new intern?" Ches asked from behind her. Alice breathed a sigh of relief she wouldn't have to keep talking to the teasing duo.

"No, of course not," Dr. Haigha insisted insincerely. "Here, have a maple twist," he said, waving to a tray of assorted donuts at the table next to them that sported a little sign saying "EAT ME."

"Um, no thank you," Alice demurred, not sure she trusted any food they'd offer.

A loud snore interrupted whatever Dr. Haigha had been going to say. Alice whirled around in surprise, spotting a nap pod in the corner with a small man curled up inside. He snored again and rolled over, muttering about a tea party.

"That's Dr. Gils. He researches insomnia; we think he's found the cure," Ches offered. "Now, come along, Alice." They led the way out the door, leaving the odd trio behind. Ches led Alice down another forest-like hallway, stopping in front of an elevator with flowers etched in the metal. She got in as the doors opened, then realized Ches had stopped short. "I have to go, but the lab is the second door to the right when you get off the elevator. Good luck. Also, if you run into Dr. Hart... actually, scratch that. Try **not** to run into Dr. Hart."

"Isn't she the CEO?" Alice asked, resisting the urge to beg Ches to come with her. They were the only friendly face she'd seen so far, and she was hoping they'd smooth the way with Dr. White.

Ches leaned in and pressed the button for the 7th floor. "Yes. Career management in charge of a bunch of scientists; terrifying prospect. Dr. Hart is between marriages at the moment, so she's in an extra foul mood. Seems she can't pretend to be a good person for longer than 6 months since that's when the beautiful young women she marries always seem to file for divorce. Anyway, catch you later, Alice," Ches said with a grin. They spun around and walked off as the doors closed with a ding, leaving Alice with more questions than ever.

The entire elevator was etched with flowers that glowed in time to the song "A Golden Afternoon" as it played over the speakers. It was strange and beautiful, like most everything else she'd seen since arriving. This part of CarrollTech looked nothing like the sterile interview room she'd seen and reading descriptions of their research hadn't prepared her for any of the scientists she'd met so far.

When the elevator stopped, she followed Ches' directions down a checkered hallway to Dr. White's lab, knocking on the door. "You're late." Dr. White said flatly when the door opened. Though a small, rather rabbity man, he was still clearly used to being in charge. "While I study chronic tardiness, it isn't a trait I like on my team. I don't think I can use you after all."

Alice felt her stomach drop. "I promise, it won't happen again."

"No, it won't," Dr. White agreed. "If you want to participate in one of my tardiness studies, I'm sure we can find a place for you as a subject. Otherwise, go find Gryph. He'll get you a new placement."

"I—" Alice started, planning to beg before thinking better of it. She looked wistfully at the lab behind Dr. White, full of its gleaming computers and state-of-the-art lab equipment. He was the foremost expert in how humans perceive time and his lab developed treatments that altered that perception. But before she could work out what to say, Dr. White shut the door in her face. She turned back to the hallway, which seemed less friendly than it had before. "But I don't know where to find Gryph," she whispered.

Dejected, Alice started down the hallway, scrutinizing the signs outside each door as she went. About halfway down, one of the doors opened, and a severe-looking woman stepped out. Her eyes gleamed when she looked at Alice, although it was possible that was just the light from the tablet she was holding.

"Now dear, do you regularly have sex?" she asked, fingers poised over the tablet.

"I'm sorry, what?" Alice blinked. She wasn't sure what she'd expected, but it certainly wasn't that. She didn't want to share that she was ace, and sex wasn't a priority for her the way it seemed to be for so many people. Whenever possible, she avoided the subject. People seemed to get weird about it and this day was already weird enough. "Er, I'm not here to be a test subject. Dr. White told me to go find someone named Gryph."

The severe woman shrugged. Her lab coat shifted to the side, revealing a tight t-shirt with 'Duchess' emblazoned across her chest. "Suit yourself. I'll let him know." She tapped at her tablet for a moment, then looked back up. "He'll be here soon. Now, are you positive you don't want to participate in a sex study?"

"No, thank you," Alice said firmly. She breathed a sigh of relief when the woman went away. But, when she was alone, the hallway seemed to stretch on forever. The longer she waited, the smaller she felt.

"Alice?" a soft voice asked from behind her. When she turned around, she breathed a sigh of relief. The speaker was a slightly built man who looked close to her age. While she noticed his feathery hair was brown and he had a beaky nose, it was his smile that put her at ease. "I'm Gryph. Sorry it didn't work out with Dr. White. No need to worry, however, Dr. Caretta has space in his lab for you. It's a good project too. He's been developing a treatment that enables people to revisit their memories."

"Interesting." Alice followed Gryph. They walked quietly for a moment. Then Alice asked what was on her mind. "Do you like working here?"

Gryph shrugged. "The benefits are good," he said mildly. "And they were supportive when I transitioned." Alice knew the statement was a test from the tightening around his eyes. It looked like he was bracing himself for whatever she might say.

She took a breath to choose her words carefully. When she spoke, she tried to match his light tone. "I'm happy to hear that, I wouldn't want to work for a place that wasn't supportive." At her answer, some of the tension melted away from Gryph. He flashed her a quick smile. She smiled back, feeling like she'd made a friend.

They went down two floors to a hallway covered in a mural of a rocky beach. Gryph led her through the third door, into another lab. Several people were hard at work at the lab benches. While the space was cluttered, she could see the same top-of-the-line equipment she'd spotted everywhere else. They found the supervisor hard at work on his laptop. He straightened up when he saw them.

Dr. Carretta was a round man who looked like he was being swallowed by his turtleneck. His eyes got misty when he looked at her. "I remember my own days as an intern! What a jolly good time that was. I even met my husband here. Now, Alice, are you ready to get to work?"

"Yes, absolutely," Alice promised as she gratefully slid into a seat next to a laptop and a mound of paperwork as Dr. Carreta assigned a lab member to show her how to help. Gryph smiled and gave her a little wave as he left.

After several hours spent reading up on the current projects, a lunch break where she mercifully avoided all the scientists she'd seen in the breakroom that morning, and several hours doing data entry, Dr. Carretta spoke up. "Nice work so far, Alice. I just got a notification asking you to head down to the security desk to sort out your credentials. Could you please nip down there?"

"Of course. Thanks, Dr. Carretta," she said with feeling as she left, heading to the security office she located on the building map Gryph had just emailed. Alice had barely made it out of the elevator on the first floor when she needed to dodge around a person carrying a box, not noticing that she was perilously close to a cart full of vials of a white liquid. Feeling like she was watching herself in slow motion, she couldn't stop her momentum enough to avoid bumping into the cart. The top flat of the vials went crashing to the ground. They shattered as they landed, sending white liquid splashing onto a woman in a red pantsuit who was passing by.

The woman's face went as red as her suit. "Who are you?" she demanded.

"A-Alice Charles," she confessed, stammering as she realized why she recognized the woman's face.

"Well, Alice Charles, you just managed to splash the CEO thanks to your clumsiness. Needless to say, you're fired. Now get out of my sight," Dr. Hart snapped. She angrily strode off before Alice could say or do anything to try to fix the situation.

Alice walked the rest of the way to the lobby in a sort of fugue state, managing to make it almost all the way there before her first tears started to fall.

"What's wrong?" asked a voice near her ear. She looked up to see Ches.

"I messed up. Dr. White kicked me out of his lab because I was late and then I bumped into a tray of vials that were in the hallway and they messed up Dr. Hart's suit and she fired me!" Alice sobbed.

"Oh, is that all?"

"What?"

"I forgot to tell you. Dr. Hart fires everyone. Don't worry, she forgets about it just as fast. Mr. Hart, her brother down in HR, never even bothers to put the paperwork through. I mean, the vials aren't great, but it's the Tweedle lab's own fault for leaving their materials in the hallway."

"I think I'm going crazy."

Ches patted her arm and flashed her another grin. "Darling, we're all a little crazy here. How else would we change the world?"

WILL YOU BE OUR ALICE?

PAUL WILSON

Editors' Note: This story contains topics some may find sensitive.

I *think I look pretty. No. Not* think. *I am* pretty.

Caleb's feelings about his appearance were not about sexuality, but rather identity. He was dressed to feel pretty, not sexy. He was dressed for himself, not an admirer. He was his own admirer.

He gazed at himself in the mirror, turning his head right then left, enjoying the coloring above his eyes. Pink. He loved the color. He loved it on him. He tilted his head up and then applied a little more gloss to his bottom lip. He smiled, batted his lashes, and giggled. He made a kissy face at himself. On the little table between the sink and the toilet, the cracked black and silver radio chimed the call letters WKAS ("The riiight music at the riiight time!") and then Kim Petras began. Caleb squealed and gave in to the compulsion to dance. He loved how his dress twirled around him, a shimmering flow of floor-length blue. His little green purse (shaped like a flower) was a lily pad undulating on the swell of his hips. To be free to dance! To dance like no one was watching, and there was no one watching—

A scream echoed up the hall and into the bathroom like a tossed grenade. Caleb opened his eyes, his smile evaporating. A shaking quake began in his stomach and he peed a little, staining his panties. He froze, hands above his head, in the bathroom doorway of the pathetic little mill house and saw his mother studying him. Why had she come back? It was mid-day! It was summer! She should have been at work for another five hours!

Her mouth was open, but no sound emerged. She tilted her head back and forth as if she couldn't fit the image of her son dressed like a girl into her brain. She made a strangled little squeal. They faced each other like gunslingers. Then the AC kicked on and she fired her first shot. She screeched. No words, just sound. Caleb collapsed against the doorway, dodging her sound bullet, but then she fired again, a single word that she transformed into a hateful slur. That one hit her target.

"QUEER!"

Caleb fell, stumbling out of the bathroom in his stolen heels. Did his mother recognize her own clothes on him? Did she remember being that young once? Had she ever danced? She screamed again, easily drowning out Miss Petras who had moved on to "There Will Be Blood."

She stalked towards him, firing her gun empty, flinging more hateful words. They pierced flesh and dress and walls alike. Caleb gathered up his ruffles, finding strength in their silky feel, and ran. He jerked past his mother, past the pictures of dead and unhelpful relatives on the wall and bolted out the door. His mother fired again, shooting him in the back with curses and questions and inarticulate sounds of horror, not a cowboy with a six-shooter now, but an enemy soldier with an automatic weapon of hate.

Caleb jumped off the porch, his beautiful long dress parachuting around him, the green purse punching him in the side. He landed and stumbled, digging up divots of grass. He ran, screaming now because the terror and sickening ease of how his world had burst open was too much. His mother stormed the porch. The screen door banged open with its usual flat *whack* against the side of the house. Caleb fled, but in contrast to the destruction of his secret and life, there was a moment of soaring freedom. He was dressed as a girl *outside*! He was out! It was exhilarating and terrifying but overlaying those feelings roared his mother's hoarse screams eradicating his joy.

CALEB RAN deep into the woods. Sunlight became a sizzling fire trail left by his escape. The shade cooled his brow and acted as a kind hand. The sensation brought him to unexpected tears. His exhilaration at being outside as his true self faded, and he was thankful to be safely hidden again. He let his dress drop so it would swish against the leaves. He loved the sound, but he walked because there was no alternative. He walked because he had to do something with the bucket of emotions slopping inside him. Maybe he could find a place to dump it out here among the trees.

The longer he walked, the more he sweated, and he hated that because it would ruin his make-up. His feet began to ache from the heels. Then he spied a friendly-looking tree. Was that a face? Wise and ancient and helpful? No, just bark with leaves for eyebrows, but he approached it anyway. He felt an absurd desire to curtsey, so he did, then leaned against the trunk and slid down to sit. Once in the soft grey dirt he closed his eyes and listened to the birds.

Maybe my life is a fairytale now and the animals will gather around to buck me up and make me feel better. A chipmunk will dry my tears with his bushy tail.

Nothing like that happened, but when Caleb opened his eyes again, he saw a butterfly bopping along and that little blob of beauty made him smile.

Okay. Okay. Now what?

Taking inventory, Caleb hugged his purse. He was glad for it, another piece of his identity. It was a silly thing, but he had loved it from the day he claimed it from the trunk in his mother's closet. It made him feel safe and calm and Caleb leaned his head back and dozed. Birds chirped and hopped above him. Squirrels played tag on the branches. The wind blew. How long did he sleep? He didn't know. When he fully opened his eyes again, his stomach told him it was afternoon.

He rose, then smoothed his hair and dress. He looked around wondering what to do. A voice spoke to him, a confident tone from inside: *A lady puts herself together before going anywhere. You were running and sweating and crying. I'm sure you look a fright! You have your purse so you can compose yourself. Do so. That's step one, Miss!*

And it was that simple. Caleb opened his purse, took out his compact, and checked his face. It wasn't as bad as he had imagined. He re-applied lip-gloss and touched up under his eyes. He didn't have mascara, but he had liquid eyeliner and outlining his eyes always made him feel better. He loved how the blue of his eyes popped. He fluffed out his hair, reassembled his purse, (after gobbling a stick of gum to quiet his stomach) and looked around himself. There were only two choices, really. Go further ahead or go back home. Which?

He walked around the tree, gliding his hand along its bark, head down and thinking, trying to come to terms with his mother's reaction. He had known this day would come. For his sanity he knew he would have to stop pretending to be a boy *sometime*, but *sometime* had always been in the future, a confrontation he now realized he had been running from because he knew she would never understand. She was too old, too set in her ways. *Rigid*, that was his mother. She was a woman who would always color the coloring pages exactly so; she would never color a purple tree or a blue sun.

His fingers encountered something warm. He gasped, jerking his hand back. He thought: *Mushroom?* What he saw caused his mouth to fall open. The wad of gum sat in the middle of his tongue like a stud.

It can't be!

But it was. The touch of it—the *warmth* of it—confirmed it.

Sitting at chest level in the thick tree, surrounded by bark and moss and leaves, was a warm pink vagina. The lips were full, perfect, and a late beam of sunlight spotlighted the moisture. It quivered and Caleb swore he heard it coo. He smiled. It was... fantastic!

It's so pretty. So pink! That's what's missing from me. I wish I had one, he thought.

He reached out and touched it again. The decision was preordained and happened with no discussion or fear. It quivered and Caleb heard that coo again, a coy and pleased trill, like Betty Boop.

I think...

The lips parted as if eager to whisper a secret, and Caleb found an opening. The hole stretched easily. He stepped up on a convenient root and was able to place his head inside. It smelled wonderful, like flowers and minerals, like a refreshing spring rain.

It's a reverse birth! I'm going back in!

Was he scared? No. He was too far delighted to be scared. Here was magic, magic like the way he felt when he put on make-up or dresses, or wigs. It was good magic. He pushed his way into the tree. The vagina was strong and accepted him. It hugged him, lowering him, but at the end the lips closed over his feet and his heels slid off, falling to the base of the tree. He went in barefoot, but he didn't care.

Caleb fell down the hole.

∼

HE DESCENDED. His dress billowed, acting as a parachute again, just like Princess Peach, and that made him laugh. Was he a princess then? That was a wonderful thought. He held the fabric all the way down. The hole was awfully deep but lit by a warm luminescence he couldn't pinpoint. Instead, he was drawn to the earthen walls where roots and foliage tangled together, but there were also clocks and ribbons and springs and shiny chains. Caleb saw jump ropes and Lego bricks and dolls, dolls, dolls! He giggled and floated down. He smelled dirt, yes, but cinnamon and baking good things, too.

He landed in a rounded brick chamber with a wooden floor. It was dry and warm and—

"Oh!"

At the mouth of a hallway, sprinkled with orange light, stood a brown dormouse wearing a deep green jacket with a pair of spectacles balanced on his nose. Its forehead sloped back, suggesting age and intelligence, but warping the image was its large jutting cock. As Caleb watched, the mouse twitched its whiskers, removed its penis, and mounted it. It winked, then took off down the hall on its cock-rocket, leaving a stunned Caleb behind.

Oh my!

Caleb followed, giggling. He wanted to see the mouse again. It was so handsome! Strange but true. It reminded him of a boy at school with brown hair, and round glasses, a boy Caleb found so pretty, that all-encompassing fantasy.

"Come back!"

The brick hallway stretched. Pictures adorned the walls, snapshots of strange family members in dusty frames. Caleb turned a corner. He saw no sign of the mouse, but he did find a door.

What's this now?

The door was heavy and wooden and ornate. There was no knob but rather a crocheted sign hanging in the middle that read: *There are no doors here, only opportunities. Every door is a jar.*

Caleb shook his head. If it was a joke, he didn't get it. He saw no place to grasp, so he pushed, expecting resistance, but instead the door swung open into a new room with a table in the center, a recliner, and a hearth. On the table were four bottles. Caleb entered the room.

THE DOOR slowly closed behind him. He turned and saw it remained, with a knob on this side. That was good. He could go back if he wanted. Carved on the keyplate was the same cock the mouse had ridden. Caleb raised an eyebrow at its detail, then turned back to the table.

The bottles were thick with glass stoppers. The liquids inside looked rich and luxurious. He thought of liquor (specifically the browns his mother kept in the kitchen cabinet that he sometimes snuck nips of, not unlike a mouse himself) but these colors were green, red, blue, and a wonderful shade of pink that Caleb immediately opened. He smelled it. It was bitter but with a sweet undertone like cake icing. His mouth filled with hopeful saliva. A label hung from the stem, adorned with the most beautiful calligraphy. It was so ornate it was hard to read. Caleb puzzled out "Drink Me" but hesitated. Was it safe?

What came to his mind surprised him. He remembered the last book he'd read—in bed, with a flashlight, long after his mother had passed out—Alison Rumfitt's *Tell Me I'm Worthless.* How he had loved that book. She had spoken to him on levels he didn't understand yet, but he had felt a kinship—a possibility of being able to discover his real self. What's more, she had made the usually seedier side of drugs seem... well, less seedy. Caleb had never thought much of the vice but with it suddenly in his hand...

He took a drink of the pink and it tasted wonderful. He drank again, a line spilling down his chin. He wiped it away with his finger, then sucked it clean. When he opened his eyes from the third gulp, he saw his face reflected in the glass bottle. His blue eyes had changed to a glowing pink. It made him feel wonderful, warm and shivery all over. He felt stronger, taller, and his whole body tingled. He bit his lip and giggled.

"Oh, I like that..." Even his voice sounded better.

Caleb looked around the room and found another door. There was a knob and a keyplate and engraved on this one was a vagina, just like the one on the tree. Caleb grasped the knob, turned it, and entered a sweet-smelling space of green crowded with cool shadows.

CALEB KNEW the artist who drew the *Alice in Wonderland* illustrations because he had researched it after having vivid nightmares from his first reading of the book. John Tenniel. A Victorian artist who—in Caleb's opinion—drew the most detailed nightmare fuel he had ever seen. So when Caleb walked through the door and found those characters talking and drinking, he froze in mid-step. When the nightmares turned to him, Caleb was sure he would die of fright as those ink-eyes needled him.

The detail in their faces was rendered in thin pencil strokes, charcoal come to life. Their heads were too big for their bodies, lips bulbous bouncing appendages, eyes heavily lidded, and hair curved to thorns protruding at every angle. They looked wild, unpredictable, and deranged, as if they would reach out at any moment and carve away a piece of him to casually nibble alongside a cup of tea. There was no way he could go further towards them.

You are no coward! Stand up straight! A lady presents herself!

So, Caleb straightened his back. At the head of the table the Mad Hatter rose, smiled, and came towards him, his oversized head seeming to float like a balloon. The other guests went back to their tea and cookies and conversation—all except the dormouse who waved and winked.

"You look..." The Mad Hatter gasped. He was clearly searching for a word. Caleb watched him try a few sounds, but he was bucktoothed, and his vowels emerged as whistles, further eroding any aura of malice. His bow tie was crooked, his shirt misbuttoned.

"What?" Caleb asked, finding his inner queen. She—he—stepped from his interior shadows and demanded: "Speak up! How do I look?"

"Enchanting. Amazing. Fantabulous! Like a princess!"

It was the best compliment. Caleb's scowl melted.

The Mad Hatter held out his hand. "I am so glad you arrived."

"You were expecting me?"

"Always my dear... Always."

"How do you mean?"

"Wonderland always calls its next Alice. As we are without one currently, you were inevitable. Your arrival... well, it is always the Alice's choice... but the arrival, the calling, always happens."

"I'm Alice?" Caleb touched his face. "I'm Alice. I... I hadn't settled on my name yet. My real name. The one I think of as myself when I dress. When I'm really me. Yes. Alice. I am Alice."

"Yes, my dear. You are. If you want to be."

"Wait. You said there have been other Alices here? Other people like me?"

The Mad Hatter chuckled, removed a windmill cookie from up his sleeve, and munched casually. "Like you, like themselves, contra-wise and similar-wise. Oh, my, yes. See there? Along the garden path?" He pointed and Caleb spied great granite statues lining a white sand road.

"There have been so many girls over the years. They all faded or grew up or grew too worldly to rule properly. At first, they wanted to be here, then they wanted to be there. Tragic." He finished his cookie, dropping crumbs liberally down his jacket. "Have you ever been of two minds about anything?"

Caleb touched his face, his hair. "Yes. For a time. Two minds, two bodies." Then he straightened his back and smoothed his dress. "But then I understood who I was and now I am only one mind. But I have had to hide that. Until today I suppose. My mother came home unexpectedly and caught me..."

"Caught you doing what? Was it naughty?" It wasn't a salacious question, only curious.

"No. I was..." He was going to say *playing dress-up* because that's how he usually thought of it, but it hadn't been playing. Dressing up was the other side of his life: wearing boy clothes and going to school with a naked face. Being the boy was the play-acting. Caleb knew it, he had just never articulated it before.

"I don't understand that," the Mad Hatter said, removing a steaming cup of tea from his pocket. "Being of two minds about something, I mean. A body only has one mind so how can there be confusion?" He sipped. "You are a girl, yes?"

Caleb didn't hesitate. "Yes."

"And so, there you go," he said. "Where is the confusion?"

"I don't know where it came from. The world? Society? I was always afraid. I had to be a boy—"

"Bah!" The Mad Hatter held an apple under his nose. A green worm wiggled at the top, near the steam. The worm admonished Caleb with a scowl and then dove back into the fruit. "See this apple? If I were to bite it—" He made to do so, and Caleb feared for the worm. "It would taste like an apple. If I baked it in a pie, it would taste like an apple. If I pressed it down for cider, it would taste like an apple. Do you see?"

"No."

"The apple, the flesh, doesn't lose its flavor no matter its body. You are the same. You are the same apple—the same flesh—despite being a pie, or cider. See?"

They walked. The Mad Hatter pointed out Alice statues along the sand path. He told her their stories. One Alice went into the forest and didn't return. One grew up and was simply gone one morning. This one's color drained away until she was only black-and-white paper, and the wind blew her to another land. Then Caleb stopped in front of a tall, beautiful blonde. She wore a short blue dress, black patent shoes, and had the most delectable smile. One hand was posed in front of her mouth as if she were about to giggle from hearing the most scandalous secret.

"Who was this one?"

"Alice."

Caleb smiled. "Yes, I mean... who was she before?"

"She said her name was Sunny before she came here to become our Alice. This one was very loving." He peered into Caleb's face. "Our Alices always find us when they need us, when this *here* is better than the old *there*. Often, Wonderland is a depository of the unwanted. Are you unwanted?"

"I would say so."

"You are welcome here, beautiful girl. You can stay with us, but that means being gone from your *there*. Becoming Alice often means running away from home and never going back. Are you sure you want that? To be gone from *there*?"

It wasn't much of a decision to make. What was left back there for him?

"Will you be our Alice? Wonderland must have an Alice, or it will grow sick and die. Will you help us?"

Caleb walked his fingers along the Sunny statue.

"We always need an Alice. This place doesn't work without an Alice."

Suddenly Caleb asked: "What was in that potion on the table? The pink one I drank?"

"It was pink for you? It's different for everyone. It was a potion to bring out your truth. You see—"

Suddenly Caleb gasped. He felt something... wonderful! He pulled up his dress, unconcerned with propriety. He opened his panties and stared down where the hated thing usually curled in a thicket of coarse hair but now... NOW! He gasped again.

"I. It. I... oh my..."

The Mad Hatter was eating another cookie and seemed almost bored with his next question. "What did you expect to find there? You said you were a girl, yes?"

Caleb raised his face; no, she raised her face. The Mad Hatter produced a compact mirror from up his sleeve. Caleb—Alice—looked, studied, and grinned. She saw the pink in her eyes. Her mouth flooded with the taste of red cake icing. "Yes."

The Mad Hatter smiled. "Up there that change is made with barbaric tools of steel. *They cut!*" He made tsking sounds. "Here in Wonderland, we can do better. I would ask if you are pleased, but the potion works on your own desires, so I know you are. The potion makes you who you really are."

"I've always known I'm a girl. I knew it. Now..."

"Now. Then. You are—were—a girl in all times."

"Now I have the correct body. It's a miracle."

"It's Wonderland. But you know if you go back, the potion doesn't work in the world up there." The Mad Hatter gazed at the sky. "Very little magic works up above anymore. So, if you go back—"

"I'm not going back."

"So that means you will—"

"Yes. I will be your Alice!"

THERE WAS MUCH REJOICING, and much merriment. The new Alice told everyone about her miracle. The tea party became a birthday party, Alice's birthday party! Later, she kissed the dormouse, and found it sweet. After that, she was given a gorgeous house made of pink bricks and found a closet full of dresses and heels and stockings and make-up and Alice was finally happy and fulfilled.

Wonderland had its Alice again. Soon Alice forgot that she had ever been Caleb. Everything was as it should be, and she never thought of the world above again, not even in dreams, because her dreams were all in pink now.

GOOD-NATURED ANXIETY FOR THE QUEER CREATURE

MINERVA CERRIDWEN

Kitty the Red, Mage of her Tower and Queen of the Realm of Gambits, was running around a meadow and wildly swinging a butterfly net. The net in question had been misnamed, as the insect she intended to catch had feathery, unclubbed antennae. The creature was also very fast, and Kitty's eyes had barely managed to focus on its fluttering wings when a light pink and blue shawl slapped right into her face.

She could only withhold herself from cursing up a storm because that would be bound to send more objects flying at inopportune times. Her actions with the misnamed net had been preceded by a very long journey. She had left her own kingdom and travelled all the way across another before finally finding herself hot on the Moth's trail—and now this. Now this! She dropped the net and flung the shawl towards the ground as well, but there was no satisfying smack; the satin hitched a ride on another breeze and daintily drifted away. The Moth, of course, had disappeared without a trace.

"Oh!" A voice skidded along the path on a pair of large, white boots. Or rather, they must have been white once—*now* the boots were smeared with mud as well as several of the more terrible thixotropic fluids one might pick up during a long walk on questionable roads. The person who had brought along both the voice and the boots didn't so much wear clothes as that she appeared to have whirled through a wardrobe filled with plain pieces of bleached linen and simply carried whatever stuck, in whatever place it had decided to stick. "Oh dear, that was my shawl!"

"I'm sorry," Kitty said. "If I'd known it belonged to someone, I'd have held on to it."

"Do you often come across shawls that *don't* belong to anyone?" the person in white asked, looking intrigued.

"It's more that I don't often come across people," Kitty replied.

"Oh." White held out a grubby hand for Kitty to shake. "I am," —she hesitated—"Snowdrop the White. But don't be mistaken!" she added hastily. "That may sound like a Mage's name, or even a Queen's, but I am a Knight!"

"I see. But then you are a Knight without a horse. Aren't you?" Kitty remarked.

Snowdrop hesitated again. "I do have a horse at home. It might have been a good idea to bring it. Just to, you know, carry all this." She gestured at all the bags of various sizes tied to the random pieces of linen on her body.

"Right." Kitty decided it wasn't so difficult to believe. Even bards and pranksters were knighted these days. In general, Knights were considered good travelling companions, eager to protect whomever joined their quest. Perhaps it wouldn't be unwise to present herself as one too. Mages like her had a reputation for being spiritless and stiff. Adding to that her royal blood— well, admitting the truth about her identity was seldom a good idea upon a first meeting. "Kitty the Red." She gestured at her pristine red dress as if she were merely adding the colour to her name in jest. "I am a Knight too. *With* a horse, but it's a little useless. Pieces go missing all the time."

Right on cue, the grinning head of a large stallion popped into existence behind her.

When it wasn't being stubborn or making a point of being mostly invisible, it was actually an extremely useful horse. The only explanation for the high speed with which she had travelled was that she had been floating on its back—never mind that a lot of the time, that back didn't seem to be attached to anything. Even so, they had never moved fast enough for the landscape around her to properly change. It was all meadows, forests, meadows again. She was terribly bored, and that was what made her suggest: "Snowdrop the White, would you care to join me? I would feel safer in the company of another Knight, and we might have more luck finding your shawl together."

"Oh, yes, we will have had so much fun!" Snowdrop replied. Kitty thought that was an odd turn of phrase, but felt pleased about the outcome all the same.

THEY TRAVERSED another stretch of forest. Another meadow. And then, to Kitty's surprise, they stumbled upon a garden: a circle of rose bushes that, considering the orderly fashion in which it grew, had clearly been planted with intent. The willy-nilly crisscross of red speckles on the white roses created an aesthetically pleasant contrast with the neatness.

Snowdrop stopped walking and set about rummaging through her bags for several minutes, setting aside various objects ranging from a collection of decorated thimbles to a small fold-out writing desk, before pulling out a handful of paint brushes, both flat and pointed, of varying sizes. She considered them for a moment before selecting a medium-sized pointed brush and tenderly moving it over the surface of the nearest speckled rose.

"Excuse me, but what are you doing?" Kitty asked, staring at the minute, tender gestures of the brush in Snowdrop's left hand.

"Oh, these are my rose brushes," Snowdrop replied, holding up her right fist, firmly clenched around all the brushes she wasn't currently putting into action. "I always bring some, just in case I run into a situation like this. And it's just as I thought: the red speckles didn't wind up on these white petals organically. Look!"

A single hair of the brush bumped against the edge of a red speckle and lifted it a little. It was paint. Red paint, flaking off the roses. A firm downpour of rain might be enough to leave them all pristine.

"Did *you* have them painted?" Snowdrop asked, gaze landing on Kitty's dress.

"Why would I want to redden roses?" Kitty asked. She wasn't about to confess that the thought of pure white roses in this particular garden made her feel vaguely sad.

Snowdrop nodded thoughtfully. "Perhaps it was the reverse. Perhaps you actually tore off the paint to add to your own Hoard of Red. Is that your business in these lands, oh Red Knight?"

"Even if it were, I've never been here before." Kitty shrugged. "I'm chasing a Moth, if you must know."

Snowdrop gasped. "So am I!"

"Did that fiend also fly into your wardrobe as if it owned the place? Nibbling holes into your finest gowns?" It *would* explain Snowdrop's current fashion choices.

"Oh, I wish it had been that easy," Snowdrop sighed. "No, I don't think I've ever come close enough to envelop it in safety. But I will!"

"When I catch it, I will imprison it and make sure it never flies into my wardrobe again," Kitty declared firmly.

"It could live in mine, if it liked," Snowdrop mused, "but never on its own. It's vitally important we preserve its species. You see, the Rocking-horse-fly has almost gone extinct, and we've already seen such a decline in the JubJub bird population. Imagine what terrible effects the loss of the Clothing Moth would have on the ecosystem! It's a relief I distinctly remember saving our environment sometime in the future."

Kitty let out an ill-at-ease hum. "Well, as long as saving it would imply keeping it contained and away from my attire, I'm all in favour of your undertaking." She searched the sky, but then sharply looked back at the rose bushes. "Moths like flowers, don't they?"

"Some might prefer chocolates or a good book, but generally I would expect so," Snowdrop said thoughtfully. "Should we pick it some?"

"No, we should inspect the bushes! It might be hiding itself here." Kitty plunged her hands between the flowers and didn't pay any mind to the fact that she got pricked by a number of thorns all at once. If she were to pay attention to every inconvenience... well, she'd start avoiding them and be more comfortable, probably. That thought was definitely too dangerous not to push away.

Snowdrop petted the roses half-heartedly, glancing more at Kitty than at the bushes.

"Go on then," Kitty encouraged her. "Two can work twice as fast as one!" She reconsidered. "I suppose they can each work at about the same speed, but... there'll be two of them, at least."

Snowdrop rocked back and forth on her heels. "You see, I remember we won't find it here. So there's not much point in searching, is there?"

"Not with that attitude!" Kitty exclaimed. "How can you *remember* something we haven't even done yet?"

"It would be sillier to remember when we've already done it, wouldn't it?" Snowdrop replied. "That would be a little backwards."

Kitty opened her mouth and closed it again. "I suppose from where I'm standing, remembering what's still to come is what would be backwards."

"How fascinating. Mind you, it's not always a blessing that I do not need to imagine what the flame of a candle is like after it's blown out. But it's not always a curse either." Snowdrop took a few steps back from the roses.

As Kitty tried to figure out what to say to that, someone called out: "Please, *ask* the blooms whether they want to be touched or not! Don't just grab them!"

Three flat, rectangular people were walking over. They had short, spindly arms and legs sticking out of the four corners of their body, and bore a single mark where Kitty would have expected a face: a black mark for two of them, and a red one for the other. Each was carrying two buckets of paint. They put them down in front of the circle: orange, yellow, green, blue, indigo, and purple.

"At last," said the Ace of Heart-shaped Diamonds, "the stars are right for our burst of creativity. Please remove yourselves. You do not want to be here for it. Things will get very messy."

"You don't mean *you* will burst, do you?" Snowdrop asked anxiously.

"We don't like to talk about it," the Ace of Book Clubs replied.

"Hold on," Snowdrop said, and she took a small glass jar out of a bag hanging off her upper arm. "This will help you clean up after you're done. It's Elbow Grease."

Kitty grimaced as the Ace of Kink Clubs accepted the slippery gift. "Wouldn't that tap over there be more efficient?"

Mounted in a TumTum tree trunk, conveniently close to the rose bushes, was a brass water tap. Above it hung a little sign from a nail: *"Rub the snout when it's mottled."*

Kitty leaned in to observe the flat front of the spout. "That could definitely use a shine."

Snowdrop slipped her hand into a bag at the height of her left thigh and pulled out a handkerchief that looked suspiciously similar to the shawl that had attacked Kitty earlier. Had Kitty not seen it fly away on the wind with her very own eyes, she might have believed it to be the same thing. Perhaps she still did, now. She was no stranger to believing impossible things.

"Together?" Snowdrop asked, and without giving it much thought, Kitty took hold of a corner of the handkerchief. The tap rumbled happily as they wiped the dried droplets and the dust off the spout, which somewhat resembled the snout of an aardvark now that it was no longer covered in grime. Even though the tap was firmly turned off, water started running out of it at such a high flow rate that the earth beneath Snowdrop and Kitty's boots was soaked within seconds.

They took away the handkerchief and tried turning the tap on and off, but the same steady stream kept flowing towards the rose garden like a creek or even a small river.

"Our art! Our art!" the Aces cried. "All the paint is washing away!"

"Stop! Oh dear, please, stop!" Snowdrop yelled at the water tap, but its happy purr persisted.

There were no fences or slopes around to contain the water, and yet the rivulet widened only gradually and had soon risen to the height of Kitty's knees. If the tap were allowed to continue running, they would have to swim to survive in mere minutes.

Kitty had to stop it, but she only knew one way, and she wasn't ready to admit she was a Mage.

"Horse, bring me my sword!" she ordered, and there were the head and body of the horse, hovering above what was starting to look like a narrow pond. Kitty reached a hand towards the scabbard attached to her saddle, wishing really hard, and pulled out a magnificent bronze sword.

She immediately pointed it at the tap's spout. "Turn yourself off now, or you'll regret it!"

Then, her voice lost in the shouts of angry artists and pleas from Snowdrop not to hurt the poor tap, it only wanted a little care—Kitty spoke a spell, and the stream of water finally ceased.

"Oh. Oh dear, what a relief," Snowdrop sighed, adding just a few more drops to the pond by wiping her brow. Her linen garments dragged heavily behind her, catching a rainbow of diluted paint streaks as she and Kitty waded to the bank, leaving the Aces to restore their work in the garden. Already, they had resumed swinging globs of paint into the air and—Kitty could only presume from this distance—onto the roses.

For some reason, Kitty felt drawn to the artistic Aces with their many colours, but it wouldn't do to dwell on those things and let the world pass her by at its terrible speed. That Moth wasn't about to catch itself, so she couldn't stay, and it didn't look as if the artists would want to come along anytime soon. No doubt her presence would only disturb their creativity.

Kitty and Snowdrop arrived on more or less dry grassland, where Kitty finished wringing out her clothes first, as she wasn't wearing as many layers. She spent a while in the shade of the trees that marked the border of yet another forest, looking down at her own reflection in the pond.

"Do you ever wonder what it would be like if the image in the looking glass matched your true self?" she asked.

Snowdrop frowned. "Is your true self someone who would imprison an innocent creature just so it could never embark upon your territory? Someone who would strike a tap for fulfilling its own purpose?"

"Sometimes I wish I could hide until I became somebody I liked being," Kitty said.

Snowdrop stopped fussing with her soaked holding bags and nodded as she gazed into the water too.

"What about *your* true self?" Kitty asked Snowdrop's reflection in the water. "Would she lock up a wild creature just so it wouldn't die at a time that's out of her control?"

"I've never been under anyone's control!" someone protested in a squeaky voice. As Kitty and Snowdrop turned around, they saw that this someone was a Dormouse, with wristwatches and fob watches attached all over his body, and two golden clock faces for eyes. "Many have tried, and I have survived several attempts at murder, but here I am!"

"Do you honestly need me to apologise for that *again*?" An Anglo-Saxon in a worn red hat stepped out of the bushes, holding a cup of tea in one hand and a piece of bread-and-butter in the other.

Time gasped. "Hatta! No, not you!"

"So you want *me* to apologise for him? That's ridiculous!" An almost identical Anglo-Saxon, save for the hat and the nibble, stepped out behind the first.

"Haigha! Why do you both keep chasing me? What have I ever done to you?" Time whined.

"Nothing," Haigha said, holding up a finger to silence Hatta. "Well, you did break Hatta's heart and drove him a little mad, but that's neither here nor there. We're only here now because we want to ask for your help, Time."

"We could save nine," Hatta added.

"Ah." Time relaxed slightly. "In that case."

"Does anyone have a needle and thread?" Haigha asked, looking up as if expecting an answer from the highest branches of the trees.

"Oh, yes!" Snowdrop said. "I always bring some. You never know."

"I thought you *did* know," Kitty replied, puzzled.

"Thank you!" Haigha said, taking the needle and a bobbin from the White Knight. "You see, a stitch in Time will save nine!"

"Oh no. Oh, no, no, no." Time made an odd little jump and fled into the forest.

"Come now!" Snowdrop called after him. "Think of it, saving nine people!"

Hatta gave her a bemused look. "We never said they'd be people."

"Nine creatures. Of any kind," Snowdrop corrected. "Surely a little sting can't be so bad if you can save nine! It'll be like, like a vaccine!"

Haigha tilted his head. "What's a vaccine?"

"Something I remember. In the future, diseases will be scared off by setting the essence of a monstrous cow at them."

Kitty frowned. "Are you certain it wasn't a monstrous *crow*?"

"Why would it be?" Snowdrop laughed. "That must be something from the past. I don't remember that at all."

"We just need to find the Time to get it done," Haigha said, and bounded after the Dormouse.

"Sometimes it's really a question of *making* Time, rather than finding him," Snowdrop remarked as they all joined the pursuit.

"Hmm... did you know," Kitty said, "that in ancient Rome, dormice used to be prepared with honey and poppy seeds to make a delicious dessert?"

An indignant screech rang through the forest.

"That way." Kitty pointed in the direction of the sound.

"I can't believe how good you are at all this Knightly business," Snowdrop said wistfully, and Kitty couldn't help but wonder if her companion remembered a future conversation in which Kitty had told her the truth.

"Give me that." Haigha stretched out his hand and plucked Kitty's butterfly net from thin air, even though both her horse and the saddlebag were currently invisible. With a mighty leap and a powerful swoop he caught Time, who had been flapping his little paws rapidly, zooming towards the treetops.

"Hold him," Haigha ordered, pushing the net into Hatta's hands. Hatta gently stroked what little of Time's fur he could reach through the mesh and the abundance of watches, and in the blink of an eye, Haigha had secured a stitch in the Dormouse's ear.

Time hiccupped. "That—that wasn't so bad."

"You could ask him now," Kitty whispered to Snowdrop. "If you wanted."

"What?"

"To fix your memory. Have you never wished that life would move the right way for you? That Time would suit you?" Kitty, for one, believed she would find it a lot more reassuring. Even before she'd fully finished it, however, that thought left a bitter after-taste. *She* might have decided that hiding the parts of her identity that might make others uncomfortable was for the best, but how could she expect the same of someone else? Of Snowdrop, the very person who'd finally transformed the landscape around her?

Snowdrop huffed. "Asking him to fit the way my mind works would be remarkably selfish. Besides, I quite enjoy remembering our upcoming shared journey!"

At that, Kitty suppressed a wince. No doubt the fact that they'd travel together long enough to call it a *journey* meant that it would take them forever to find the Clothing Moth.

"Oh, go away, silly Moth," Haigha muttered. "It must have been drawn to the thread of the stitch."

Kitty and Snowdrop froze.

Then Kitty yelled: "Run!" and the two of them bolted after the brown smudge fluttering between the trees.

~

JUST OUT OF THE FOREST, they could see colourful mountains in the distance.

"The Carpethians," Snowdrop whispered. "Piles and piles of wool carpets. That's what paradise must look like for a Clothing Moth."

"Do you think," Kitty said, neither of them ever slowing down their run, "that this specific Moth is a Business Attire Moth? Or a Casual Wear Moth?"

"Judging by the speed, I would bet it's a Sportswear Moth," Snowdrop answered.

Wild apple trees were scattered over the plain leading towards the mountains, and finally they got close enough to see the Moth resting on a branch near some small, juicy red apples.

"Quiet now," Snowdrop instructed, and they both crept closer. The Clothing Moth, it turned out, was wearing very little in the way of clothing: merely a set of pale lace underthings.

"A Lingerie Moth," Kitty whispered, in awe.

"YOU FOUND IT!"

"CONGRATULATIONS!"

"AND A HAPPY UNBIRTHDAY TO YOU TOO, LITTLE MOTH!"

Time, Hatta, and Haigha came rushing in, twigs cracking and grass moaning under the hasty onslaught of their feet.

Kitty grumbled in frustration, expecting the Moth to fly off again, but instead, the insect plucked Snowdrop's pink-and-blue shawl from the twig above her and wrapped herself up.

"I am appalled!" the Moth complained. "I do not appreciate the male gaze! I do not exist for the male gaze to appreciate me!"

"Hey!" Time protested. "My he/him pronouns do *not* mean I'm male! My clockfarse is non-binary, you hear me!"

"You shouldn't have to cover up from how you feel comfortable, Mite," Haigha said soothingly. (He pronounced the name the French way, not as if he wanted to imply the Moth had an extra pair of legs.)

"Yeah, and there's nothing we haven't already seen. We all know you're hiding quite a *behemoth* of an aedeagus in those panties," Hatta commented with a smirk. (He, on the other hand, *was* alluding to something vaguely resembling an extra leg.)

"Oh! OH! JAIL!" Mite screeched. "Jail for Hatta for one thousand years!!!"

"Oh, not again," Hatta groaned. Long chains rose from the ground, clinking and rattling, and wound around him until he resembled a metal sausage with a hat.

Snowdrop smiled. "Well, Mite, it looks as if you can stand up for yourself. I no longer seek to catch you."

Kitty nodded in agreement, quietly celebrating the fact that no one seemed to be shocked about Time being non-binary. All anyone ever said about him was that he could heal all wounds. Perhaps not being one or the other wasn't something she needed to keep hidden after all.

"I quite like your spirit, Mite. The world is better off with you flying around in it, and you'll always be welcome in my house. As long as you only munch on the clothes that cause dysphoria."

"I may hope," Mite said coolly, "you two do not expect my gratitude for the mere fact that you no longer intend to rob me of my freedom."

"Good point," Kitty and Snowdrop muttered.

With a final huff, Mite tied the pink-and-blue shawl around her neck so it billowed behind her like a cape, and flew off.

"Wherever she's going, I hope she'll have a whale of a time," Haigha said earnestly.

"Oh no. Don't say that!" Time begged, but it was too late.

The Dormouse stretched and its fur turned a bluish grey before it all fell out.

"Quick!" Haigha yelled. "He needs water! Knights, help!"

"Oh, er... oh, this is terrible!" Snowdrop stammered. "I can't remember how we solve this! Should we, oh, I mean, er, should we, should we push him towards the sea?" She glanced around as if hoping a sea would pop up out of nowhere.

"Erm, er, maybe my horse can pull him back to the pond?" Kitty suggested.

"But we don't have a rope!"

"Not a single piece, in all your bags?"

"How would you lift a whale with a *single* piece of rope?"

Kitty had to admit that would be challenging, at the very least. "Would Time even fit inside a pond?"

The Whale stared at them imploringly, his skin wrinkling in dehydration even as he kept growing larger: he was running out.

"Hold on, Time," Kitty said, chewing her lip as if it would release a solution if she only bit it hard enough.

"Oh, curses! I have no clue what to do!" Snowdrop wailed. "I'm not a Knight! I'm a Mage! And a Queen, technically."

Kitty gasped. "You lied!"

"I wanted you to think I was worth your company." Snowdrop suppressed a desperate sob.

"So... so did I..." Kitty confessed. Then she suddenly clapped her hands together. "We should stop trying to think like Knights. Snowdrop, we can just turn him back!"

She grabbed both of the other Mage's hands and looked her in the eyes, receiving a resolute nod in return.

The Whale was still expanding towards where Hatta lay helpless in his chains under an apple tree, unable to move away from the crushing weight. An orange orb of shimmering magic materialised between Snowdrop and Kitty, at first contained inside the circle of their arms, but then it hovered up and over to encapsulate the Whale. Turning pink, the shell of magic seemed to press in on the Whale's sides, making it smaller and smaller until it once again became a Dormouse, fur and all. The watches lay at its feet, all intact and waiting to be strapped back in place.

"Phew," the Dormouse said. "Thank you."

"It appears you two can do more when you admit you are Mages than when you attempt to be liked by others." Haigha gave them a pointed, rather judgemental look.

Kitty and Snowdrop glanced at one another and then quickly looked away again, but they were both smiling a little.

"We really should treat our Time more kindly," Kitty admitted.

"I remember we can teach each other exactly that, without forgetting to stand up for ourselves." Snowdrop softly took Kitty's hand in hers.

"Before you go," Hatta said quickly, "please, Your Red Majesty—take my hat. Old as it is, it's still fit for a king, and it'd only fade away in jail."

"There's a door right there in the mountainside," Time told them. "You might want to use it."

And so the Queens said their goodbyes and walked through, discovering on the other side of the wooden door a low hall with more doors of every imaginable size, all made of reflective glass. Kitty admired how she looked in Hatta's red hat. It was indeed fit for a king, or a queen, or for neither and for both. She tapped it so it sat at an angle and felt a spark.

Perhaps the hat didn't serve a specific purpose, and perhaps someone would tell her in the future that it was only a burden that might fly away. But it still felt exactly right.

"I can see my true self a little better now, I think," xe said softly.

In the mirror image, Snowdrop smiled, standing right beside xem. "I can see it too. And I quite like the view of us together."

"Would you mind continuing our adventure as a team?" Kitty asked.

"Let's," Snowdrop said, but then she hesitated. "Do you think we are doing the right thing by letting the Moth go? We should probably still make sure the environment allows her to thrive."

"We will," Kitty said. "Just as soon as we discover what's behind this door."

Xe pointed at a medium-sized sliding door. It didn't matter where exactly it would lead. The two of them were stepping through together.

~

A caterpillar, once a moth
was still awaiting Time
to feed her off the scrumptious cloth
and speak to her in rhyme.
Once she'd lived in confidence
and spread her wings to rise;
the beating of a cruel pretence
reverted her in size.
When she regained her self and wings
it was not Time's sole feat:
community supports and brings
one's glow back from retreat.

OF TUNNELS AND FALLING THROUGH THEM

KATIE ARNETT

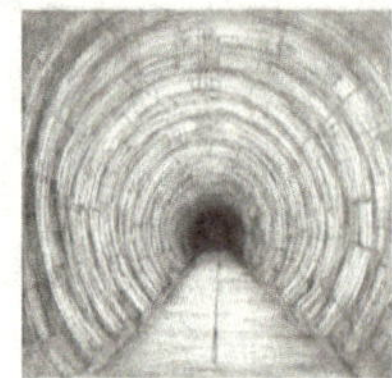

It takes a long time to learn how to find your way in Wonderland.

Everywhere you look, there's a strange mix of modern—maybe even futuristic, depending on who you ask—technology and unkempt nature, wild and untamed. Giant computers with screens partially hidden by hanging ferns, ancient gardens tucked away behind coded gates, that sort of thing. It's a strange mix, and you never *really* stop questioning it.

And even once you've managed to move on from that, learning to recognize individual pathways and places provides its own challenge.

There are dozens of different directions to turn, dozens of places to be. The patterns—however minimal they are—tend to be slight and hard to notice, and it's no surprise that it's a bit of a maze.

Privately, Aleks has always said that Wonderland got its name because it's a wonder anyone ever found their way to where they were going.

Still, she's had time to learn her way through the mazes and labyrinths, turning it into a game of sorts. There are tunnels and hidden paths—though Aleks is sure she's not the only one to use them—that she knows like the back of her hand. Back when she'd first arrived here, she'd made it something of a challenge, getting from place to place as fast as she could.

Now?

Navigating Wonderland is just another walk in the park.

In times like these, that familiarity is a blessing, because Aleks may or may not be running late to her meeting with the Hatter.

Fine, she *is,* in fact, running late, but the Hatter—she knows his name is Decker, she really does, but everyone else calls him the Hatter, so why should she be any different? It's a title that fits, after all—he has always been generous with his time, and his gatherings are known for being chaotic.

She turns a corner, running down the corridors to make it in time. Even if the Hatter is late, it won't do her any good to be. Not when she's already got a reputation for it.

Aleks wonders who else will be there.

It's not unheard of for the Hatter to only invite one person to his little domain, though that's usually just a sign he wants someone to test one of his brews. Aleks hasn't had the dubious honor of such an occasion—from what she's heard, his new brews are either a delight or something terrible—and while she isn't against the idea, today she has the feeling that's not the case.

She's proven right, unfortunately.

By the time she arrives in the Hatter's corner of Wonderland, there are already two people crowded around the table. Every inch of the surface is covered in knick-knacks and decor and, of course, porcelain teacups painted with delicate patterns. All of them are chipped, used far too many times to be in perfect condition, but that only adds to the charm.

The rest of the room is just as messy, though Aleks will never say that out loud. Think it? Sure, because there are towers of books on the verge of falling over, cards spilling across the floor, bolts of fabric laying everywhere you look, and that's not even making a dent in all the things Aleks sees. But saying it? Never.

As far as she's concerned, the Hatter's space is a cozy one, so why would she want it to change?

Across the room, Red snaps her fingers. She's glaring, impatience written on her face for anyone to see. "It's about damn time."

Red, for all of her charm and prowess, isn't the kind of person that gets called patient. Brilliant, yes, no matter how much Aleks hates to admit it, but far from patient. If you pay attention to the exaggerated rumors and stories, then you've no doubt heard of Red making her way through the outer tunnels—the ones that link with other worlds—in a handful of hours.

Most people find her inspiring. Personally, Aleks just finds all the stories about her to be overdone.

But Red is her partner, regardless of her feelings on the matter, and when the Hatter is smiling like *that*—eyes fever bright, hands clapped together tightly, his grin wider than what should be possible—it's a clear sign something exciting is about to occur.

"Good!" The Hatter says. "We're all here then."

Red scoffs at Aleks. "How do you always manage to get lost? I don't understand how you can live here so long and still not get to where you need to be."

Aleks flashes her best grin and gives her a mocking bow. "Sorry to disappoint, Your Majesty," she says, "but it's a special talent of mine."

Before either of them can get another word in—history shows that the two can bicker for ages if no one cuts in to stop them—the Hatter clears his throat. "Dear girls," he says, not unkindly, "I do believe we have something to discuss?"

And, well, he does have a point.

Rather than sitting down—the chairs are comfortable, but it's fairly common for there to be things piled up on them—Aleks leans against a wall. It's not the most comfortable position, but it's better than shoving a pile to the floor. Out of the corner of her eye, Aleks sees Red doing something similar, adjusting her position near the door.

The Hatter untangles his fingers, only to bring his hands together with a resounding *clap*. "Now then! Let's get started, shall we?"

And so they do.

The Hatter talks and talks. Each word is just as unpredictable as the last, a seemingly endless mix of long-lost references from his home world and scientific rambling related to portals and how to scout one out, as though neither of them had ever done it before. There's something endearing about it, something familiar, and if Wonderland had something as mundane as mentors, Aleks wonders if the Hatter could be hers.

"There's a tunnel, you know, one of the outer ones." His grin widens ever so slightly. "It would be very much appreciated if the two of you could clear it out. Make sure there's no obstacles in the way, and nothing's lurking where it's not supposed to be, the usual sort of thing."

Aleks certainly isn't going to say *no*.

Rushing through a tunnel is an exhilarating experience, regardless of what you happen to find in them. There's something thrilling about not knowing what you'll encounter, whether you're chasing your partner through winding corridors and mazes, or darting in and out of a fight, the wind in your hair and blood on your hands, and—

For better or worse, Aleks loves it.

"I'm in," she says. The grin she's wearing is a wild thing, one Aleks sees mirrored in Red's face. And she doesn't mean it as a challenge, she really doesn't.

Red still flashes her a fierce smile. "If you think I'm letting you go in alone, you're dreaming."

And there's something to be said—perhaps others had said it—about unspoken challenges and endless bickering, and perhaps something about partnerships, but honestly? Aleks doesn't care much for poetry, and she never has.

"Excellent!" The Hatter says, looping an arm over each of their shoulders. "Why don't we get the two of you to our dear Chess, hm? Perhaps take a walk towards the Looking Glass, if you know what I mean."

As you can guess from Chess's name, Wonderland's communications master is a bit of a trickster.

It's a gamble simply trying to find them, given their penchant for disappearing out of the blue, only to reappear in front of your eyes. It should be impossible how easily they do it, with their bright blue hair and practically glowing eyes, and that's not even mentioning their echoing cackle.

They're great at what they do, and Aleks would go as far as calling them the best at it.

Chess's home realm—they haven't told anyone its name, or what they'd done there, but that was hardly outside of the norm—has far more advanced technology than any other Aleks has come across, short of the technology built into Wonderland itself. It only makes sense for them to be good at—or so they like to say—walking people through labyrinths and mazes and whatever else the tunnels throw at you.

Chess is undeniably interesting, no matter how disconcerting they may be at times, and Aleks *does* enjoy their company, but their disappearing act is beyond tiring when you're trying to find them and they've fucked off to who knows where.

The Hatter—the only person who's supposedly been here longer than them—claims that he knows all of their hiding spots. Says, *don't you know? They tend to lurk near the Looking Glass, these days.*

The Hatter is right, of course. Despite all his eccentricities, or maybe because of them, he's seldom wrong.

The Looking Glass is a beautiful thing, all stained glass and flowering vines and glimpses of the rich, bronze frame. The air around it sings, dancing to a song no one can hear, and there's no denying that there's something magical about it.

True to the Hatter's word, Chess lingers on the ground in front of it, fiddling with a box in their hands. They don't look up until Aleks is a few steps away from them, Red trailing just behind. When they do, there's a playful expression on their face.

"Fancy seein' you here," they say, rising to their feet. "A little birdie told me you two were going for a run?"

Red steps forward. "You heard correctly."

Chess laughs, and then they're throwing the box into the air. It's an uncoordinated throw, almost falling short before Red catches it. "There you go, little travelers. Two sets of earpieces to keep us in touch."

Red opens the box, taking her pair, before handing it over to Aleks. She gives them a quick look, a careful one, but honestly? Aleks trusts Chess's expertise, trusts that her equipment will work. Out of the corner of her eye, she sees Red slip the earpieces in, and Aleks does the same.

"You already know how they work, so I'm not gonna waste our time explaining," they continue. "Head through the Looking Glass, and I'll be here to keep an eye on you." Chess's smile sharpens, flashing dangerously. "Someone's gotta make sure you idiots don't end up dead, hm?"

And maybe the comment is a *little* harsh, a little unnecessary, maybe even a little cruel. But it isn't unheard of for people to die out there, to fall through Wonderland and never be heard from again. More often than not, Chess was the one with them, talking over their ear, guiding them through the tunnels, telling them where to go.

There's a reason for Chess's borderline cruelty, and after all these years, Aleks understands it.

"And we appreciate it," she says, smiling. The words are true, after all, and Aleks has never found reason to lie about such senseless things.

Red gives a nod, confidence seeping from every motion. "Is there anything we need to know?"

Chess shakes their head, purple hair obscuring their face. "Nope!" They say brightly, looking back up at them. "Nothin' on my end is showing up as unusual, so consider it a run-of-the-mill exercise!"

As though there was ever a simple trip through the tunnels.

And Red gives her a *look*, the kind with a honey-sweet smile and narrowed eyes. It's not a look Aleks is unfamiliar with, in fact, it's quite the opposite. She sees it before every run, before every challenge, before every goddamn word that falls from Red's lips, and—

"Ready, darling??" Red asks.

Aleks grins. "You know I am."

She takes a step forward and presses her fingers to the Looking Glass, all too aware of Red's lingering gaze, and she's—

Falling.

It's a strange sensation, slipping between the realms.

It's something like flying, or maybe swimming, that weightless feeling when your feet have left the ground and your heart is in your throat. It's disorienting, at first, like the world has been flipped on its head, and in a way, it has.

Each realm is different. Each one has its own laws, its own

rules, its own set of forces that govern the way it runs. Why should the in-between be any different?

There's no way to know how a tunnel will look or to guess its rules—even when you have access to Chess and their technology —and it only adds to the thrill of it all. It's dangerous, of course, not knowing what you're diving into, but isn't that part of the point?

The moment the world stabilizes, everything is *still.*

There's no sound to be heard, no flashes of movement from further down the tunnel, not even a glimmer of light for them to see with. If it weren't for her own heartbeat thudding in her chest, echoing in her ears, and the soft exhale of Red, Aleks would've thought she was dreaming.

But if she focuses, she feels Red behind her—eyes on the back of her neck, someone shifting their weight, a hand brushing against her own.

That doesn't stop the stillness from being unsettling.

There's something unnatural about the silence that seeps into her bones. In all her time in Wonderland, Aleks has never seen anything like this before, never even *heard* of it.

"Chess?" Aleks only gets static in response. "Chess, can you hear me?"

Nothing.

There's a sigh from behind her, and then Red's hand grabs onto hers.

"Come on," she says, and then Red is pushing past, walking forward into the darkness. "There's no point in just sticking around here, not if we want to get out of this mess."

And, well, it's not like she doesn't have a point.

So Aleks keeps walking. She doesn't miss the fact that Red doesn't let go of her hand, even as they're walking in the same direction, towards the same place, however unknown it may be.

"So," Aleks says, unable to keep the cheeky grin off her face, "feeling clingy today, aren't we, your majesty?"

Red laughs. "In your dreams," she says, though if Aleks didn't know better, she would almost call her voice *fond*. "You get lost running through Wonderland. I'd rather not have to chase you down in a place like this."

And there's no reason for laughter to be spilling past her lips, but Aleks can't stop it. Doesn't think she would even if she could. "You love me."

"Maybe I do, and maybe I don't," Red says from somewhere in front of her. "Can we *please* talk about this when we aren't preoccupied?"

Aleks doesn't make another comment—it would *not* be helpful, but damn it all if she isn't tempted to—and continues walking, one foot in front of the other. It's disorienting, not being able to see where she's going, especially when she *knows* what can lurk in these tunnels.

They're still holding hands.

She doesn't mention it.

And it's strange, walking in the dark. There's no end in sight, and even if there was, they'd still need to make it there and clear out the tunnel and make it back to Wonderland, and well, there's a bit of a checklist.

It's fine.

It's fine.

Maybe Aleks isn't the most fond of places like this, of the darkness and silence and utter stillness of it all, not after she fell into Wonderland. She loves Wonderland, she really does, loves running through its corridors and talking to Chess and the Hatter, and even Red—though, she refuses to admit it to her—but *really*, ending up there?

Because there was a fall, years ago, one that lasted far too long and—

Humming.

Red is humming something, a song Aleks hasn't heard before. The melody isn't a constant one, speeding up and slowing down however she sees fit, her voice low and warm and somehow, soft. There aren't any words, nothing except for that warm, warm melody, but it's comforting, nevertheless.

And Aleks starts talking.

Starts saying words that mean nothing at all, and somehow, everything. Pointless little stories to fill the time as they wander— hands still tangled together—through the dark. Random things, like the time that she and Chess—back when Chess still spent their time running headfirst into danger—had managed to get themselves stuck in a tree. Or how she'd *almost* ended up as the Hatter's last tester for his brews, if it weren't for a sudden mishap on the other end of Wonderland.

But Aleks talks and Red's humming doesn't stop, not unless Aleks manages to drag a laugh out of her, the sound never failing to bring a smile to her face.

She wonders if this is part of the challenge.

Simply *being,* trusting in whoever's with you.

Trusting that, no matter how long it takes, you'll get to the end of the tunnel.

"Aleks," Red says, "open your eyes, *idiot.*"

Aleks opens her eyes—when had she shut them? She doesn't know—just in time for Red to shove her forward. Aleks throws out her hands, trying to balance or, if it comes to it, catch herself before she hits the ground.

There's a door under Aleks' hands, the wood twisted and worn. It doesn't give when she pushes it, and in the dark, she fumbles, searching for something different. A lock, perhaps, or a bump on the surface.

Or, Aleks thinks, feeling cool metal against her skin, *something as simple as a doorknob.*

That should be all of it—

All that's left is to turn it—she doesn't feel a place for a key, and the real test seems to be making it this far—and step outside, step into somewhere new, step into—

Red takes her hand, calloused fingers tangling with her own. "Go on, then," she says, and Aleks gets the feeling that she's smirking. "Open it."

Aleks slowly twists the handle, as though doing it fast could end with something terrible, and—

It's beautiful.

Sprawling green hills dotted in giant flowers, and towering mushrooms. The sky is a brighter blue than Aleks has ever seen, and it seems to go on for an eternity.

"Aleks?" Chess says, after a long moment. "Did you two get through all right?"

Red squeezes her hand, gives her a wild smile, one that's warm, *oh so* warm as she nods. She steps closer, raising Aleks's hand as she presses a kiss to her knuckles, before backing away with a smirk on her face.

Aleks can't help but return the grin.

"Yeah, Chess," she says, not looking away from Red's dark eyes, "We're more than all right."

AUTHOR BIOGRAPHIES

ALICIA K. ANDERSON

Alicia K. Anderson has a Ph.D. in Mythological Studies and Depth Psychology from Pacifica Graduate Institute. Her stories have been printed in several magazines and anthologies, all of which can be found on her website at https://aliciakinganderson.com/

KATIE ARNETT

Katie Arnett is a teen author from Temecula, California, currently living in the San Francisco Bay Area. She is a speculative fiction writer, primarily on the fantasy and sci-fi genres, focusing on writing queer stories for queer people. She has written for various small publishing presses, such as Black Hare Press and Eerie River Publishing.

CHRIS BANNOR

I am a writer of speculative fiction. I work in both novel length works and in short stories. While I'm still polishing up my first novel for publication, I have a number of short stories and micro stories that have been published in the last year. Check out my books page to learn more about those.

Why speculative fiction? I adore fantasy and science fiction. I am truly terrified by a good horror story. I suppose the real reason is that life is all about the 'why's and 'what if's. It just so happens that when faced with a dilemma, my brain says... what if this happened... in space!! Wouldn't my co-worker's behavior make so much more sense if ... they are actually an ancient wizard? Why hasn't the zombie apocalypse happened yet? When are those aliens finally coming to abduct me?

Until then, I'm just a writer and the mother of two teenagers doing my best to wrangle my kids, my words, and my imagination into something presentable to the world.

EVAN BAUGHFMAN

Evan Baughfman is a Southern California teacher, author, and playwright. A number of Evan's plays are published through Heuer Publishing, YouthPLAYS, Next Stage Press, and Drama Notebook. Evan has also found success writing horror fiction, his work found recently in anthologies by No Bad Books Press, Improbable Press, and Grinning Skull Press. Evan's short story collection, *The Emaciated Man* and *Other Terrifying Tales from Poe Middle School,* is published through Thurston Howl Publications. His novella, *Vanishing of the 7th Grade,* is available through D&T Publishing. D&T also published his novel, *Bad for Your Teeth*. More info is available at amazon.com/author/evanbaughfman

ANNA BUSHI

Without a time machine, Anna Bushi spends her day traveling to medieval India, avoiding prowling tigers, trampling elephants, and hiding from scheming royalty. She keeps trying to leave, but every time she gets close, she realizes she forgot her notes on sword fighting or the secret to casting a spell.

Visit her at AnnaBushi.com to get updates about her books.

K.R. CERVANTES

K. R. Cervantez is the author of *Mischief's Game* and has done several short stories with different anthologies, including The Mirror. She happily married with an amazing family. She has a young self-proclaimed spider expert for a daughter and an adorable dog named Karma. When she's not writing, she is enjoying a good book or watching some of her favorite shows. She's wonderfully nerdy in all the best ways, She likes anime, mangas, and comic books. Coffee, chocolate and pickles are a way of life for her, just not always at the same time.

MINERVA CERRIDWEN

Minerva Cerridwen (xe or she) is a neurodiverse genderqueer aromantic asexual author from Belgium. Xe enjoys baking, drawing, and learning languages. Xyr queer fairy tale novella "The Dragon of Ynys" came out with Atthis Arts in 2020. Find more information about Minerva's writing on xyr website: https://minervacerridwen.wordpress.com/

KATHRYN DIAZ

Kathryn Diaz is a writer, teacher, and native Houstonian. Her work has appeared in the Cincinnati Review MiCRo series, Anathema: Spec from the Margins, and Glass Mountain. She holds an MFA from Cornell University. Currently, she lives in New England with her cat, Potato.

THERESA HALVORSEN

Theresa Halvorsen has never met a profanity she hasn't enjoyed. She's generally overly-caffeinated and, at times, wine-soaked. The author of multiple spec-fiction works, including *Tiny Gateways, Warehouse Dreams, Lost Aboard,* and *River City Widows,* Theresa wonders what sleep is. Because she didn't have enough to do, she also started No Bad Books Press. When she's not writing, editing, publishing or YouTubing with the Semi-Sages of the Pages, she's commuting through San Diego traffic to her healthcare position. In whatever free time is left (ha!), Theresa enjoys board games, geeky conventions, and reading. Her life goal is to give "Oh-My-Gosh-This-Book-Is-So-Good!" happiness to her readers. She lives in Temecula with her amazing husband, occasionally her college-age twins, and the pets they'd promised to care for.

DONNA KEELEY

Donna Keeley has been writing for years but is only recently getting her works to print. A long-time science fiction and fantasy fan, along with historical novels and mysteries, Donna enjoys crafting stories that are complete in a single volume. Her Paranormal Mystery Series features real, haunted locations and uses the documented ghosts as part of the fictional mystery story.

A resident of San Diego County since 1986, Donna has embraced the culture and history of the region, which is reflected in the first book, "Having a Whaley of a Time". The story features the ghosts of the famous Whaley House and appeals to mystery readers, lovers of ghost stories, and cats. Upcoming locations for stories include the Queen Mary in Long Beach, California, the Alamo in San Antonio, Texas, and Loretta Lynn's haunted plantation in Hurricane Mills, Tennessee.

LMZ

LMZ (they/he/she) is a writer and a drummer (and a percussionist, poet, photographer, and composer). They self-published their debut novel, "Nautila," in 2020 and are editing their soon-to-be second novel, "Boyish." They have been published on 101words.-com. They love biblichor and glam-punk. Their piece, "Alex Down the Meerkat-Hole," was inspired by the work of Lewis Carroll.

EVE MORTON

Eve Morton lives in Waterloo, Ontario, Canada with her partner and two sons. She reads tarot cards and coffee grinds for fun, while teaching university classes on the dangers of too much and not enough media consumption. Find more updates at author-morton.wordpress.com.

MORRIGAN PUHR

"Happiness is a perfume you cannot pour on others without getting a few drops on yourself." Ralph Waldo Emerson's quote encapsulates my appreciation for all those who have shared their kindness and their stories. Great stories push and pull us through the ups and downs of what it means to be human until the aroma of wisdom and joy escapes like a wild breeze, filling the air with a touch of joy and a hint of reflection.

As a co-founder of the Semi-Sages of the Pages, I am proud to participate in a community of kind and brilliant people. In our cozy YouTube and Discord corner, we gather to build a positive space for all people who have a story to share. My involvement in co-founding Flair Educators and Bone-a-fide Books further reflects my passion for creating supportive networks of connection where opportunity doesn't just knock; it comes rushing in.

I am a happy public school teacher, and no, that is not an oxymoron (at least not today). Nothing is more magical than the bright eyes of a student passionately connecting with literature, especially when it's an academically dense text, heavy from the weight of its own wisdom.

My happiest adventures are with my husband, three kids, and four horses. We are often found indulging in waterskiing, riding in the wilderness, or hanging from the side of a thousand-foot cliff. In facing my own mortality I connect to the most important adventure of all: living each moment with as much courage and compassion as I can.

LS REINHOLT

LS lives in Denmark. When she isn't teaching maths, languages, or drama, she spends most of her free time writing science fiction and fantasy. Her latest published work was "The Bound Heart", a short story co-written with Minerva Cerridwen in the queer horror anthology *Skulls & Spells* (Artemisia's Axe, 2022).

ROBERT RUNTÉ

Robert Runté is Senior Editor with EssentialEdits.ca and has edited over 35 traditionally published books, primarily science fiction and fantasy. A former professor, he has won three Aurora Awards (Canadian SF&F) for his literary criticism. He currently reviews for the Ottawa Review of Books. His own fiction has been published in over forty venues and six of his short stories have been reprinted in 'best of' collections, such as Canadian Shorts II and the first Metastellar print anthology.

STEPHANIE SANDERS-JACOB

Stephanie Sanders-Jacob writes horror and weird fiction. Her debut novel, *Singing All the Way Up,* came out in 2023 from No Bad Books Press. Her short fiction has appeared in Hearth &

Coffin, Books of Horror, Mixer, Mosaic, and Ether Arts. She can be found at sandersjacob.com.

CHRISTINA TANG-BERNAS

When not out exploring the universe, Christina Tang-Bernas lives in Southern California with her family. Her work has appeared in Radon Journal, Twist in Time, A Quiet Afternoon 2, and And If That Mockingbird Don't Sing, among others. Find out more at http://www.christinatangbernas.com.

C.N. WHEATON

When she isn't playing around in fictional worlds, C.N. Wheaton can often be found teaching science to semi-reluctant teens. Her short stories have recently appeared in *The Fantastic Other*, *Humour Me*, the *Beach Shorts* anthology from Speculation Publications, and *The Initialization of Briar Rose* anthology from Manawaker Studios.

PAUL WILSON

In October 2023, I have a story appearing in the Queer Sci Fi Anthology *Rise*. I have two stories published in June 2023, one at *Discretionary Love* and the second at *Tales From the Moonlit Path*. I have a story in issue #62 of *The Sirens Call* magazine early July 2023. I have published over thirty-five short stories in both magazines and anthologies, as well as two novels, and a short story collection. I won the first annual Aiken Community Playhouse playwriting contest that produced my comedic two-act play. I have written nine novels, countless articles, reviews, essays, plays, and over 150 short stories including horror, sci-fi, fantasy, satire, and comedy.